UNWRITTEN

JEN FREDERICK

SUMMARY

After years of trying to hit it big with his band, Adam Rees' dream is finally about to come true. A new lead singer brings with him a hot tour invite, but with a catch—his sister has to come with them. Despite an off-limits edict, Adam is instantly attracted the smart and beautiful Landry. But if he wants to claim his woman, it might be at the expense of all his ambitions.

Landry Olsen has had success at every stage of her life, except when it comes to men. She's put her heart on the shelf, but one look at Adam and she's a goner. The hot rocker heats her from the inside out, and she wants him as much as he wants her. The only thing standing in their way of their happiness is Landry's brother—she ruined his musical hopes before, and she won't do it again. Even if it means saying no to the one guy who makes her believe in love again.

There's no fruit more tempting than the forbidden kind...

Check out the other books in the Woodland series:

Undeclared
Undressed, *a novella*
Unspoken
Unraveled
Unrequited
Unwritten

ALSO BY JEN FREDERICK

PRAISE FOR JEN FREDERICK

"Unwritten is another of Jen Frederick's swoon-worthy reads."

— New York Times Bestselling author Elle Kennedy

"Jen's books will make you ache in all the good ways!"

— New York Times Bestselling author Katy evans

"[G]enuine, steamy, and creative... This story is written with breathless intensity, and Frederick portrays the seriousness of anxiety and phobias without reducing her characters to walking collections of diagnoses. The secondary characters add enjoyment, giving readers updates on past starring couples and anticipation for stories to come."

— Publishers weekly on "Revealed to Him"

To Jeanette Mancine,
You're the type of friend that comes along once in a lifetime. Thank you
for allowing me the privilege of knowing you.

1

ADAM

The Beginning

So this is how my single state ends. How all the casual dating, random hookups, and fucking around grinds to a halt because of one girl. A girl I haven't even laid hands on. A girl I haven't heard speak. A girl whose green eyes—they must be green to go with that red hair—are bright enough to light up the whole damn bar.

"You all right, man?" Ian Turner, my drummer, asks as he muscles by me with a snare in one hand and his throne—aka the stool—in the other.

I wipe a hand across my jaw. It comes away dry. No drool is a good thing. "I'm fine. Why?"

"You look like someone hit you with a baseball bat," Ian explains.

That sounds about right.

"Just happy with how we played," I improvise, not entirely ready to admit to my downfall.

He buys it. A huge grin spreads across his face. "We killed it tonight."

We did, indeed. After only a month on the local scene, my band—Fuck Marry Kill—is slaying it. I hoist the bass drum onto my shoulder and gesture for him to lead. We need to clear the stage for the next band.

Part of me wants to run back out there and play another song or ten, but one of my old man's mantras was to always keep the audience wanting more. Rock their clothes off (sometimes literally given the band's infamous collection of underwear collected over the years on tour) and they'll be hungry to see you again.

The rest of me wants to hunt down the redhead. I figure she's in the bathroom now because the corner of the bar near the door where she hid for the three final songs has been filled by a couple of hipster guys with carefully trimmed facial hair and plaid shirts tucked into dark jeans.

"You see Mica Hollister is here?" My bassist Rudd careens around the corner, barely stopping before crashing into me. His eyes are hot and excited. Ordinarily, the only things that turn Rudd on are women and a sweet guitar riff. But Hollister would get his dick hard, too. Hollister's a regional promoter with sticky fingers in a dozen pots.

"I saw. I heard he's setting up some big city tour for new bands?" I give Davis, our new front man, a nod as he holds the door open for Ian and me.

Rudd trails behind like an overeager puppy. "Not just new bands—any bands with a decent local following. It's called the Under the Radar tour. He wants to use it to build a big social media following and then launch the best one into big-time radio play."

"Hollister's always full of ideas." There's not a promoter in the business who doesn't think he has the next Coachella up his sleeve. Making those ideas into something concrete is the challenge, and I haven't seen Hollister put together anything bigger than a local festival of a couple thousand people.

Ian shoves his throne into Rudd's empty arms. "Hold this." He piles the bass drum on top and hops into the back of the van. We start handing stuff inside. When the band is playing on a regular basis, there's zero need to get to the gym. Lifting the instruments in and out of the back of this vehicle three or four times a day is all the workout I need.

"You should hear him out," Rudd urges.

I shake my head at Rudd's persistence. Talking to Hollister is the last thing I want to do right now. I head inside for more of our equipment. Sooner we get this done, sooner I can hunt down the redhead. There's probably a dozen dicks pointed in her direction, and I need to get out there and stake my claim.

"Hollister's a blowhard," Ian declares. "He's the kind that strokes your dick with one hand while robbing you with the other."

He's not wrong. Hollister's been around for ages, even when my dad was touring. He's always trying to put something together, and although he has contacts, he's disorganized, which means most of his big ideas end up being huge fuckups. Plus, he's known to employ shady tactics, skimming money off the top of a band's take, meddling with the makeup of a group, and being a general asshole. I steer clear of him.

"I don't care who's stroking me, as long as I get some loving," Rudd replies.

"That's the most honest thing I've ever heard come out of your mouth," I grunt. Behind me, Davis cough-laughs. He's new, so he doesn't hassle Rudd as much as Ian and I do, but he'll catch on. The only way to live with Rudd's gigantic ego is to constantly punch it down to size.

"We sign up for Hollister's deal and we're going to be huge. Roadies will be doing the heavy lifting while we're in the green room getting some post-concert loving."

"Except for you, Rudd. No one wants to fuck the bassist," Ian ribs.

"Fuck you, man," Rudd retorts. "Lots of chicks love the bass guitar."

"Name one famous bassist."

I roll my eyes.

Davis nudges me. "They always like this?"

"Always," Ian confirms.

"Always." I nod. Rudd and Ian have been friends for a while, and this is an ongoing debate—whose instrument attracts the most chicks. "I think it's numbers over quality, though."

"Nothing wrong with that," Davis says.

"So is this gig better than filing reports at CloudDox?" I ask, only half joking. Davis's day job is some kind of data engineering at a local cloud computing company. This particular incarnation of my band will only go as far as our singer takes us. I can write the songs, the music, get the gigs, but without a front man, we're in the shitter, which is where my band dreams have been since high school. I've had other lead singers before, but Davis is hair-raising good. There's something special about him. I feel it and tonight the crowd experienced the magic, too.

The guy's voice is a rare one—great range and a little gravel for the girls. He stepped in to cover for a friend at a concert series last summer. He only sang backup, but the minute I heard him, I knew. He had *it*. A few beers later and Davis was officially part of FMK.

"Fuck, yeah," Davis replies. "So what's next?"

"We've got a Thursday night gig at the farmer's market followed by a two-hour set at Gatsby's. Saturday, we're driving to Layton to do a half-hour set opening for a local college band."

Davis makes a face. No one likes to be the opener. Depsite our success tonight, we're still so fresh from the garage you can smell the exhaust. Still, we're burning that all off.

"Don't worry. A few more nights like tonight and we'll headline bars all over the state." Other states as well, but I keep that ambition to myself. I'm not sure he's ready.

Davis is big on going home at nights. Rudd thinks he has a honey stashed away, but if he does, she hasn't shown her face around here.

"Or we can go on the road with Hollister, make some decent cash, get our sound heard by a shit ton more people than we played in front of tonight," Rudd persists.

"Hollister can wait." I squint toward the back of the bar. The redhead still looks absent, but if I don't get over there soon, some other guy's going to make a move. Then I'll have to get rid of him, and despite the owner of Tonic House being a long-time friend of my father, that might get me kicked out.

"What if he asks someone else, though?" Rudd says.

Ian clears his throat and tosses me a look that says I better go talk to Hollister or Rudd will be riding my dick all night. With a sigh, I mentally hit pause on my plan to find my dream girl. Turning to Rudd, I say, "If I talk to Hollister, will you stop hassling me?"

He grins. "For tonight."

"Jesus Christ. Go inside and find a girl who's too desperate to say no, will you?"

Rudd doesn't immediately do as I ask. As if sensing an imminent explosion, Davis collars him around the neck. "Come on, Rudd, I'll buy your first drink. The girls inside are thirsty, and I'm man enough to admit I can only handle a couple of them."

"I knew I liked you from the first moment I saw you," Rudd says.

"I thought the first words out of your mouth were, 'Who is this douchebag and why is his khaki-covered ass in our studio?'"

"As I said, liked you from the first."

Ian chuckles as he follows them. I don't get two steps inside the backstage door when Hollister pops up, like a whack-a-mole. The guy might have had hair once, but I don't remember the last time he looked like anything other than a pale, bald light bulb.

"Adam Rees, that was a righteous set, my man. Righteous!" He slaps me on the back as if we're old, old friends. "You played like a motherfucker up there."

I stifle a sigh. "Nice to see you, Hollister."

"I'm getting a tour together."

"I heard."

"We need you."

"You don't need to butter me up, Hollister. Just give me your spiel and I'll consider it."

He rubs his hands together, like some comic book villain. "I'm taking five bands on tour, including Threat Alert. Crowds like the variety, but we charge more—for everything. For booze. For food. For merch sales. Each band gets a share after management."

Interesting. Threat Alert is a rockabilly band with a bluegrass sound. They were just signed to a small indie label and had one song on the Billboard Top 100 chart. "What's your role?" I ask warily.

"My job is to set up the gigs and Right Stuff will take care of the rest."

I perk up. Right Stuff is a legit outfit. They ran a big tour out east a year ago and two bands of the seven that worked the coast ended up playing at big summer festivals.

Damn. This might be the real deal.

I don't ask how Hollister hooked up with the promotional firm, because it probably involved shit that wouldn't make me happy. "How long?"

"Five months."

I whistle. "That's a long damn time."

"I know. But all you got to do is show up. I swear the thing is going to pay for itself. Look at the crowd tonight."

Over Hollister's head, I take in the venue. People are lingering by the stage, as if they're afraid if they move they'll lose that euphoric feeling that engulfed them while we were playing.

Hollister presses me. "Four hundred people paid a twenty-dollar cover tonight. They're spending a ton on booze and I bet if you checked with your merch man, you sold a bunch of CDs."

It's never been about the money for me, but that's not true for the rest of my guys. Ian's got a new baby. Rudd lives in a trailer with three other guys. And if I'm pulling Davis off his cushy desk job, I'll need to dangle a real carrot in front of him.

"Don't know. I'd have to talk to the band. Davis, my singer, has a day job."

Hollister grimaces. "Well, he's going to have to quit that."

"It's a real job. Benefits and all."

"We need a big name, Rees, and yours is the biggest around here."

"You mean my dad's name is the biggest around here," I correct.

He shrugs. "Same thing. Last I checked, you're still Adam Rees."

"I'll think about it," I say, not wanting to get into a big argument about using my last name rather than my music to gain success.

"All I ask." Grinning, he pulls an envelope from inside his jacket. "The details are in here, including the Right Stuff management contact. You've always wanted to tour without using your old man's connections. This is it."

I fold the envelope and stick it into my back pocket. "I'll let you know."

"Don't take too long," Hollister warns. "There are a dozen other bands that would kill for this."

Try a thousand other bands, but there's no point in showing Hollister that I'm eager. He might have questionable ethics, but he's sharp. Pretending lukewarm interest is the right play because any excitement will be leveraged against me. "Like I said, I'll let you know."

Hollister purses his lips in frustration. He wants an immediate commitment, but that's not going to happen. I want to investigate this deal, but most of all, I'm not going to commit to a five-month tour of anything until all the guys are on board. I stare implacably back at him. When he realizes he's not going to get an answer tonight, he gives me a sad shake of his head. "You're going to be a headache on this tour, aren't you?"

"You've known me forever, Hollister. Did you think I wasn't going to question everything?" I've spent my entire life keeping one eye out for people who wanted to take advantage of me—my money, my skill, my parentage. Because of that, I've cultivated a close set of friends outside of the music industry, kept my achievements to myself, and learned to rely on my gut instinct. Despite a few missteps here or there, my system hasn't failed me.

And while I love the idea of this tour, agreeing to it can wait. Tonight is about paying attention to my gut and finding the redhead before someone who isn't distracted snatches her up.

I make my way down the back hall to the door that leads to the front and spot her back in the corner. *Bingo.* Our eyes meet. I drink in what I can see from this distance—her red hair framing an oval face, a slender neck, the delicate slope of her nose. She raises a hand to tuck a strand of hair behind her ear. A flash of gold winks at me.

My feet start moving in her direction.

"Adam! Over here! Adam! Adam Rees, get your ass over here."

I want to ignore Rudd's shouting, but if I don't go over there and tell him what Hollister had to say, he'll hassle me all night. Better for me to get my business out of the way so I can spend the rest of the night with her.

I'm coming to you. Hang on. I try to telegraph. When she doesn't move, I make a beeline to the bar.

"What'd Hollister have to say?" Rudd asks when I reach the counter. All three of my bandmates look at me with expectant eyes.

I hand the envelope to Ian. He pulls out the contract while I explain the deal. "We've got an invite to go out on tour with Threat Alert and two others. It's being partially underwritten by TA's new label. Bad news is it's for five months."

"That's not bad news!" cries Rudd. "That's fucking awesome!" He punches his fist in the air.

"Ian?" I ask.

"Is it even a question?" His smile is so broad the corners of his mouth might reach his ears. "I'm in. I'm so in."

"What about the baby?" Ian and his wife just had their first kid.

"Berry will be as psyched as anyone, plus, her mom will help. Is this the real deal or another of Hollister's pipe dreams?"

"It sounds legit. I'll vet it tomorrow, but if you guys want to go, I'm down with it."

Five months playing music with a decent band isn't a hardship for me. I have plenty of money to take care of us if the tour craters, but while Ian and Rudd are willing to throw five months of their life away for their music, I don't have the same confidence about Davis.

He peers at me over the top of his glass before draining the contents. Slamming the empty glass on the bar, he hails the bartender.

A girl trots down immediately, her white T-shirt damp from work. "What do you need, babe?"

"I'll take four shots of the top-shelf whiskey," Davis orders.

"We celebrating something?" I ask, cautiously.

"We're going on tour," Davis answers with a crooked smile. "That seems like something to celebrate, no?"

Rudd and Ian bust out the cheers. They body slam each other. Across the room, Hollister catches my eye. I give him an affirmative chin nod and a thumbs-up for good measure. He salutes me.

I pick up my just-delivered shot and raise it. "To FMK."

"To FMK," the boys cheer.

The whiskey burns as it slides down my throat.

"Christ, man, it's all coming together," Ian crows, slamming his shot glass onto the bar top.

"Can you imagine the road pussy?" Rudd claps his hands together.

"Do you ever think about anything but sex?" Davis jokes.

"Yeah, music. Which is the same thing, ain't I right?" Rudd asks me.

"Can't argue." Speaking of sex and women, now that I've arranged the band, I have other matters to take care of.

"Give us another round!" Rudd shouts over his shoulder. To us, he says, "I'm going to hit the head. None of you motherfuckers touch the glasses until I get back."

Hurriedly, I toss a few bills on the bar to cover the bill. "I'm out, too."

My band finally coalescing? Check. An undiscovered talent like my new singer found hiding in an office cube? Check. Big tour on deck? Check. Girl I'm supposed to spend my future with waltzes into a random bar and stares at me for nine minutes straight like I'm the incarnation of every wet, dirty fantasy she's ever had? Check. Check. Check.

"Where are you going?" Ian asks.

"To meet my future," I answer.

2

LANDRY

I broke my glasses an hour ago, but from my vantage point in the corner of the bar it looks like two arrows are slicing through the thick crowd of drunk, hyped people, heading right toward me. One of them looks like the hot guitar player who was onstage with Davis. The other looks like Davis who was slamming drinks at the bar.

"What're you doing here?" Unfortunately, it's Davis who reaches me first. The stench of whiskey on his breath is strong. I wonder how much he drank before the set, or hell, during the set.

"Can't I come see you play?" I counter, trying to downplay my unease. After all, can I really lecture him about bad choices after the night I've had.

"Yeah, but—"

Thankfully, before Davis can say anything else, Rock God steps forward.

"Who's this?" he asks, his voice rich and deep.

Our eyes meet—a collision of green against brown causing a shower of electricity to spark and cascade around us. My breath catches at what I see in those dark pools. I don't have a ton of experience, but it looks like lust and it's directed toward me.

The minute I stepped into the bar, he drew my eyes. Who wouldn't look at him twice? He's gorgeous. Sandy brown hair, strong jaw, high cheekbones and searing eyes that could hook you a mile away. There's a piercing at the corner of his right eyebrow that somehow only emphasizes his good looks. His smile made all of the women and half of the men want to climb on to the stage and press their mouths against his lips to see if the smile tasted as amazing as it looks.

His body is muscled perfection—not the thick necked stuff that screams *steroids*, but the defined, proportional goodness. He looks strong and sturdy, like a thousand pieces of emotional baggage could be flung at him and he'd be able to bat them away like some super hero. He's taller than Davis by at least two inches and Davis stands six feet.

But it wasn't his looks that captured my attention. It was his intensity and focus.

As he played and performed with passion I hadn't seen before, I began to wonder what it would be like if I were the object of his attention, what it would feel like if his fingers worked their magic on my body instead of the frets, what his tongue would taste like if it were making music with my mouth. Given the number of screams directed toward him, I wasn't the only one having inappropriate thoughts.

His dark eyes laser into mine, rendering my mouth dry and other parts of me wet. I now understand why Davis thinks his new band is going to be a huge success.

"My sister. Landry, Adam. Adam, Landry." Davis waves a casual hand back and forth, completely oblivious to the sexual tension simmering in the air.

At least...I think it's sexual tension. I'm partially blind, having left my broken glasses in the car, and it's been so long since I've had a man between my legs that I've likely regrown my hymen. Maybe Adam's just a super intense guy, and I'm reading too much into it.

My nerves are frayed thin. I could be misinterpreting everything right now. Lord knows, my instincts aren't worth shit.

"Landry," he says slowly, as if enjoying the feel of my name on his tongue.

"Hey," I choke out, reaching for the wall behind me so I don't collapse in a puddle at Adam's feet.

He smiles and that's it. I'm slain. Roll me into a grave and throw some dirt on me, because I'm all done.

"Glad you could come tonight. Did you enjoy the show?"

I nod vigorously. "It was good."

Davis laughs out loud. "Bullshit. You hate live music."

Adam arches his eyebrow in surprise, a stray strobe light glinting off the upper ball.

"I've never said that," I protest. Suddenly it's important that everyone within listening range believes I love music. That it's my life.

"You kind of did. Last month I invited you to see a show and you said, 'I'd rather cut my ears off.'"

His eyebrow creeps higher while I turn beet red. *Brothers are the worst.*

"I'm sure I didn't." Although that was probably an exact quote by Davis. It's not that I don't like live music, per se. It's more that I prefer to sit at home in sweatpants, watching re-runs of *Real Housewives*. I like my glamour and excitement secondhand. My face throbs, reminding me of what happens when I go out.

"I'm pretty sure you did," Davis counters. I wish the floor would open and swallow Davis. Or me. Both of us would also be an acceptable option. "Anyway," he continues in the oblivious way older brothers can be, "since you're here now, come and meet the rest of the guys."

He grabs my arm, and I yelp in pain. Jumping back, I manage to knock my injured elbow into the table behind me. The beer glasses to tip and a bunch of people to shout in dismay.

"What the hell?"

"Are you all right?"

"Goddammit!"

A rush of cold beer spills down my back.

Laughter mixes with curses as Davis hauls me off the table, causing me to cry out in pain again. I cradle my arm against my body. Crap, it hurts. Tears spike behind my eyes.

"She spilled my fucking beer," some drunk guy yells.

There's a jostling and more cold liquid spills down my back and into my jeans. About the only thing that could make this evening worse would be for me to get my period. I close my eyes for a second and wait for my body to betray me. Nothing happens. I tell myself to be grateful for the small things in life.

"Are you okay?"

I flick my lids up to see Adam leaning over me.

Davis's face appears in the periphery.

"Hey, did you hear me? She spilled our beers."

"I'm—"

"Seriously, man, that was a twenty-dollar pitcher."

Adam straightens quickly and slams his hand on the table. "Here's your fucking twenty. Buy a pitcher and shut your pieholes before I shove the bills down your throat."

"No need to be pissy about it, man."

"I'm fine. Really." I tug on Davis's arm.

"Is there a problem here, Adam? Do you want me to kick these guys out?"

I look up to see an older man with straggly hair hanging down to his waist glaring at our group. A crowd of people stares in our direction.

Davis clears his throat. "There's no problem, Mr. Hill. I slipped."

The old man slaps Davis on the back. "Told you to call me Kenny."

"Davis," I say quietly but urgently. "I'm okay. Really. I'm going to go—"

"Kenny, this is Davis's sister," Adam interrupts. "She got a bunch of beer down her shirt. I have an extra one in my kit. Do you mind if we use your office so she can change?"

"No, no, of course not." Kenny pulls a huge set of keys from his front pocket and slaps them in Adam's hand. To the angry beer boys, he says, "You folks okay?"

"Yeah," the one who Adam threatened concedes glumly.

"We'll get you a new pitcher," Kenny promises, hailing a waitress.

Adam jerks his head. "Come on."

I close my eyes. How do these embarrassing things happen to me? Better yet, why?

I came to Davis's show tonight to hide, and ended up making a big scene. "Sure," I agree sullenly. My new silk shirt sticks to my back, and my panties are now wet because of beer rather than something else.

"What happened to your arm?" Davis asks as we follow Adam down a dark hall past the restrooms. "And where are your glasses?"

"Broke them," I mumble.

"And you drove here?"

"I held them to my face and left them in the car." It sounds as dumb as it felt when I was doing it.

"That's inventive," Adam remarks. His lips are twitching as if he's trying not to laugh.

Davis groans. "Or stupid."

"Thanks, Davis. I love you, too," I snap.

Adam releases that laugh he was holding. "You guys sound like siblings."

He stops at the last door and unlocks it. Inside, he throws on the lights and that's when the danger of this situation hits me.

It was dark in the bar, lit only by colored strobe lights that concealed more than they revealed. I don't want a bright light illuminating every dark cranny—or in my case, bruise and cut.

"Come on in..." Adam's voice trails off as he stares at me. "Fuck me. Who did that to you?"

I stick my tongue in the corner of my mouth, feeling the cut and tasting the copper of the blood, and desperately wishing I were home. Was it possible to run away? "Does it look that bad?"

Davis spins me around. He takes one look at me and jumps to a conclusion. "Marrow."

There's no sneaking home now. I drag my palm down my face. "Let's go in and I'll tell you about it."

~

FOR ONLY BEING TWENTY-FOUR, my life has held a multitude of humiliations. I ate a worm in kindergarten because some punk in fourth grade told me it was a piece of candy. It was as gross as you can imagine. When I was fifteen, I went for an entire period with my skirt tucked into the back of my tights until a teacher, not even one of my damned friends, pulled it out for me. On my first day of college, I tripped over a nonexistent wrinkle in the tile and spilled a Venti Frappuccino all over the cutest guy in my dorm.

Then there was the time I attracted the unwanted attention of some psycho stalker and had to tell everyone in my life about him—along with an innumerable amount of police officers, detectives, investigators, and judges—so I could be safe again. And tonight? I'm sitting in a dingy office with a fat lip that I caused myself, watching my brother pace and rant while a tatted and pierced god glowers at me.

"Here," says Adam, handing me a towel. The tattoos on his arms meld together in one bold but blurry black shape. He takes a step back, away from me and out of Davis warpath.

"Thanks." The ice cubes scrape against each other as I lift the damp towel to my lip. Sighing, I sink onto the cushions of the sketchy leather sofa, cracked in places and sticky in others. The first contact I've had with a hot guy in a long time is when I have a busted lip and my brother is railing on me for my stupidity. How unoriginal.

Also, why I can't berate him for drinking.

"I can't believe you didn't call me." Pace, pace, pace. "What kind of friends just leave you at your house alone?" Stop and turn. "I swear to God, next time I get my hands on that motherfucker, I'm going to kill him. I don't care how long I spend in jail." Pace, pace, pace. "Why didn't the alarms go off?" Stop. Glare. Turn. Commence pacing.

"You probably don't need stitches," Adam observes.

I tongue the cut. "No, I don't think so."

I squint, trying to bring Adam's face into focus. Damn my far-sightedness. Davis's big, blurry head appears in my line of sight instead.

"You being straight with us? That you hit your face on the side of your car?" he demands.

"Unfortunately, yes." It's humiliating, but the truth. "I thought I heard something." I still believe I did. A dark shadow slunk around the side of the house, and it wasn't a dog, like Penny suggested, or a shadow, which is what Gail insisted. "I was startled, bumped into Gail, and twisted my ankle on a rock. When I tried to right myself, I stumbled into the car, cutting my elbow on the handle." I raise my elbow up. "I've a bruise, I think, but the cut stopped bleeding."

"And the face?"

"Well, as we both know, I'm a klutz so I face-first into the mirror." I tap my cheek. "It looks worse than it feels. I mean, it only hurts when I laugh and smile."

"I'll keep the jokes to a minimum, then," Adam quips—which, of course, makes me laugh.

"What's funny about this?" Davis barks.

I slump back against the cracked cushions. "Nothing."

Adam raises his palm. "Just trying to lighten the mood."

Davis's jaw tightens and I sense he wants to tell Adam off, but won't, because Davis loves being in this band too much. Yet my showing up here with my banged-up body and banged-up face is pushing him over the edge.

Suddenly I'm exhausted. The adrenaline rush from listening to the band has worn off. Davis has every right to treat me like a child. Instead of investigating exactly what—or who—was lurking around the house, I ran straight to my brother. I need to start dealing with my own problems.

Besides, I've already ruined one band experience for him. I don't want to do that again. No, I correct. I *won't* do that again.

I knuckle my eyes and get to my feet.

"Where the hell are you going?" Davis demands.

"I'm tired. I'm going home."

"Not without me, you're not." He turns to Adam. "We done here?"

Adam straightens. "You need some help? Because I'm all in for whatever you need."

"The police won't do jack shit, if that's what you're asking," Davis informs Adam. "They were useless before, and they're going to be useless now."

At the word *before*, Adam's pierced eyebrow shoots upward. My cheeks grow hot again. In my head, I know that being the victim isn't something I should be ashamed of, but my head doesn't control my emotions very well.

"There was nothing to call about," I say. "Gail and Penny swore I was imagining things, so it's not like I had good eyewitnesses."

"Those two brainless twits were probably too drunk to recognize their mothers," Davis rants.

I bite my tongue to prevent a bark of laughter from spilling out. Davis's characterization isn't far off the mark. Penny and Gail are pretty, but the elevator doesn't go all the way to the top for them. Still, they were fun to barhop with, and I'd been stuck in the house for far too long. "Another reason not to call the police."

"You should've called," Davis insists. "You've got the restraining order. They would be bound to follow up on that."

"Do we have to get into it right now?" I flick a gaze toward Adam, who rises to his feet. I hate that my dirty laundry is being aired in front of him.

I direct a frown in his direction. Doesn't he have anything better to do? There were about a dozen girls trying to crawl onto the stage. In fact, he had to shrug a couple of them off as he was leading us back here.

"Why not?" my brother says.

Davis can be so damn obtuse sometimes.

"I think she means that she'd rather not talk about it in front of me," Adam offers. He turns to me. "I want to help, Landry. Davis is part of the band and what affects him affects all of us."

I'm sure that was meant to be reassuring, but it only serves as a reminder of how my stupidity can screw things up for Davis.

"I'm fine. Really. I just want to go home."

"Do you think that's a good idea? Going home alone? Davis, if you want to stick around here, I can run your sister home."

My stomach flips in excitement, closely followed by dread. I don't need to be in close quarters with this man. I'll end up doing dumb things. I shoot a pleading glance at Davis. For once, he reads me clearly.

"Nah, I better get going. Let me know about the tour thing, will you?" Davis moves toward the door.

"What tour thing?" I ask.

"We've been invited to go on a five-month, multi-city tour with four other bands, including Threat Alert," Adam explains.

"Threat Alert?" I echo. The name doesn't sound familiar.

Davis snorts, one hand on the doorknob. "She has no idea. Landry listens to the *radio*."

He says *radio* like it's a dirty word, but it's true. I listen to pop hits. What can I say? I'm a pleb.

"'Destiny's Here?'" Adam supplies. At my continued blank look, his lips twitch slightly and then he hums a few bars. "'I ran away, afraid to stay, now destiny's here.'"

The words barely register as I stare at his beautiful mouth.

"Landry?" my brother prompts.

I jerk my head toward Davis. "Yeah?"

He frowns. "Didn't you hear what I said?"

"Um..." What were we talking about? Oh yeah, the tour with the other band. "I don't recognize it."

"It's a new song," Adam reassures me.

"If it's not in the top forty, I doubt she's heard it." Davis clucks his tongue in dismay over my musical ignorance. "I'm going to get my gear. Stay here. I'll be right back."

"Okay," I start, but he moves so quickly I end up talking to his back.

The door closes slowly behind him, leaving me alone with Adam.

I brush a nervous hand over my hair. I slapped on some lipstick in the car, using the parking lot lights for illumination as I peered through my broken glasses at my reflection in the rearview mirror. My hair is stick straight, but the last time a brush made contact was about six hours ago. I probably look less appealing than gum at the bottom of a shoe.

All those hot looks I thought I'd read in Adam's eyes were probably ones of horror mixed with concern.

"Shit. I forgot why we came back here." Adam heads over to the desk and leans down, rummaging through a bag sitting at the side. Standing up, he holds out a worn gray T-shirt with a little U logo. "It's clean. I promise."

"My shirt's dry now," I lie. It's sticky and damp as hell, but I'm not about to admit that.

"You sure? It can't be comfortable."

"It's fine."

His hand slowly lowers to his side. Something almost like disappointment flits across his face, but I chalk that up to my crappy vision.

"So, Landry, if you don't like music, what does get your engine running?" He dumps the shirt into the bag, then leans his butt against the desk and folds his arms across his chest.

My eyes drop to his forearms, which are nicely defined. Every part of him is nicely defined, from his biceps to his broad shoulders to his narrow waist and solid legs. If I could put together my ideal man shape, like some sort of sexy Mr. Potato Head, it'd end up looking exactly like Adam. And now I'm about to tell him that I'm a nerd.

"I write code. Computer code."

He gives me an encouraging smile. "That's cool. You must be smart."

"Um, I guess?" I never know how to respond to that. When someone compliments Davis on his singing, he invariably says something cocky like, "I know." I need to adopt that attitude. If I had his confidence, I'd sashay over to Adam, drag my hand down his muscled chest and lick the sweat off his neck.

But I don't have that confidence. My limited experience with guys can be categorized into two columns: the jerky one I dated in college and the scary one who stalked me after I got out.

"No guess about it." He pushes to his feet and approaches, stopping only a step away.

I can feel the heat of his body, smell the clean sweat of his under-the-lights workout. This close, I can make out details of his upper arm tattoos —bold lines and elegant swirls glide together in harmony. It shouldn't work, but it does. The tattoos serve to highlight his sexy body, making me want to trace my fingers and tongue along the lines until I reach—

"You know, now that Davis is in my band, I consider him family." A finger tilts my chin up until I meet Adam's dark eyes. "And there's nothing I wouldn't do for family. Give me the name of whoever hurt you, and I'll take care of it."

I lick my lips. "I just got scared over nothing."

"You don't look like someone who scares easily." His thumb rubs gently across my skin.

I don't have a good response, because I want to agree, but I don't think that's the truth. Someone who didn't scare easily wouldn't be in my shoes. Someone who didn't scare easily would've chased after Marrow. Someone who didn't scare easily would lean forward, raise her face, and kiss this man.

"You ready?" Davis bangs the door open.

I jump back from Adam's touch and dart a nervous glance in Davis's direction. But he's too impatient, gesturing for me to scoot out the door, so he doesn't notice how close I was standing to Adam or sense how charged the air is in this small office.

"Yeah, I'm ready."

"You sure I can't do anything?" Adam offers once more.

Davis shakes his head. "We got it."

I briefly meet Rock God's eyes. "Nice to meet you, Adam."

After a beat of hesitation, he nods. "Yeah. Same."

Adam's gorgeous and talented. Another time, another life, I'd be all over him, but for so many reasons, taking him up on his offer would be disastrous. So I hurry out of the room with the heat of his eyes on my back as I walk down the hall.

Out by the car, my brother shoves his guitar case in the backseat while I get into the passenger seat.

Once he's in the driver's seat Davis picks up my mangled glasses. "You did a number on these, didn't you?"

"Yup."

"That asshole. I wish I'd..." Davis trails off, swallowing what I imagine are very murderous thoughts. We've gotten into a dozen arguments about what he was going to do to Chris Marrow. I wanted Davis to stay away. Davis wanted to carve him up with a dull spoon.

"I know what you wish, but it was probably nothing." I fiddle with my seatbelt as Davis pushes the button to start the car. When he shifts into drive, I wiggle in my seat.

"I only had two shots the whole night," he says tightly.

"I'm sorry," I say. "I wasn't checking up on you."

"You sure about that?"

I pat my face. "Real sure."

Davis grunts, but pulls out. We both fall silent. He's probably dwelling on my idiocy while I'm multi-tasking—worrying about him and me at the same time.

When we arrive home, it's completely dark. He keeps the lights on and hits the garage door opener. "Stay here," he orders.

I get out.

He sighs.

I scamper inside the garage and find a flashlight, which I hand to him because if I don't I'm sure he'd rip it out of my fingers.

"Where'd you see him?"

"By the side door to the garage."

Davis shines the light in front of him, and we go investigate.

"Looks like someone was standing here."

I peer down. The snow melted off last month and the ground is soft and springy. There's a slight depression in the old mulch my dad laid around the sidewalk and trees, but there's no shoe print. No glaring evidence that says, "STALKER WAS HERE."

"I'll call Pressley in the morning," I relent with a sigh. Detective Pressley is the woman who was finally assigned to my case after months of me getting the runaround from the cops. She's the reason Marrow served any time at all, even though three months of an eighteen-month sentence seems grossly inadequate.

"For all the good that'll do." Davis flicks off the flashlight and hands it to me. "Go inside and I'll park the car."

I'd like to tell Davis to go home, but I don't want to be alone in this big house tonight, which is yet another reason why kissing Adam would've been a huge mistake.

My head's already a mess. I don't need to screw up my heart, too.

3

LANDRY

"H e's lying!" Davis fumes the next morning.

I drop my head in my hands, the frames of my spare glasses digging into my temples

"I know, but right now, what we have are two people who swear he was with them. You say that you saw a shadow. The girls you were with believe that it was either an animal or just the wind." Detective Pressley gives us a regretful look. "I want to help you, but the evidence isn't there."

Which is why I didn't call her last night.

"Can't you just present this stuff to the judge? He's texting her and now he's creeping around our house. Who else would it be?"

"We don't have any evidence—no witnesses, no physical evidence, nothing—to show he's violated the terms of his probation."

"So I just wait for him to attack Landry again?" Davis interjects bitterly.

I slump farther down in my chair and poke a tongue at my sore lip. On Earth Two, my alternate life, Adam's walking into my bedroom wearing nothing but a smile and carrying a cup of coffee. We just had the best sex of my life, and he's eager for more.

Sadly, I'm on Earth One.

"I'm sorry. There's nothing we can do. We have to catch him in the act." She taps the printout of messages I brought with me. The text messages look less ominous on the page, almost fake without the green and blue bubbles.

Where are you?
I forgive you.
I'm making plans. Don't you worry.

"Catch him in the act? Like you want her to lure him to her house and have her get beat up again?" Davis is incredulous.

"Davis, stop it. I tripped and fell." Besides, Pressley would never ask me to serve as bait. She's the one who gave me the info about the self-defense class I took a year ago.

"This is bullshit," Davis repeats. He abruptly gets to his feet and stalks out of the small room.

Pressley and I stare at each other in silence. My eyes drop to the cuff of her crisp white shirt. You can tell how long Pressley has been up by the condition of her shirt. At the start of her shift, it's crisp. At two in the morning, it's as crumpled as a wadded-up dollar bill. I like crisp Pressley best. You never want to see a detective late at night. It always means bad things.

"I hope you know I'd never suggest you put yourself in danger," she says softly.

"I know." I take a deep breath and rise. I shove away the fantasy of Earth Two and pull myself together. "I'm sorry for Davis. We're frustrated."

"I am, too," she says. "I wish I could do something more for you, but I can't trace these texts. We don't have the budget for that kind of thing, even if it's possible to trace them. Until we have proof that these messages are from him or we see him violating the restraining order, there's nothing we can do. The law presumes that he's innocent until proven guilty. Have you thought about changing your number?"

"This is the fourth number I've had in the last six months. But yeah, I'll change it." I try hard to keep the frustration out of my voice. This isn't Detective Pressley's fault, I remind myself in an effort not to completely lose my mind and lash out at the one person who's provided actual help to me

"When he screws up—and he will—we'll get him." Her gaze flicks to the scar on my cheek—the one that Marrow left when he whipped a coffee mug at the side of my face during the attack that sent him to prison for the brief three months. "We're not going to let you get hurt again." She walks around that big desk of hers. "You have your safety kit?"

"Yeah, I have it." I have a can of pepper spray, an alarm on my keychain, and an app on my mobile that calls 9-1-1 and with the press of one button sends my location to a bunch of people in my phone: Davis, my parents, and my best friend, May. Sadly, only one of them is in town. May is in Mongolia and my parents are in Turkey.

"And you took those self-defense classes."

"Yes." For all the good that did me. Last night, I froze like a timid rabbit and then ran to hide behind Davis's guitar.

"Good. Be alert and try to stop worrying so much." She hesitates with her hand on the door. "Maybe you should try to get out of town for a while. Put yourself outside of Marrow's reach. He's required to stay in the state per his probation requirements, but you don't have to stay put, Landry. Go to a beach, meet a nice guy, have some fun."

I should've gone with May, I think for the hundredth time since my best friend took off on her backpacking trip across the world. Except for the fact that I didn't want to backpack or spend days without showers. May's idea of a good time is to pretend she's an extra on the Bear Grylls survival show.

"I'm going to eat bugs, Landry! Isn't that cool?"

"No, May, I don't think that's cool at all."

"Did you know that ants are full of protein and some of them taste chocolate-y?"

"That sounds terrible. I'll stay home."

I tell none of this to Pressley, though. Instead I give her a brief hug and say goodbye.

Davis is out in the lobby, a regretful look on his face. "Sorry for losing my shit in there," he mumbles.

"Don't worry about it." I drag my purse strap higher on my shoulder. "You ready?"

"Yeah. Mind if we stop at my condo first so I can grab some stuff?"

I frown. "What stuff?"

He shrugs. "Just clothes and shit. I'm staying with you until Mom and Dad get back."

"You don't have to do that," I object. "I'll be fine."

He gives me the Look. The one that says *I'm your big brother and I'm going to protect you until my dying breath so don't bother arguing with me.*

Normally I find it sweet, and sometimes it's annoying. Today, I feel almost...ashamed. I know I'm not to blame for this Marrow situation —or for what happened to Davis's afterward. I didn't even know Marrow had a thing for me and I didn't ask Davis to mete out a revenge beating that fractured three bones in his hand. Those things happened, though, and it's hard to shake the consequences of it all.

For all my good fortune—the business success, Mom and Dad rekindling their marriage, Davis in his new job and his new band— the past still has a hold on me.

I don't want that for Davis. He has a job, a life, and—the tour. Damn it, he has an opportunity to go on tour and maybe even hit it big.

"Just for tonight," I say firmly.

Davis gives me the Look again. Biting my lip in exasperation, I follow him out of the police station.

"IS THAT...A SNAKE HEAD?" I adjust my glasses in hopes that my vision is distorting things.

"Yes!" May's excited voice blares out of my laptop speakers. "We had snake for dinner when we were riding in Kharkhorin. That's the old capital of Mongolia," she explains. I don't even know what the current capital is but I smile and nod. "Anyway, the meat was chewy, if you were wondering. They let me keep the head which I'm bringing back with me. Isn't that amazing?" She shakes it again, and it bounces up and down on the Skype screen, the dead eyes watching me no matter where I moved in front of the camera.

"Amazing," I say faintly, my stomach roiling. "So where are you exactly?"

"Close to Ulan Bator. I visited the Gandan Monastery—it was gorgeous."

Ulan Bator...the name rings a bell. Oh, I think that is the current capital. I remember reviewing May's itinerary, which seems to change by the week, and thinking it sounded like a *Tomb Raider* game with May playing the part of gun-wielding, acrobatic Lara Croft. "How long are you going to be there?"

"Only a day." She leans forward. "I hooked up with another tour to ride into Amarbayasgalant Monastery. It's for three weeks."

Yup. Lara Croft, take two. "Find any ancient treasures or curses?"

She giggles. "Thankfully, no, but I am practicing my backflips." Her eyes sparkle with happiness, which in turn fills *me* with happiness. Before she left, May was miserable. We'd sold our app and made out like bandits, but our lives took a weird turn. Instead of being the happiest people ever with our big, fat bank accounts, Marrow came into my life and May fell for the wrong guy. Now she's riding ponies, eating snakes and ants, and having the best time of her life.

"Are you going to spend the rest of your life riding ponies in the desert?"

"Maybe?" She shrugs. "Look, we both know I was a mess when I left. I needed distance and being out here, meeting monks, learning to meditate, it's all helped me heal."

"I should join you, then, because my life is just as untidy."

She wrinkles her nose. "Nah, you'd hate it out here. Besides, there's no way for you to get to me. I'm leaving tomorrow."

I try to keep the relief out of my face. I love May, but we're so different. Working together is one thing. Vacationing together would break our precious bond.

"Be safe," I tell her.

"I will. Love you, Laundry Basket." She waves at the screen.

"Love you, too, May Day." I blow her a kiss and then she's gone.

I drum my fingers on my desk. It's quiet in my parents' house. Upstairs, Davis is in his old bedroom, playing "Come Alive" on his guitar. It's been two days, yet he refuses to leave me and go back to his condo.

If he won't leave me alone in the house, how's he going to go on tour? Joining May is not a possibility. And I won't interrupt my parents' trip—they're on a second honeymoon, trying to save their marriage.

What happened the last time Davis had to quit a band makes my stomach cramp. I'd eat a mouse and a snake before letting him travel down that dark road again.

So that leaves one option. I try the bait thing, luring Marrow out in the open and trapping him somehow. The notion makes me want to vomit, but I can't allow my situation to stand in the way of Davis's dreams.

Not this time.

4

ADAM

"You bang those cupboard doors any harder and they're going to fall off," my roommate Bo says as he strolls into the kitchen.

"Where the fuck are we keeping the coffee these days?" I grouch. The problem with living with four other guys is that shit keeps getting moved.

Bo reaches for a can behind the coffee pot. "Here. By the coffeemaker."

I grab it and rip off the lid. "Well, it used to be in the cupboard next to the sink."

"I moved it," a new voice volunteers.

I look up from spooning grounds into the filter to see my best friend Finn amble into the kitchen. He and Bo work together flipping houses. They must be on their way to a job site.

"What's up your ass?" Finn asks, opening the refrigerator door.

"Band shit."

"Thought you were happy with it. Mal said you got an offer to go on tour. Want some?" he asks, pointing a carton of eggs in my direction.

I nod eagerly. I'm going to miss the bastard and his mad cooking skills when he moves out.

The whole dynamic of the house is changing. Finn's buying a home with his girlfriend, Winter. Bo and Noah are graduating from college and moving to Chicago. It's going to be Mal and me in this big fucking place and neither of us can make anything more than coffee.

I slap the lid of the coffeemaker down and join Bo at the table.

"Where's AnnMarie?" I ask. AnnMarie is Bo's girlfriend and probably his future wife. Every one of my friends is hooking up, and I'm still chasing girls at bars.

"She's sleeping."

"Is Noah over at Grace's?"

Bo nods. "And Mal's in his study. He never sleeps, does he?"

"Nah, insomnia's a bitch." Mal's past has him by the balls and won't let go. I'm hopeful that he'll shake loose, someday.

Bo takes a deep draw from his coffee mug. "So what's the problem with the band?"

"My new front man's sister showed up at the bar the other night. She had a cut on her lip and a nasty bruise on her arm."

Bo sets his mug down carefully. Finn swings away from the stove with a deep frown on his face. Neither of them like the idea of some girl getting hurt.

"Her brother is knocking her around?"

"No, she said it was an accident. That she thought she heard some intruder by her house, got startled and fell against her car."

"You believe that?" Bo looks skeptical.

I wave for Finn to check on the eggs. He flicks me off but returns his attention to the stove. "Her brother bought it, but it sounds like she might have a stalker. Guy by the name of Marrow." I pull a sheaf of paper from my back pocket. "Mal looked it up and there's a Christopher Paul Marrow who was arrested for harassment, assault and battery a few years ago. He got sentenced to eighteen months and got out after serving three at a minimum-security prison."

Bo plucks out of my hand the criminal rap sheet that Mal printed off. He scans it quickly. There's not much information there, but what few details exist make me want to crush Marrow's head between my hands until his eyeballs pop out.

"Shit," Bo mutters.

A plateful of eggs lands on the table. Finn takes the paper from Bo, reads it, and says, "We should go check him out."

"We?" I echo, pretending the fluffy eggs are the only thing I'm interested in.

Finn gives me a look of disbelief. "You never get up before noon, yet here you are, slamming cupboards and making coffee before the crack of dawn."

I shrug. "Fine. So maybe I was going to find Marrow and see what was what."

"We'll all go," Bo says.

"You are only allowed to watch." I point my fork in his direction. Bo loves to fight, but if anyone gets to hit Marrow, it's going to be me.

Landry's a tiny thing. The top of her head barely reached my chin. The thought of some fucked-up bastard bruising her makes my blood boil. I barely held it together the other night, seeing her delicate mouth marred by the cut.

Shit, she's beautiful. I stayed up all last night and the night before because I couldn't stop thinking about her. Every time I closed my eyes, I saw her green eyes staring at me with a healthy dose of lust in them. She wanted me and if it weren't for her brother, I could've given her exactly what she wanted—to lay her back on the sofa and kiss her until we were both breathless. I wouldn't have taken it any further than that, though.

She's like one of Finn's skittish colts that need a slow, gentle hand. Well, I can be slow and gentle. Even if it means my balls might turn permanently blue.

But first, I need to get rid of Marrow so that I can go on this damn tour. When I spoke to Davis yesterday, he admitted that he's still staying with Landry at their folks' place, and that he doesn't feel comfortable leaving town right now. Fortunately, we have until the end of the week to give Hollister an answer, and the tour won't kick off until the week after that, so there's still time to change Davis's mind. Or, rather, there's still time to put Davis's mind at ease, along with making sure Landry is safe.

Then I need to figure out how I'm going to stay in contact with her. Starting something with a girl before I kick off on a five-month tour through a dozen states is stupid, but there's a connection there and I'd be a fool not to follow through. My friends are settling down and finding real happiness while I stumble in and out of beds, feeling more unfulfilled than ever.

Allowing Landry to slip through my fingers because of some fluke of timing would be stupid. I've been called a lot of things in my life— selfish jerk, man child, musically obsessed—but not stupid.

I gobble down my breakfast. After Bo finishes, he runs upstairs to say goodbye to AnnMarie. Finn and I wait for him outside.

"You sure you want to buy this place?" Finn asks.

I fiddle with the cigarette I've tucked behind my ear. "Yup. Not ready to let go of it yet."

I don't have someone to make a new home with like Finn, Bo, and Noah have. This is my home, and I'm not ready to give it up.

"It's hard for me to let go, too," he admits with a wry smile. "We put a lot of time and effort into this place."

Finn and I bought this huge house several years ago when the real estate market crashed. Finn's dad was the builder, and when the market took a header, the buyer walked away. Finn talked his dad into letting us buy the five-bedroom glass-and-timber home, and Finn and I finished the interior by ourselves.

"I'll grant you visiting rights, but I'm taking full custody."

"Fair enough." He holds out his palm, which I slap.

"What're we making a deal about?" Bo asks, coming out of the house.

"I'm granting Finn visiting rights to the house."

"Shit, man, some of my best memories happened here in the house. I better get some visiting rights, too."

"Because you lost your virginity here?" I tease. Bo, a reformed player, likes to maintain that he never had another woman before AnnMarie.

"Damn straight." He throws open the door of his truck. "Climb in. Let's go do some reconnoitering."

The address on the printout leads us to a new development on the south end of town.

"You sure we have the right place?" Finn says.

The homes here are nice. Real nice. For some reason, I thought Marrow would be a dipshit hiding in a rundown apartment. Instead, his digs are as swank as mine.

"What's Marrow do for a living?" Bo asks.

"The asshole just got out of prison. I'm guessing nothing." A memory pops into my head.

"What revs your engine?"

"Code. I write code."

"Maybe he's into computers," I suggest.

"That might explain this."

This is a low-slung modern ranch. Like our house, this one has a lot of windows. In the driveway sits an orange Porsche Targa with a white racing stripe.

"I know that's a six-figure car, but how much do you think the crib set him back?" Bo wonders.

"Half a million, easy," Finn offers.

"So she has a stalker with a lot of money and more than a few brain cells. I'd be scared of shadows at my house, too," Bo says. He glances at me. "What do you want to do?"

"Go inside, drag the guy out by his hair, and hot glue his balls to his car's exhaust pipe?"

Bo grins widely. "I'm in for that."

"Mal probably has a better idea," Finn interjects. "Why don't we go home and see what else Mal can find out about him?"

"Party pooper," Bo grumps.

"I agree with both of you. That Finn sucks, but we should go home and check in with Mal." He can find out anything about anyone. People tell him shit. He's like a bartender, only he doesn't need booze to loosen tongues. You sit down with him and find your-self spilling secrets you wouldn't tell a priest. Don't know how it happens. It just does.

Finn pulls out into the street. Halfway down, I tap on his shoulder.

"Wait a sec. Pull over. I recognize that car."

Finn does as I ask, sliding to a stop. Across the street is a familiar silver Passat. The driver has his eyes glued straight ahead and doesn't even notice Finn's truck.

I hop out and knock on the Passat's window.

In the driver's seat, Davis jumps and curses. His hand fumbles for a button on the door, then the window rolls open. "What the hell are you doing here?" he demands.

"Probably the same thing as you." I jerk a thumb over my shoul-der. "This Marrow's place?"

"Yeah. How'd you know?" he asks with narrowed eyes.

"One of my roommates is an information junkie. He did some googling and figured it out. What do you know about Marrow?"

Davis scrapes a hand through his hair. For the first time I realize he's got red highlights. His sister's hair is darker and richer than his, but I'm starting to see the resemblance. "He was in college with her, a computer science major. They had some courses together, but they weren't friends. Landry swears she never said more than a couple words to him the entire time she was in college. And I believe her. Landry spends most of her time with her nose glued to her computer. She's oblivious to how guys see her."

My eyebrows shoot up. Girl is a total smoke show. How can she not notice the stares she gets? "How is that possible?"

"She was a late bloomer. No one paid attention to her in high school. She had some acne problems. Braces. She went to college, lived in the computer lab for four years, and graduated looking like she does now." He gives me a wry half smile. "It was a hell of a lot easier when she was this awkward teenager who guys mostly left alone."

And now she looks like a wet dream. Oval face, with that red hair and green-gold eyes. A tiny waist and a sweet set of tits that would rest perfectly in my palms. I don't envy Davis's position.

"So this guy asked her out and she turned him down?"

"No. He made up this whole fucking relationship in his head." He does the hand and hair thing again. "Landry and her friend, May, worked on this project all through college. A few months after they graduated, they finished it up and sold the code. I encouraged both of them to get a life. Landry started going out and...I guess it triggered him. She began dating and he felt like she was betraying him. He attacked her in her apartment one night." Davis drags a finger along the side of his cheek. "The mug broke and cut her. She still has a scar."

All my humor's gone, replaced by a boatload of guilt.

"It's not your fault, man," I try to reassure him.

He shakes his head. "I know that, but I still can't stop thinking about how I was the one who told her that she was wasting away in our parents' basement. That she should get out and have some fun." He turns a sad face in my direction. "I can't leave her behind."

My heart sinks, but I think I knew this was coming.

"Fuck. I get it." I stuff my hands in my pockets. If it were my sister, I couldn't leave her behind, either.

"Sorry, Adam. I wanted this. I really did."

"I know."

With a bleak look, he rolls up his window and drives away.

5

ADAM

"You think he'll go for it?" Finn asks.

I check my messages again. Nothing. I shove my phone into my back pocket.

"He was downing celebration shots faster than Rudd when I told them about the tour invite. He wants to go, but he can't leave his sister behind. I'm hoping that he'll look at the tour bus and be shocked and awed." I pick up the sledgehammer and whale it across the eighteen-year-old cabinets. They come down with a crash that's not as satisfying as I thought it'd be. What I'd really like to do is take the hammer to the side of the head of the asshole who hurt Landry Olsen.

"Can't they just report this yahoo to the police?" The sink goes out the door, followed by the fixtures and the basin of the old shower. "You sure it's not about his job?"

My initial fear about asking Davis to be part of FMK was that he was too much of a desk jockey to put in the practice time, but he surprised me by showing up every night we asked of him and offering every spare minute on the weekends. He's been as committed as

Rudd and Ian. Maybe even more than Ian, since the drummer has the new baby in his house.

"No, it's the family drama." I wouldn't leave sweet Landry alone, either. This idea of mine is inspired. For a few months I'll get Landry in close proximity to me, where I can wear down any resistance she might have, and I'll play with my band all over the country. It's the definition of a win-win.

"Maybe get a different singer? One without so much baggage." Finn staples a bunch of cords to the ceiling. We're renovating the entire bus, from the electrical and plumbing to the new leather seating areas and mahogany paneling.

"Nah, Davis is it."

"Oh, the old Adam Rees intuition." Finn points the side of the staple gun against his temple.

"I did tell you to ask your old man to buy this house," I remind him.

Finn cocks his head. "Fair," he concludes.

"And I suggested we invite Noah and Bo to be our roommates."

"True."

"And that you should break up with your psycho girlfriend, Ivy."

He raises his arms in surrender. "Okay, okay. You've got good gut instincts."

"My gut knows things." Like when a song I write is going to be a hit, when a singer has enough charisma to carry a band to the next level, or when you see the girl you're supposed to spend the rest of your life with. It also knows you don't sit on your ass and let those opportunities flow to someone else. "Besides, you've watched him. He's the real deal."

"Yeah, he's good, but the band will only go as far as you take it."

"And I'm taking this one all the way." I'll drag everyone else with me if I have to.

I'm hauling the last of the garbage out to the rented dumpster when Davis drives up in his Passat. Bought with his data-farming money, no doubt.

"What's all this?" the singer asks as he steps out of his car. He gestures toward the black bus.

"My dad's old bus. We're renoing it for the tour." I pull off my gloves and shove them in my back pocket. "Finn's probably got an extra pair of work gloves if you want to lend a hand."

Finn waves from inside the bus.

Davis's jaw drops a fraction, and I feel a surge of hope. Most small bands, particularly ones that play on the local level, use touring vans because a bus is a six-figure behemoth. The band members sleep on couches and floors belonging to wait staff, local bands, friends, friends of friends, or even in the van itself. That's what Davis thought he'd signed up for.

But most band members don't have world-famous rock musician fathers who happened to keep their old tour buses for sentimental purposes.

I do, and I'm willing to use every bit of leverage I can to achieve my goals, including bribing a singer with a luxe ride.

"We're touring on a bus?" He brushes by me to run up the stairs.

"Yeah. This is Bessie. Dad used it on his last tour in the States. He couldn't bring himself to get rid of it." I rub a hand across the new counter we're installing.

Davis does a sweep of the interior. There's a nook over the cab that the bus driver uses, a small galley kitchen and seating area, four bunks, and a bathroom. Beyond the bathroom is a U-shaped sectional that forms a king-sized bed. It's where my dad slept on the last tour because he and the other members of Death to Dusk weren't speaking to each other at that point. The bunks were used by Dad's manager, their merch guy, and a few groupies.

I lost my virginity to a groupie on a bus like this when I was fourteen. She fucked me to impress my dad. I probably participated for the same reason. I wanted to show my old man I was a grownup.

"Four bunks." Davis notes, dismay in his voice.

I hide a grin behind my hand. There's only one reason he'd be upset that the bus only holds four bunks, given that we only have four band members. "And a main bedroom in the back."

"Yeah?" He perks up. "For you?"

I shrug casually. This needs to be his idea. "Or anyone. I figured we'd rock, paper, scissors it."

"Hmmm." He nods. "This can work, I think."

"What can work?"

"My sister needs to come with."

"Yeah?" Again, I strive for a noncommittal tone.

"My parents are on the verge of divorce, and to save their marriage my dad retired this year and booked a three-month excursion around the world. Landry's best friend is riding ponies in China." He turns around, a fierce expression on his face. "I can't leave her behind. I swear, she's not making it up."

"Hey, never thought she was."

Davis sighs heavily. "We went to see the detective who put Marrow in jail the first time around, but she says that without any evidence, we can't charge him with squat. Detective Pressley sent out his parole officer to check up on him, and a couple junkie friends swore up and down that Marrow and them were playing video games all night."

"So the cops aren't going to do anything," I conclude.

He gives a grim shake of his head.

"Okay." I pause as if I'm mulling over the idea, when it's all I've been thinking about since I woke up this morning. "Then Landry should come with us."

"No way. She'll ruin it," Rudd predictably proclaims a few hours later.

I shoulder him aside as I carry in the flat screen that will go in the front of the bus. The new tile is down. The cabinets are up and now we're installing the finishing touches.

"It's not up for negotiation, Rudd," I tell him, dropping the television onto the bench seat.

"Unless she's a troll, we're going to hook up, but we all know I don't do relationships. When I'm done hitting that, she'll be angry every time I bring some other chick back to the bus."

The thought of Rudd sleeping with Landry makes me want to choke him, so I keep my mouth shut.

"Why would she want to fuck you?" Ian pulls the wires through the wall and threads them around the frame of the bracket that'll hold the TV.

"Why wouldn't she?"

"Because she has actual taste and doesn't want to get syphilis?"

"Those were warts, man," Rudd yells. "I've told you a million times, that's a genetic condition."

Ian and I exchange a smirk.

"Why can't he just go to jail?" Rudd whines.

I grab the screwdriver from the seat cushion and attach the anchor plate for the TV.

"He was in jail," I reply. "He served three months of an eighteen-month sentence." When Davis told me all the gritty details, I wanted to string this Marrow guy up—not just because he was messing with my plans, but because it wasn't right that the dude only served a fraction of his sentence. What was the frigging point?

"But if he screwed up again, can't he just go back?"

"They don't have any solid evidence that he was there, and he's got douchebag friends backing up a fake alibi."

"How do we know it was fake?" Rudd asks with an arch of his eyebrow.

I twist the last screw in and toss the screwdriver onto the counter. "Davis believes his sister, and I believe Davis. You got a problem with that, take it up with him. I know it's not ideal, but we've got the space here."

"Where's she gonna sleep?" he demands.

"In the back."

"The big space? Thought you would take that."

I hoist the screen and fit it onto the wall anchors while Rudd sips on his beer. He's the laziest son of a bitch. "Like I said, we've got the room."

"What's she going to do on the road? Make us sandwiches?"

Davis appears at the door. "You guys talking about Landry?"

Rudd scowls. "Yeah, man. I don't like it. Women only mess bands up."

"Ian's married," Davis points out.

"So? Ian's wife isn't coming on the road with us." Rudd's growing belligerent, and Davis's face is getting red.

"She's only coming for two months," Davis tells our bassist.

"Two?" I ask, feeling strangely disappointed. "The tour's for five."

"My parents will be back in two."

That changes my timeline a bit but will help to appease Rudd, I hope. "It's two months. Learn to love it. Davis is our lead singer. He wants his sister to come. End of story," I say tersely. To Davis, I ask, "What can your sister do? We don't need someone to run the merch tables. Hollister is going to handle that." He's also taking a ten percent cut, but if the tour is as profitable as he thinks it's going to be, then his manager fee will be well worth it.

Davis shrugs. "What do you want her to do?"

"I've got some ideas," Rudd says slyly.

Davis stiffens. "She's off-limits. No one here touches her."

I don't immediately stake my claim. I haven't figured out how to break it to him that his sister and I are going to be a thing. He's understandably protective of her, and during the short time he's played with the band, he's likely developed a few misconceptions about my attitude toward relationships.

Davis clears his throat.

Ian raises both hands, palms up. "I'm married, dude."

Rudd petulantly crosses his arms. "What? All I'm saying is if we're going to have a single, attractive female on the tour with us, she might as well sleep with me."

Davis scowls. "She can clean, get the food, do whatever it is that needs to be done. Take care of the books, track the per diem, that sort of shit."

Rudd looks like he wants to protest, which Davis won't like, and soon the two of them will be rolling around on the new flooring. That's not the best way to build band camaraderie. Besides, they'll both find out soon enough that the only guy who'll be sleeping with Landry is me.

I clap my hands together. "Great. Now that that's solved, let's get the rest of this shit on the bus and get ready to go. We've got a tour date to make."

Mention of the tour predictably cheers everyone up. Everyone but Davis, that is. Ian and Rudd tumble off the bus to help Finn carry in the rest of the gear. Davis lingers behind.

"Need something?" I ask, trying for a light tone even though part of me wants to bust Davis's chops for making this more difficult than it should be.

"You need to keep Rudd away from Landry. She's had enough to deal with. I don't want some poon hound sniffing around her twenty-four seven."

"Rudd will keep his hands to himself."

"He better," Davis says darkly. "Because anyone touches her and I'm gone."

"She's a grown woman. Let her make her own decisions."

Davis grabs my arm. "Adam, I really need you to help me on this. She's vulnerable. It makes no sense for me to bring her on this tour to keep her away from Marrow if all I'm doing is exposing her to a different kind of danger."

"Maybe she falls for one of the guys on tour and they live happily ever after," I suggest.

He snorts. "Pigs will fly before then. We both know that bands are mostly made up of horny shits who will sleep with anyone who offers herself up. I'm no choirboy and neither are you. That's not what I want for Landry. She's my sister."

"I think you need to let her make up her own mind." How protective is he?

His jaw hardens. He releases me and straightens. "If you won't help me, then I'm not going."

My jaw drops. "Are you kidding me?"

"No. Promise me that you'll make sure no one touches her while she's on tour."

I scrape a hand across my chin. I can't make this promise because I have all kinds of plans to touch her.

"Adam?" he presses.

"I'll back you on this unless she pursues someone. I'm not going to babysit a twenty-four-year-old woman."

After a fraught minute of silence, Davis gives an abrupt nod. "Fair enough."

Then we shake on it, which means I've given my word not to seduce the one woman I can't get out of my head.

Perfect. Just fucking perfect.

6

ADAM

A week later, all the reno is done and we're ready to roll out. Ian and Rudd are playing with Ian's new baby when Hollister shows up with a bunch of paperwork. Davis and his sister haven't arrived yet. I hope that doesn't mean they're backing out.

"Sweet wheels, man. This your dad's?" Hollister jerks his head toward the bus.

"Yeah. From *The Crows* tour." Dad's last album was an homage to Hitchcock. The cover was a bunch of black crows, and the band's stage costumes had more feathers than a pillow factory. We were finding feathers in shit months later.

My stage costume is a version of what I'm wearing now—jeans, T-shirt, boots. I shake my head ruefully. Music in the 80s and 90s was a lot different for bands than it is now. We can't all be Daft Punk and wear helmets nonstop, although I think Ian would love that.

He breaks the crazy drummer mold. He can bang the rack with the best of them, but partying isn't his scene. He's got a few deviant tastes—ones that he shares with his wife, though. Voyeurism doesn't make much sense to me. I like doing, not watching. And exhibitionism gets old after a while.

I grew up watching people fuck. I'm too jaded to be titillated by that shit. But Ian and Berry are big fans of it and that's how their marriage works. Given that they've been tied together since high school, I can't judge it.

"Mind if I go in?" Hollister asks with bright eyes, handing me a sheaf of papers.

I nod, scanning the info sheet. Our first stop is Kansas City. They have amazing barbecue and the crowds aren't half bad. It's a bigger city, so the bar will attract a variety of folks, not just college students.

As Hollister pokes his head inside, I call out a warning in case he's hoping to catch a glimpse of how Dad traveled years ago. "We renovated it. There isn't much of anything original left in there."

He doesn't appear to care. The interior turned out great. It helps that Finn builds for a living. He could probably construct a bus from the wheels up. I doubt that any of the bands are going to have digs as nice as ours. The downside is that everyone and their fucking cousins will want to party in our bus every damn night.

By the time we make it out of Kansas, the place will be trashed. I wonder what Landry will make of the bus, the partying, the whole degenerate scene. Some girls are really caught up in it. Even for the no-name bands, there are folks—mostly female—who will do just about anything for a guy with a guitar.

I didn't get the sense that was Landry. Our short encounter felt more personal...or I could be spinning fantasies out of nothing. *No,* I shake my head. Girls have pursued me all my life—mostly because I play a guitar and have a fat wallet. There was no materialistic vibe coming from her. It was lust. One that I returned in full.

This morning, I woke up with my hand around my dick and the image of a naked, trembling Landry grinding down on my face. And my hand is the only thing that's going to be around my dick for a long while unless I can persuade both Davis and Landry to my way of thinking.

Like I told Ian, Davis is the key to FMK's success. Bands have broken up over smaller things than one bandmate screwing the wrong woman.

Hollister reappears. "Nice digs," he says, coming over to join me. "You're lucky because Threat Alert's new label is springing for a tour bus, too. If yours had been the only one on the tour, every sucker would be squatting in here. Still, TA's bus is half the size, so I suspect yours will be party central. Make sure you get rid of all the weed and shit before you get on."

"I know the drill." Bands are a magnet for police. They get an instant hard-on seeing us motor down the road and can't wait to pull us over. Drug use is acceptable only at the venues, not while the wheels are turning. "Nice locations you've got here." I jiggle the sheet. There's a surprising number of untraditional venues designed to hold a couple thousand rather than the bars that max out at a few hundred. Hollister has come through.

He grins. "We do well for the first two months, I can see extending this into the summer. Maybe Europe."

My eyes snag on a weird detail under a number of the clubs. As with most tour itineraries, this one has the dates, location details, and check-in times, but several have the name of a female in bold lettering. The music scene is still a sausage fest, so this is a surprising number of female promoters.

"Who are these?" I point to the first name: Anna Cairns.

"The promoters' girlfriends. Don't touch them." He pins me with an accusing stare.

"Dude, that was years ago, and I had no idea who she was."

"You should've."

I grind the back of my teeth together. Not because Hollister is wrong, but because he's absolutely right. Fucking the promoter's woman is a huge no-no. Sometimes fucking their ex is just as bad. I learned this lesson the hard way.

When I was twenty-one, I had a band made up of guys from college. We did a small regional tour with bars no bigger than the one we played the night Landry walked in. On an extended Chicago stay, I hooked up with a Mrs. Robinson-type—a thirty-something yoga instructor who could fold her body in half like Gumby.

The next afternoon, I showed up for the gig and was told to go home. We were booted off the rest of the tour because Mrs. Robinson was the promoter's longtime girlfriend, and he'd planned on asking her to marry him. Worse, he told all his buddies, and I ended up blacklisted from the Chicago music scene for years.

Turns out that my old man had dicked over a friend of this guy, and the two of them decided to repay a decade-old grievance by freezing me out. Since I didn't have the same star power as my dad, I couldn't flex any muscle. The band folded soon after.

I'm fairly certain that is part of what's driving Davis's fear for his sister. Sex can ruin a good thing fast.

"Yeah, I know. Look, I'm not new to this. We're not going to tote around drugs on the bus, and we're not going to screw any ladies who the promoters have their eyes on." I tear off the bottom corner of the itinerary. "Got a pen?" I ask.

He produces one from his shirt pocket.

"Speaking of off-limits ladies, put this on your list." I scribble Landry's name on the list. I know I can't fuck her right now, but that doesn't mean anyone else should be either. For Davis's sake.

Hollister takes my slip of paper. "Landry Olsen? Who the hell is she?"

"Davis's sister." I return to the bus. My phone's here, and I want to see where the hell the Olsens are.

Hollister's hot on my heels. "You're bringing your front man's sister on tour with you?" He begins shaking his head. "No. No. No. No."

"You sound like Rudd." I duck inside and check my messages. There're two from Davis.

We're running late.

And then fifteen minutes later.

JFC she's trying to bring the entire house.

Hollister's not done. He follows me, complaints still spilling out. "Jesus. I can't believe I'm agreeing with Rudd of all people. You know what the rules are. No one who's not part of the band goes on tour with you."

"My band. My bus. My rules."

He snatches the paper back from me. "Five bands. Five bands—twenty-some horny guys—and one chick? This is a recipe for disaster. Please tell me she's ugly."

I run my tongue across my teeth thinking about the perfection of her tight body and how likely it is that I'm going to plant my fist in someone's face for looking at her wrong. The probability is high.

"Guys will have to learn a little self-control. It builds character."

Hollister's not amused. "It only takes two of you wrestling over her like a bone for this whole thing to go into the shitter."

"You disinviting us?"

He glances over at Ian and Rudd, who are playing with Ian's three-month-old kid, then back to me. We both know he's not doing that. Part of the reason we're being invited, despite only being together for a few months, is because I'm Sydney Rees's son. The name still carries weight with promoters. I'd bet my left nut that we wouldn't have gotten some of these venues if the Rees name weren't on the press kit.

Right as Hollister opens his mouth, Davis's Passat rolls down the long driveway. Everyone stops what they're doing to watch Davis and his sister exit the car. Okay, to be fair, we only care about Landry. Everyone here knows Davis. Landry's the mystery.

Out of the corner of my eye, I see Hollister's jaw drop open. He sighs in defeat, slapping the crumpled tour list against my chest. "She's your problem. Don't screw up."

Rudd races over, beaming. "I'm in love. Seriously, madly, deeply in love. I take back everything I said about Davis's sister not being welcome on the bus. She's so welcome, I'm going to let her sleep in my bunk."

"And where are you sleeping?" Ian mocks.

"In the same bunk, of course. Hollister, man, you're welcome to crash in the extra space," Rudd says generously. "Just don't open my curtain. We'll be busy inside."

The promoter glares at him, but Rudd's already moving off, down to introduce himself to Landry.

"Hey, beautiful. Let me carry that for you." He rips the bag off her shoulder and practically knocks Davis down in an effort to grab Landry's other bag.

"This going to be a problem?" Ian murmurs in my ear. I reach over to grab the little one, propping Jack against my shoulder.

"Depends on her response. If she shuts him down, then no. If they end up sleeping together, then yeah. It'll be a big fucking problem."

7

LANDRY

M ay gave me three rules for this trip.

1. Do not sleep with any guy who plays an instrument.
2. Suck up to the bandmates.
3. Be open to new experiences.

I told her that these rules sort of contradict each other, but she waved the snake head at me until I capitulated. She was right, though. Screwing around with a guy I'll have to see every day for the next two months is a disaster waiting to happen. I'd catch feelings when all he wanted was sex.

Case in point, my brother. I love him and he's a genuinely decent guy, but he could sleep with a dozen girls in the span of a week and not care one iota about them. Whereas I sleep with one guy and think we're going to get married.

That's what happened when I was in college. I did have one hookup after college, but then Marrow happened so who knows. Maybe I am capable of emotional-free sex, but I'm not counting on it.

It's probably best that I keep my attraction to Adam under wraps so I don't spend the next two months miserable as he samples the female population from here to California.

"The bus looks nice," I chirp. Nice is an understatement. This thing looks like it could be on the front cover of some magazine, if there are magazines about buses. It's all shiny lacquered wood and black leather. Tiny lights on the floor form a pathway down the center.

Davis unpacks a grocery bag of stuff I bought last night. At the bottom, he finds a pan of brownies, which he hands to Rudd. "Pot brownies, Landry? Really?"

"I'm trying to suck up," I protest. Pot's the one thing I don't wouldn't mind if Davis took up. I mean, if he has to have a bad habit why not that one?

Rudd sniffs the brownies. "Too bad we can't eat this."

"Why not?"

He takes the pan and sets it outside. "We can't have pot on the bus. Cops are always pulling these things over for one bullshit excuse or another."

I grimace. "Oh crap. I didn't know. I'm sorry."

"Yeah, I know. Just...don't try so hard." Davis pats me awkwardly on the head.

I bat his hand away. "Got it."

His face softens, probably sensing my anxiety at this whole situation. "Come on. I'll show you the rest of the joint."

He drags me down the hallway pointing out all the features. Right behind the driver's cab is a long black leather sofa. Across is another small seating area comprised of a table and a cushioned bench on either side. I presume that the table lowers and the whole thing becomes a bed. I could sleep on either the sofa or this contraption.

A press of a button and a door swishes open. Four bunks, stacked two by two, are next.

"This is like a spaceship," I marvel. "Is it hydraulics?"

"Who knows?" Davis shrugs. He doesn't care how the sausage is made, only that there's meat on his plate. "Here are the bunks." He waves a finger to either side of the bus. Each bunk has a small screen folded against the ceiling of the bunk and a short, stiff black curtain that pulls closed, giving each occupant some semblance of privacy. "This is where the band sleeps."

We stop at another door with another push button entrance. To the left is a small hallway and a door.

"Bathroom with a shower." I catch a glimpse of more black and stainless steel. "Door." He gestures to the exit door across from the shower. "Back here is the lounge, I guess." It's a U-shaped seating arrangement. He kicks his foot against the base and an empty drawer pops open. "You can put your stuff here."

"Where am I sleeping?" I drop my shoulder bag that I've rescued from his bandmate, Rudd.

"Back here." He taps a silver switch recessed into the side of a cabinet. "Press this and the couches will fold out. There are sheets and pillows in the cabinets above."

Crap. The biggest bed? The most sequestered space and it goes to me? This set up isn't going to endear me to the band. Instead the guys will think I'm a spoiled princess, always needing the best.

"Wait. I can't sleep back here," I protest. "This is the biggest room. Give me a bunk. Or the sofa in the front. Heck, I'll sleep on the floor. Please." When he doesn't immediately shut me down, I know he's wavering. I press harder. "Seriously. If I'm going to spend eight weeks with you guys, treat me like one of the guys."

"I don't know." Davis runs his hand through his hair—an action he does when he's uncertain or frustrated. "This is Rees's gig, and he said you should be back here."

I suck in my lower lip. I hate seeing Davis in any mood other than serene. In the past, the ruffling of his hair was the precursor to more troubling behavior. "Was there something I said"—*or you said?* I think —"that made him believe I needed this?"

Davis looks everywhere but at me, his guilt on clear display.

I press my palms together, prayer-like. "Davis, you need to get along with these guys and so do I. If this is Rees's gig, as you say, then he should have this room. I'll take whatever bunk the rest of your band doesn't want."

"Fine. I'll go get Rees." Davis stalks off.

I glance around the room again. Is eating snakes really that bad?

Adam appears a minute later. His handsome face looks as angry as it did the other night. "Is there a problem?"

I open my mouth to deliver a firm rebuttal of his plans when my ovaries melt and my knees go weak. Since I'm finally wearing my glasses, every inch of his beautiful frame comes through with perfect clarity. I place a hand against the back of the sofa so I don't fall over. His big tattooed arms, made strong from all the practice he does, are holding a tiny baby clad in a sunshine-yellow onesie with the words "shit happens" lettered on the back. The forearms flex as he pats one long-fingered, talented hand along the baby's back.

Those wonderful fingers. They could soothe me anytime. My core tightens. I'm so going to hell for entertaining dirty thoughts while in the presence of a baby! *Get your act together*, I sternly order myself.

"Is he yours?" I manage to squeak. I'm torn between utter enchantment at seeing him so tenderly hold the baby and dismay that he's taken. But why wouldn't he be taken? He's so damn gorgeous and so damn talented that it'd be crazier if he were single.

Do not sleep with a musician, May chastises me in my head.

"No, this little guy is Ian's. What's the problem here?"

"It's too good for me," I explain, battling back a wave of unnecessary relief that Adam isn't taken. "I don't need this. I'll sleep in the top bunk over Davis and you or Ian or Rudd can sleep in here."

"Is that right?" Adam looks over his shoulder to my brother.

Davis shrugs. "I don't care where she sleeps."

Adam turns back to me. "You're sleeping back here, not because I think you're some precious piece of porcelain that needs to be coddled. You're back here so the boys can fuck who they want, when they want, without having to worry that you're going to judge them. Now if you want to sit in front and watch because that's what gets you off, then be my guest. Otherwise, you'll sleep here."

Okay, then. "I'll sleep in here," I concede, a blush creeping across my cheeks. "Thank you. I'll just pay a greater portion of the rent then."

"Rent?" Adam sounds confused.

Davis props his forearm against the wall and leans his head against it, as if I'm so wearying that he can't stand upright. "She wants to pay her own way and she wants a job."

"I'm right here." I wave my hand. "But, yes, I'm not going to be a leech. I'm paying my own way. Food, gas, shelter. The whole shebang."

I pull out my wallet. I made Davis stop at the bank before we came, so I have plenty of cash. But instead of taking my money, Adam's frowning.

"No. You'll get a per diem like the rest of us. The money that comes in will go toward the gas and paying the driver."

"Please. I insist."

"Trust me," Davis interjects. "She can afford it. And if you don't take the money from her, she'll hassle you every spare minute of the day."

That garners a raised eyebrow from Adam.

I clear my throat. "In college, a friend and I wrote an app and we sold it for a good amount."

By now, the entire band has crowded into the small hallway outside of this back room.

"What app?"

"Peep," Davis supplies.

"Peep?" Rudd exclaims from behind my brother. "I was on tour last year with Domestica and used that app every day. It's the only way I survived that fucking snoozefest. You made that?"

"Me and my best friend May wrote it together," I admit.

"Two girls while you were in college?" says Rudd. He sounds astounded, although I'm not sure what's more surprising—that it was two women who wrote code, or that we did it in college.

"Peep? Isn't that a porn site?" Ian asks.

My cheeks heat up. "We didn't develop it for that purpose. But, yeah, I think it's mostly used for amateur porn these days." The code itself is licensed to a number of different companies, but the app was sold off to a media corporation that later turned around and sold it to an adult film company. Which is why I only ever say that May and I wrote an app, not the specific one we wrote.

"Best app ever." Rudd muscles by Davis to throw an arm around my shoulder. "Goddamn. I would've taken more computer science classes if I knew chicks like you were there."

"Well, that's where we were hiding out," I concede.

"You share anything on it? Maybe I've seen your work." He waggles his eyebrows.

"Nope. I'm more of a behind-the-scenes kind of gal." Show my naked body to strangers? I'd rather be shot and quartered.

"You could make a fortune if you had your own channel. I would totally sign up for that."

"Rudd," Adam says sharply.

"What?" He blinks innocently. "I'm trying to get to know our newest bandmate."

Someone growls, which makes Rudd laugh.

"It's fine. It's all fine." I pat Rudd awkwardly on the back and set a few boundaries. "Rudd and I are going to be BFFs. Right?"

"Abso-fucking-lutely. At night, we can throw slumber parties back here and rub each other's"—another deep growl rumbles and this time I pinpoint the source as Adam—"feet," Rudd finishes with a smirk.

"I thought our friendship would be more of a mental connection. Like a metaphysical one. It'll be meaningful and longer lasting than any physical relationship," I say airily.

"Bummer," Rudd says, but his eyes are twinkling in a way that lets me know he doesn't mind that I'm not falling into his bed.

"We good here?" Davis jiggles the keys in his pocket impatiently. He's done with all the introductions and wants to be on the road. He was like a kid at Christmas this morning, shouting to see if I was ready every five minutes. "Because I want to get the rest of my gear."

"I'm great. After all, I get to sleep back here while you all get the tiny, tiny bunks."

Before anyone can give me a smart-ass rejoinder, a feminine voice hails us from the front of the bus.

"I'm back, baby. Got the medicine."

Ian swivels around. "Hey, babe."

"That's Ian's baby momma. Berry. As in strawberry," Rudd explains. "Ian has asthma and Berry wanted him to take an extra dosage along."

The rest of the band files down the hallway toward the newcomer. Berry's a stunner. Dark hair, dark eyes, and a huge smile. For a woman who just had a baby, she looks surprisingly chic in her navy-and-white striped top and navy capris.

"Is Strawberry her name?" I ask.

"Naw. It's Beryl. Family name, I guess. Weird as fuck, don't you think?"

"I like it." We women need to stick together. "It's unusual. Is she coming on the tour with us?" It would be awesome to have another woman traveling with us. Plus, I'm itching to get my hands on the baby that's still snuggled against Adam's chest. Or was. Berry pulls the baby from Adam's reluctant grasp. The baby voices a protest, whimpering as he's transferred to his momma.

I can sympathize. I wouldn't want to move from Adam's arms, either.

"Hey, I was holding him," he objects.

My ovaries clench again. Why is a man with a baby so damn sexy?

"Is it the baby or Adam?" Rudd asks softly.

I jerk back. "What? I...what?"

He winks at me. "You sighed."

"I did not."

"You did. You sighed like a girl at her first concert."

"It was the baby," I proclaim. Inwardly, I cringe. I've got to do a better job of hiding my rapidly developing crush.

Rudd chuckles. "It's alright. I'm not going to tell anyone. We're besties, so your secret's safe with me."

"It's the baby," I repeat.

"You keep telling yourself that." He draws away. "Berry, come and meet our new bandmate. This is Landry."

Grateful for the interruption, I smile at the dark-haired woman. "Hi, Berry. Your baby is so adorable."

She shifts her tiny son to the side before reaching out and grasping my hand. "Jack? I know. He's a peanut. So how do you feel about traveling with these jokers?"

"I'm sure it's going to be awesome."

She busts out laughing, which causes Jack to cry a little harder. "Girl, let's go to the back so you don't choke on all the lies you feel obligated to say in front of them."

Before I can blink, Berry brushes by a protesting Ian and grabs my arm, hauling me toward the back room we just abandoned.

"Isn't this thing amazing?" she raves. "Finn and Adam did such a great job fixing it up. Before, it was a rotted dump. I swear you could still smell the vomit and shit from the last time Adam's dad took it out on the road."

"Adam redid it himself?" Obviously, he's a man of many talents, particularly talents with his hands. That thought leads to another, naughtier one, and suddenly it's very warm in the back of the bus.

"Yup. Him and Finn. You know Finn?" The baby starts fussing loudly. Berry plops down on the edge of the sofa and pulls her shirt down. "You don't mind, do you?"

"Nope. Feed away."

She gives me a small smile of appreciation and proceeds to expertly flip her breast out and into little Jack's mouth. He immediately clasps his lips around the nipple and starts to suckle. I take a seat opposite of her. The black leather feels soft as butter under my hand.

"Finn O'Malley runs the O'Malley Construction company with his uncle," Berry explains.

"Oh wow. I've seen their signs around." Everywhere from construction at the Capitol to big projects in the suburbs.

"Right. So Adam and Finn are old friends. Since grade school. I think they ate sand from the sandbox or something. Anyway, the two of them bought the house over there." She jerks her head in the general direction of the timber and glass structure just beyond the bus. "And they live there with a couple other guys who go to Central. Or maybe they're done with Central." Central's the fancy private college in town. Berry continues, "I don't really know. When Adam got the invite for the tour, he told Ian that they were going to take the bus. Ian, as you can guess, is thrilled."

"These are nice digs," I admit. "You coming with us? I bet Ian would be so happy if you were here and I'd love another woman. Look at all the room we'd have." I wave a hand around the space. "You, me, and Jack. It'd be perfect."

She laughs. "You've never had a kid, have you?"

I shake my head. "No. Never."

"I can tell. A newborn is like a bus full of these guys at their drunkest. Impossible to control and incredibly loud until you give them the tit."

I grimace. "Do you have any other coping techniques? Because I'm not down with the whole giving-them-the-tit thing."

"They're pretty much giant kids. Ignoring Ian works. He hates the silent treatment. Rudd needs constant attention, and Adam, it depends on his mood." Berry doesn't give me a chance to ask what she means by that. "I'm moving back in with my mom and dad while Ian's gone. I have plenty of support, and this is Ian's big chance. Besides, being on a tour is terrible. I rode with Ian for two weeks during a summer break between our junior and senior year of college. It was miserable. Of course, we were in a twelve-seater van instead of a bus like this one, but the stench." She shudders. "I couldn't do it again. 'Course, it sounds like you don't have a choice."

"Ian told you about my stalker?" I shift uncomfortably in my seat. I hate that's the only thing some people will know about me. Oh, there's Landry Olsen. The girl with the stalker.

"Only that you had one and that Davis didn't want to leave you behind, which Ian totally understands." She eyes me speculatively. "Old boyfriend?"

I sigh and rub a finger where the bruise once was. The cut is scabbing over and I have to force myself not to scratch. Revisiting Marrow's attack is more embarrassing than painful. "I wish, because then it might be a little understandable, but no. Just another student who built up a grand romance in his head. When I didn't acknowledge him and started dating someone, he felt..." I push up my glasses and struggle to find the right word. "Betrayed? Hurt? I don't even know. Anyway, my therapist said that his focus on me wasn't about me, but what I represented."

"That sucks. You'll be safe here. I can't imagine that with all these guys around, he'd try anything."

I hope that's true, but my stalker doesn't think like a rational person. In fact, if he finds out I went off with a bunch of guys, it'd probably set him off. Hopefully he doesn't find out. Pressleytold me she asked Marrow's parole officer to check up on him and give him a little reminder about the terms of his early release.

"Honestly? I'd be so much happier if there was another woman on board. You sure you don't want to hang around? Even for the first week or so?"

"You'll be fine." She hesitates, running a hand down little Jack's body. "Can I give you a piece of advice, though?"

"Absolutely."

"My number one piece of advice is to not catch feelings for Adam. I know it's going to be hard because he's hot as sin and as sweet as candy, but he's not even close to settling down."

"No warnings about Rudd?" I joke.

She gives me a knowing look but doesn't call me on my obvious bullshit. "Rudd's harmless. Adam, on the other hand, would cause a nun to sin. Put him onstage with a guitar and it's impossible not to be turned on. Oh, I can see that you're a little confused since I'm married to Ian. Ian and I have been together since we were sixteen. Can you believe it?"

"No. I can't even remember half the guys I went to high school with."

Jack pops off the boob and without even looking, Berry switches her baby from one side to the other. Jack latches on immediately and

Berry continues talking. "Ian's my one true love and this little guy makes us even closer, but I've got eyes and a working vagina. Adam's got star power or charisma. Whatever *it* is, he has it. That's why Ian's been playing with Adam for the last five years. One of these days, Adam's going to catch fire and Ian wants to ride along."

"Ian's a great musician," I say, although I don't know what makes a good drummer versus a bad drummer, but Adam sounds like he's very particular so Ian must be good.

She waves a hand. "Of course he is. And he's ambitious. But he doesn't write lyrics or compose music. And while he's crazy—all drummers are—he's also shy. He prefers sitting behind the wall of drums and cymbals. Adam's different. You know the difference because Davis is your brother."

She's right. Both Adam and Davis have some quality that draws the eye. "I'll be careful," I promise. I bring up another subject that has me worried. "What about drugs?"

"What about them?"

"In Davis's old band scene, there was a lot of hardcore use. Not weed, but other stuff." I study my nails, as if this isn't important to me.

"What's music without coke?" Berry jiggles Jack lightly. "It's there. Just like it always is when you get a bunch of people together late at night who want to do nothing more than play music and party. The guys here aren't into it, because that's a quick way to ruin your career. But there'll be plenty of temptations on tour."

"As there are everywhere," I grimace.

She gives Jack another pat. "Yup. The other piece of advice I have is to stay the hell away from Hollister."

"I don't know him," I admit.

"He's the promoter slash manager who set up this whole tour." Jack finishes gnawing at Berry's poor boob. She swiftly tucks everything away and flips the baby onto her lap. "Grab me a towel, will ya?"

I reach inside the small bag she threw onto the table and pull out a Winnie the Pooh printed towel, which she places on her lap. Turning the baby to face me, she performs a strange series of pats and thumbs against the baby's back. Jack's tiny mouth opens and he gives the cutest burp.

"Hollister hates it when the guys hook up. He thinks that the relationship drama fucks up the chemistry of the band. All the boys should be focused on one thing—music. If there's a distraction, then the entire band isn't firing on all cylinders. Women—or guys, depending on the band member—belong in the category of booze and drugs. To be done recreationally but not so much that it interferes with the music."

I stare in fascinated horror. "What about female bands?"

"Hollister doesn't like them and actively avoids booking bands with women. He's a total misogynist. If anything goes wrong on tour, it'll be your fault. Stay as far under the radar as possible."

"He sounds like a real prince. Anything else I should know about? Things to watch out for?" I try to hint at whether she wants me to report back to her any shenanigans involving Ian.

"You mean, do I want you to make sure that Ian doesn't stray?" Her dark eyebrows arch over pretty brown eyes.

So much for delicate hints. "Not that I think he would, but would you want to know?"

"If I don't trust him, I shouldn't be with him. I should definitely not be having babies with him. The music scene is tiny and everyone's a huge gossip. I guess that's a third piece of advice. If you hook up with someone, everyone on the scene will know about it. Some guys have bigger mouths than others. Just keep your ear to the ground. You'll know which ones are which. Call me if you need anything. I have years of dealing with these guys. Keep them preoccupied. Remember, they're like children."

"So give them someone else's tit?" I joke.

"That's the spirit," she encourages.

As she packs up Jack's paraphernalia, I want to ask her to sit down and tell me more about Adam. Where does he fall? In the loudmouth category? Is he a manwhore like Davis?

I don't ask any of these questions, though, because that would violate rule number one.

Don't catch feelings for Adam Rees.

8

LANDRY

On the Road

The band's been brainstorming their set list. Adam and Davis have their guitars out and they've been playing on and off for the better part of the trip so far. They didn't exactly kick me out but they weren't welcoming, either. So I came up front to sit with the bus driver, Ed, who gave me a dirty look when I attempted to move stuff off the passenger seat.

I abandoned that idea, sat my ass down at the little banquette behind the driver, and pulled out my laptop. While May's been traveling around the world, I've been noodling around with a small bit of code to develop a ride share app for women. Since it's not something I'm passionate about, it's hard to stay interested.

What intrigues me is about thirty feet away. I thought the bus would seem claustrophobic, but instead it's too long. There's too much space between me and Adam Rees. Oh yeah, I shouldn't think that way since I'm not supposed to fall for him, but...it's been so long since I've felt even a flutter of attraction that I can't help wanting to fan it.

Marrow's stalking did a number on me, scarring me mentally and making me wary of all penis owners. A boatload of therapy has helped, but I haven't met anyone who moved me. I guess it's not surprising that a guy who Berry said could tempt a nun to sin is the one who catches my eye.

My therapist would probably say that's because he's unattainable and therefore a safe focus for my crush. He's not going to like me back, let alone develop an unhealthy obsession for me.

Sooooo...crushing on him isn't a bad thing, right? It's the opposite, really. I won't take it to the next level. I'll keep it to myself and enjoy the flutters in my stomach and the way that his presence makes me both hot and cold. And maybe at night, when the band is bedded down for the night, I can play out a few fantasies. That wouldn't hurt anyone.

As long as I keep it to myself, my little secret won't have any effect on Davis.

"What's the smile for?"

I jerk up my head to see Adam leaning against the small kitchen counter. A smile lurks at the corners of his mouth. My heart rate speeds up and my face grows hot. He definitely notices the latter, because the smile gets broader.

Stupid pale skin. Every bit of awkwardness I experience is broadcast across my stupid face.

"Nothing." I try for nonchalant and gesture toward the screen. "Just a piece of code."

He saunters over. "Must be an interesting set of commands you're writing if it gets you this worked up." He reaches out and tucks a bit of my hair behind my ear.

If possible, I blush even harder. My heart is thumping so loud, he must be able to hear it. "Um, what can I say?" I stammer awkwardly. "Code turns me on." Oh God. Code turns me on? *This* is my idea of flirting?

He rubs a few strands of my hair between his fingers before

letting it fall back to my shoulder. "I get it. You're passionate about your work. I get lost in my work, too."

He's so close to me that his hip is rubbing against my shoulder. If I turned my head, I could probably lick his zipper. It takes so much effort not to turn my head. So. Much. Effort.

This never happens to me. I'm a computer geek—I don't go around fantasizing about licking a guy's zipper. This attraction to Adam is starting to freak me out. It hasn't abated at all since the night at the bar.

"Uh huh," is all I can manage as I blindly stare at the computer screen. Since I don't trust myself not to touch him, I pin my hands under my thighs.

There's a moment of silence, then I swear I hear a small sigh before he backs away. "I came out to tell you we're stopping in about fifteen minutes at a gas station. It's a big one and has a restaurant, bathrooms. Take your time. We aren't playing until tomorrow."

I give a small nod, unsure what to say.

There's another beat of silence before he moves off. I wait until I hear the swoosh of the door, a sound I missed when he first came in, before pulling my hands out from under my legs.

I should've spent more time in clubs than in the computer lab.

WE PULL into the gas station minutes later. I shut the laptop and nearly break a nail trying to open the door before I realize there's a fancy button that releases the latch. Davis and the boys spill out of the second door across from the bathroom.

Adam doesn't spare me a glance, but Ian and Rudd wave in my direction, and Davis walks over to check on me.

"How's it going?" he asks.

"It's going." I don't want to complain, especially since we're only three hours into our first day of a two-month road trip. "I'm going to need to do some running in the mornings or whenever it is that we stop. I can feel my butt getting bigger as every mile passes."

We walk toward the entrance of the gas station. Davis says, "The guys were telling me that you sleep whenever you're able, shit in every can that's not attached to the bus, and try and eat some decent food from time to time."

"Maybe I could learn to cook," I suggest.

Davis rears back in horror. "Nah, let's order out."

"Come on. I'm not that bad."

He continues to stare at me in disbelief.

"Fine." I roll my eyes. "I'll keep my dirty hands off the camp stove."

"Good. You can come to the back and listen to us jam."

I make a face. "I don't think Adam wants me back there."

"Let me ask."

He moves to open the door, but I grab his arm. "No. It's fine. Really, I'm completely fine." I don't want Adam to think I'm some spoiled brat who is forcing myself on them.

"There's no reason you can't hang with us in the back," Davis insists.

He has that look in his eye that says he's not changing his mind. It's the one that he had when he threatened to leave the band unless I came on tour with them.

"Fine. Do what you want." I drop his arm.

After I use the bathroom, I wander around the store. It has everything from a snack aisle to an open cooler selling specialty meats and cheeses. There's a whole wine section in the back. Is this what truckers do? Eat brie and crackers and wash down the whole thing with a glass of red wine? I buy a bottle of water and a snack pack before moseying over to Rudd, who's staring at a menu board with a serious expression on his face.

"Want something?" I ask.

"Yeah, but I haven't decided. Hey, Ian. Want to split a pizza?" he calls over his shoulder.

"Sure. No black olives, though," Ian yells from the other side of the store.

"You want some, princess?"

I wrinkle my nose. "Princess? What's wrong with Landry?"

"Dunno. You don't seem like a Landry to me." He gives me a cheeky once over.

"I have a feeling that whatever I say is going to set me up for some naughty remark for your benefit," I answer, taking my purchases and backing up.

"All my remarks are naughty, and they're for *your* benefit, not mine." He winks.

Not touching that, either. "I'll see you back in the bus."

"See you later, darling."

I flick my middle finger up, which makes him laugh. Outside, both bus doors are open, but the only member of FMK around appears to be Adam. He's got one leg bent at the knee, his foot flat against the side of the bus while he lights up a cigarette. Jesus. *Why is that so sexy?*

I take some comfort in the fact that he's not running away at the sight of me. But he's not waving me over, either. Still, my feet point in his direction and I find myself stopping in front of him.

"Hey," I say stupidly, because I can't think of anything else to say.

He gives me a cool nod and all that nervous anxiety I had when I was a nerd in high school bubbles up in my throat and I start babbling like a fool.

"So thanks for allowing me to come along. The bus is gorgeous. I didn't even know a bus could be that nice. They should have a different name for them, like limobuses."

"Coach."

"What?"

"It's called a luxury coach."

"As in football coach?"

"As in." The left side of his sexy mouth quirks up. "But it's just a bus. In a few weeks, you'll hate it. It'll stink. You'll get tired of looking at the same interior for hours at a time." He takes another drag. "You'll be so used to having an engine under your ass that you'll feel the phantom vibrations for hours afterward."

"That last one doesn't sound so bad," I assure him.

"Going on tour sounds fun, but it's a long grind."

"Well, um, thanks anyway for having me. I know you didn't like the idea of me coming."

His eyes darken and his fantastic lips turn down at the corners. "I like you just fine. Who said I didn't? Davis?"

"No!" I exclaim. I don't want him to get the wrong idea and be mad at my brother. "Davis never said a word about you. I could just tell. I mean, that you didn't like me here because, you know." I wave a finger at my lips, trying to indicate that he hardly ever smiles around me. Except for the fact that he'd smiled just now, and I ruined it. "I'm going to shut up now."

"It's fine. You're fine. Having someone on the bus who's not part of the band is unusual, but we'll get used to it." He inhales again until the cigarette is nearly all ash. "Davis says you're bored." He lifts one eyebrow. "And we're only a few hours into the trip. Doesn't bode well for the next two months."

I feel myself blushing again. "I'm not bored."

That eyebrow shifts higher. "So your bro is lying?"

"No. I mean, I *was* bored before, but mostly because of the boring code I'm working on. Not because of you guys or anything."

"Well, like I said, the tour is a long grind. If you want something, speak up and ask for it. If you want to come back and hang, do it. The bus is your home, too."

Either I'm imagining it, or there's a glint of heat in his eyes as he says that.

"As long as it's not a bother," I murmur. "I'll be so quiet that you won't even notice I'm there."

He drops the cigarette on the ground. As he grinds the stub out with his boot, he says, "Right. Like that's possible."

I don't know what that means, but it makes me hot all over.

9

LANDRY

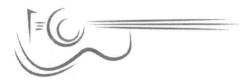

Next Stop: Lexington

I don't go to the back and join the band. I crawl into Davis's bunk, pull the curtain closed, and force myself to nap. It turns out to be a good skill to acquire.

When Adam told me that the tour was a grind, he wasn't kidding. The first stop was exhilarating. The band played in a huge club with an actual stage. The biggest crowd Davis ever sang to was at the Central City summer festival, and even then only a few people were actually listening. The rest were off getting food and drink or standing in line for the portable toilets.

At these clubs, the crowds are pressed right up to the stage, shouting the lyrics along with him. And at each stop, it seems like the audiences are getting bigger.

Davis's band plays second-to-last, with Threat Alert closing out the night. Personally, I think FMK should be the closing act. They get people out of their chairs and onto the stage. Threat Alert has only the one song that anyone appears to like.

I'm a computer nerd, not a musician, so I keep my observations to myself, but Rudd makes the same observations each time we kick out the last of the partiers.

"Why don't you ask Hollister to move us to the end of the rotation?" he says to Adam as we roll toward Evansville, Indiana. Three shows are behind us: Kansas City of the great barbecue; Springfield, the birthplace of Lincoln; and St. Louis, where we stopped so that the band could take pictures next to the base of Arch.

"Time's not right," Adam answers cryptically.

I shoot a questioning glance at Davis, who shrugs. He doesn't know any more than I do.

After Evansville, we move on to Louisville.

"Threat Alert's bringing the whole vibe down," Rudd complains over breakfast.

Adam merely shrugs and continues eating his pancakes.

The sixth show takes place in Lexington, Kentucky. The accents here are thick and charming. I spend an inordinate amount of time chatting up the bartender as the bands set up, mostly because I'm so thrilled to be out of the bus. So thrilled that, for the first time, I'm not nervously waiting for Marrow to waltz through the door.

It helps that I haven't gotten any text messages from him since I left, which means he doesn't have my new number and quite possibly still thinks I'm in Central City. Besides the monotony of the miles that pass between tour stops, I'm the most content I've been in a long time.

The band gets along great. When they're not sleeping, they either play music or cards or video games. The bus has satellite so we can watch Netflix at any time. It's pretty much a rolling hotel. Food's not great. No one on the bus can cook much of anything and after I burned some toast, Davis won't let me near any of the appliances.

I wrinkle my nose. I don't blame him. The smell of burnt food didn't leave the bus for two days. The only person not hassling me about it is Adam.

Adam. I sigh moodily. I had hoped that in close quarters, with so much forced closeness, I'd end up hating him. At the very least, I'd be irritated by something he did. Like he'd talk too much or he'd be moody or he'd pick his nose. I pray for some dirty habit, but one hasn't shown itself yet. He's been nothing but generous and kind and thoughtful. He's always checking in to see if I'm bored—as if he's worried I need entertaining. I've pretended that my current project— one that involves debugging an update for Peep—is all-consuming, when in reality I can't concentrate on anything but him.

"Don't like your drink?" Scott, the bartender, asks me.

He wipes down a nonexistent spot next to my hand.

"No. It's great." I take a giant sip to show my approval and end up choking on it.

Scott smirks, but drops the cloth to pour me a glass of water. "Here you are, slugger."

"Thanks," I sputter. I pat my throat. "Went down the wrong tube."

"It happens." He settles his meaty forearms on the counter. "How's the tour going?"

"Good, I think, but I don't have much to compare it to."

"First tour?"

"Yeah. My brother's the singer," I feel compelled to add.

"Threat Alert?"

"No, FMK."

"Ah. Adam Rees's band. They're good."

"You know him? Adam, I mean."

Scott's mouth quirks up knowingly. "Got a crush on Adam? They all do."

All? I hide my wince by taking another sip of water. "No. You've seen these musicians. They're all little boys once they put their instruments down." I lift one shoulder. "Once you've been on tour with them, all the magic is gone. The music scene really isn't my thing. I'm more into the guys wearing suits and ties than ripped jeans and T-shirts."

Scott straightens, his warm face growing noticeably cooler.

Okay, I took it way too far. I try to salvage things. "I mean, he's like a brother to me."

"Who's like a brother to you?" Adam says from over my shoulder.

"You," Scott says. "We've found one girl who hasn't fallen for the infamous Rees charm. She says she prefers businessmen to rockers. She must not know about the size of your wallet, Rees."

Adam cocks his head. "She's got plenty of her own cash, Scott." It's a mild rebuke but enough of one that Scott tosses his rag down and pretends someone else needs his attention down the bar.

"Was he hassling you?" Adam says quietly after Scott moves away.

"No. Not at all. I was...caught off guard and said some dumb stuff." I can't look at Adam. I'm too embarrassed.

"I doubt that." He shifts slightly, as if he's about to run down Scott and demand an apology.

I reach out to grab his wrist and then back off at the last minute. "No. Seriously. I was asking questions about you and he said I must have a crush. I told him no and then decided to add an asinine bit about how I prefer the office types over the band types."

Adam's face is impassive. Unlike Davis, whose every emotion is readable from a mile away, Adam's expressions are hard for me to decipher. Is he offended I

"And is that true?" he says.

"No. I don't have a type. I—" I break off because my entire experience with the opposite sex was two awkward attempts at dating with the Marrow episode sandwiched in between. I know that none of those experiences give me a healthy outlook on relationships, men, dating, or romance in general.

"Because of Marrow?" Adam guesses.

He's too damn intuitive for his own good. I scrub my finger against the lacquered bar top for a second before answering. "In part. But even before then, I've never been good with guys." My finger pops up to adjust my glasses. "Marrow only made it harder."

"He's not here now. You don't have to be afraid."

"I'm not. Actually, I—"

"Afraid of what?" A new guy pops up. "Hey, Scott, grab me whatever you got on tap. The good stuff, though. Not any of that watered-down shit."

Scott waves a hand of acknowledgement. The new guy is one of the musicians in Threat Alert's band. He plays the same kind of guitar that Rudd does. The guitarist turns around and leans his elbows against the bar top. I've heard them call him Albie, short for Fat Albert. I had to look that up on Wikipedia and I still don't know where the connection comes from. Albie is short, thin, and mayonnaise white.

Adam's normal poker face holds a mild hint of annoyance.

"Rees," Albie says, tipping his thin chin up. "Landry, right?"

I nod and stick out my hand. He gives it a dismissive look before addressing Adam. "Hollister thinks we should play a joint song. Kind of ease from one band to another. You guys can play 'Fine Games' with us."

"We can, can we?" Adam says. The chill in his tone is enough to send goosebumps skittering up my arms.

Albie doesn't even notice. "Yeah. After all, the crowds are coming to hear us. They'll want you to play one of our songs." He spins around. "Where's my drink? Scott, buddy." The bassist tips his hand toward his mouth. "Need my beer. Shit," he shakes his head. "The wait staff here sucks." He stomps down to the end of the bar to confront Scott directly.

Adam slides his hand under my elbow and helps me off the stool. "Not all musicians are assholes like Albie, Landry."

"I know," I say in surprise.

He sighs. "Do you?"

I don't know how to respond to that so I keep my lips zipped shut.

Adam only sighs again.

TWO DAYS LATER, we're on the road speeding toward Charlotte. The guys are sleeping. May's somewhere in eastern Mongolia. An unfortunate number of places there do not have any internet access.

I'd go talk to the bus driver, but I don't want to bother the guys. They need their sleep. The last couple of shows haven't gone as well.

Albie keeps bugging Adam about doing some cross-band stuff. Adam keeps putting him off.

There's also a weird tension in the air between Adam and Davis. I don't know exactly what it is, but it makes me nervous.I find myself watching Davis more closely. The post-show parties in the buses are getting wilder. Last night, while Adam was talking to the bar owner, I trailed Davis into TA's bus. I don't know what the capacity of that thing is, but there were wall-to-wall people.

I suppose that explained why so many of the partiers were various stages of nudity. Girls were down to their bras. Guys had their shirts off. A couple were having sex in the corner of the bunk where Ian and Rudd were sitting, sharing a joint.

Davis kept himself occupied by drinking. A lot. But that was better than him joining the crew in the front that were snorting lines of coke, passing out Molly, and chasing the pills down with shots of Jägermeister.

Davis was stiff and unhappy that I was there watching him, but I couldn't leave. It didn't get better when Adam showed up and the half-dressed girls tried to press up against him. To his credit, he ignored all the offers and spent the rest of the night by Davis and me. He probably felt the waves of tension and wanted to make sure the Olsen siblings didn't get into a fight in front of all the fans.

When we finally left, Davis was drunk and I was weak from anxiety. As for Adam, I think he was confused. He tried to talk to me, but I didn't have any energy for him. I stumbled into the back and threw myself on the bed.

On the positive side, I'm not stressing about Marrow any longer. Instead I'm filled with worry about Davis, about the band, and about my inconvenient attraction to Adam.

There's a knock on the door. "Landry? You awake?" Adam says softly.

I shove my laptop to the side and hurry to the door. With a press of a button, the door slides open to reveal a sleepy Adam, wearing sweatpants and one of those tanks that are open on either side. Slices of his golden skin flash enticingly at me as he walks in.

He's carrying a mat under his arms. "Do you mind if I do a few stretching exercises? I haven't lifted in a couple of days and I think my muscles are atrophying."

I stare at his biceps. "I hadn't noticed," I reply dumbly.

He flexes. I clench my jaw so it doesn't drop open in lusty appreciation.

"Well, I can feel it. I'd do it between the bunks but I don't want to wake anyone up."

I step aside and wave a hand toward the couches. "Be my guest."

I hurry over to grab my laptop off the table. He tosses the mat to the side and presses a button and the table slowly lowers to level with the floor.

The muscles in his back bunch as he flicks the mat open.

"You can sit on the couch if you want," he offers. "Won't bother me."

I crawl onto the cushion and scoot over to the corner.

"You managing the boredom okay?" he says as he lowers himself to the ground. He places his hands in a diamond shape and begins a series of pushups. This is stretching?

"Yeah, I have my work." I pat my laptop absently. I can't take my eyes off his body. Since he's face-down, I don't have to. I take the opportunity to catalogue every muscle, every inch of exposed skin. Everything about him is impressive.

My tongue creeps out to lick a slow path along my lower lip. I'd give my entire seven-figure bank account to be able to touch him. Just once. My fingers curl against the top of my laptop.

Desire unfurls, heating my blood, quickening my heartbeat.

Beneath me, just inches away from my fingers, Adam's body moves in one smooth and steady motion. Up and down. Up and down. I fantasize about my own frame—smaller, lighter, softer—positioned under his. I imagine that he touches me as he does his guitar —with reverence and knowing. I dream about him kissing me, his beautiful mouth forming my name instead of lyrics.

Need throbs at my neck, my wrists, between my legs. I draw a hand down my throat, pressing my fingertips against the wildly beating pulse point. I feel the echo of that pulse in my core. God, it's been so long.

So long since I've felt the tender, intimate touch of anyone. I want Adam. I want him so much I'm afraid that it's going to be the ruin of me.

I jump up and race out of the room.

"Landry?" he calls in bewilderment.

I slam the door to the bathroom shut and shove a hand down my pants. I lean against the bathroom door and touch myself, imagining that it's Adam's long, talented fingers instead of my own, working me until I have to bite my forearm to keep from crying out.

Shit. This is no good.

No good at all.

10

ADAM

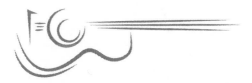

"Come over and sit your sweet ass next to mine, honey." Rudd pats the cushion beside him and gives Landry a devilish grin.

After our fifteen-minute rest stop, we're back in the bus with only a few more hours to go. A few more endless hours given how close Landry is to Rudd. An inch to her right and she'd be sitting on his hand.

"So it's honey now?" she teases as she nudges Rudd's shoulder with her own. Her glasses slip down her nose. "What happened to darling and sweetheart?"

"You didn't seem to like those, so I'm trying a new one out. How's it working?"

She pretends to consider it while pushing her frames back into place. "Honey's not bad, but I don't think it fits. Keep trying."

Don't encourage him! I want to growl. I glance over at Davis to see if he's going to put a stop to this, but his nose is buried in the sheet music I handed out earlier.

Ian also appears completely unconcerned that Rudd and Landry are a few seconds from mashing their lips against each other.

"Hey, buddy, you might want to ease up on your fret or you're going to lose a few fingers," Ian murmurs beside me.

I look at my left hand with surprise and realize I'm gripping the strings so tightly that they're leaving marks. *Get it together*, I order myself.

Then I hear a giggle. I slap my hand against the guitar and glare at the two snuggled in the curve of the U-shaped sofa. "You going to practice, Rudd, or make moves on your singer's sister?"

Rudd's head jerks around, an innocent look on his face. "Dude, just trying to make Landry comfortable. No reason to get your panties in a bunch."

He reaches between his legs to pick up his guitar. I watch in satisfaction as Landry is forced to move closer to her brother to avoid the neck of Rudd's instrument.

Ignoring my drummer's look of speculation, I start playing the first song in the set that we're performing tonight. Rudd, for all his faults, is a total professional and immediately joins in, although he does wink one last time at Landry, who responds by rolling her eyes.

Does she know that her hard-to-get attitude is exactly the right way to play it with Rudd? He's got women throwing themselves at him all the time. We all do. It's one of the very real, albeit clichéd, perks of being in a band. There's something about music and instruments and stage lights that make panties drop—literally.

My dad's band used to keep a drawer in the tour bus full of panties and bras they'd been given. At the end of a tour, Moet, the drummer, took it back to his house. I don't know if he still has it. I prefer to leave that as one of the mysteries of the universe.

There hasn't been a girl I've met or fucked whose underwear I wanted to keep—or even see, for that matter. I've always subscribed to the theory that underwear looks best on the floor, not the body. But I can't help but wonder what Landry's looks like. Does she have frilly lacy panties or is she more of a boyshorts kind of gal? Is there a thong covering her sweet pussy or maybe she's going commando?

It's shit like this that keeps me up at night or makes me do stupid things like a bunch of pushups in the back of the bus. Sure, I need to stay fit. Tours are long and physically exhausting, but did I need to do them in front of her? Damn me, but that was juvenile. An act thirteen year-old me would've cringed at.

But I wanted—scratch that—I needed a response from her. Any kind of glimmer that the pull between us still existed. I know she's not ready to act on it, but, I'm not prepared to beat my friend and bandmate into a pulp if she's moved on to him.

I examine the two of them. They're friends, I decide for my own sanity. She flirts with him because Rudd's safe. And she runs away from me because she knows I'm not.

It's a good thing that the song we're playing is a fan favorite and that I know it so well, I could play it drunk, stoned, high, or maybe even comatose. Because right now, I can't concentrate on anything but Landry. My jeans have shrunk a size and I'm grateful I have a guitar in my lap, although Ian, who's next to me slapping his hands against his thighs, could probably see my hard-on if he glanced my way.

I ponder how serious Davis was with his threat of leaving the band if any of us make a move on his sister.

The song ends, and before I can start the next one, Davis clears his throat.

"What is it?" I snap, more harshly than I intend.

He hesitates, tapping a finger against the sheet music. "We're playing this song a little fast, don't you think?"

"And maybe a mite too angry," Ian adds with a smirk.

Goddammit. He *did* look my way.

I shift the guitar. "I hadn't noticed." I was so wrapped up in speculating about Landry that I hadn't been paying attention to the beat.

"I'm concerned if we start the set out too fast that we won't be able to keep up the intensity of that first song throughout, but maybe we could do it a half beat faster." Davis taps out the rhythm and starts to sing again. Rudd joins in and soon Ian's hands are slapping against his knees.

It's slightly faster than I have it written, but I like it. For the next twenty minutes, I force myself to keep my attention off Landry and on the band. It's not easy, though, as a stray bit of sunlight streams over her shoulder, highlighting her creamy skin. I manage not to screw up too badly, and after the fifth song, I call for a break.

"You going to make it until she leaves?" Ian asks under his breath. "Because if being around her for a few hours turns you inside out, I'd hate to see what you're going to be like in two months."

"I have no idea what you're talking about," I mutter back.

He rolls his eyes. "If that's the way you want to play it."

"Are you all hungry?" Landry asks, drawing my attention away from Ian. She couldn't hear us, I hope, but she senses a bit of tension and is instinctively trying to dispel it. "I could make dinner for us. Something light before you go onstage."

"No way." Davis jumps to his feet. "I'll make it."

"Seriously, Davis, I can make a salad or something." Scowling, she hurries after Davis.

Rudd makes a gagging sound. I'm in full agreement. Lettuce isn't my thing, either. But I set the guitar aside and follow the two siblings down to the tiny galley kitchen. My body doesn't care what it eats if Landry's cooking.

"What's the problem? We're not going to force Landry to cook if she doesn't want to," I say. She's here to escape a bad situation, not to do chores for us assholes.

"She's a terrible cook. If you want to miss our next show, then by all means, let her at the stove," Davis says.

"Davis, I'm not that bad." Landry punches her brother in the arm.

"You poisoned the family."

Poison? I can't help grinning. She gives an exasperated huff, blowing a lock of hair away from her face. Fuck, she's adorable. "It was an accident."

Davis looks over her head at me. "She nearly overdosed us on sodium. She put like half a bottle of table salt in a pan of water, forgot it and boiled it until it was nothing but a few drops of water and a hunk of salt. Then she dumped tomato sauce in it." He shakes his head. "Face it, Landry, you're too easily distracted to cook. I'll make us something."

The look she sends her brother's way is murderous. I smother a chuckle behind the back of my hand.

"What's so funny?" she asks indignantly, hands on her hips.

"I've heard of the saying 'She doesn't know how to boil water,' but didn't realize it could actually be true." As she continues to glower at me, I add, "We've all got flaws."

She purses her lips, the juicy lower one forming a very suckable bit of flesh. "Well, let's hear yours."

"How much time do we have?" I lean against the fridge.

"Two months," she fires back.

"Not nearly enough time."

"Now you're stalling."

No, I'm enjoying the hell out of sparring with you.

A bang of a pot against the stove has me straightening up. I'd forgotten that Davis was here. Hell, I think I forgot anyone else was here but me and Landry. She looks just as disconcerted, jerking away from the counter and backing up to sit in the banquette just beyond the stove.

Davis looks over his shoulder at me. I give him a bland smile. *Just making friendly with the sister. Nothing to see here,* I try to convey.

Ian wanders down, a shit-eating grin on his face. He knows me too well, the bastard. But he's a friend, and he keeps his mouth shut as he slides into the booth next to Landry.

"What're we talking about?" he asks, as if he wasn't hanging out near the door listening to the entire conversation.

"Adam is going to list all his flaws for us," she says.

Ian swivels around to face me. "Wow. Do we really have enough time?"

I flick him off. "That's what I told her."

"You both say this, but I haven't heard one flaw yet," she points out.

Ian opens his mouth, but I wave him off. "Let me ease into this before you start revealing all my deep, dark secrets." I consider my list of extensive shortcomings and opt to go with the one that Ian would probably start with. "I'm a perfectionist."

"He has a temper, too," Ian adds.

"And he's more stubborn than a mule." Rudd ambles down the hall to peer over Davis's shoulder.

Terrific. They're making me out to be an inflexible asshole who always has to get his way.

"You got any complaints?" I ask Davis.

"Nah, it's all good. Besides, none of those things has killed your family like Landry's cooking almost did. We were one meal away from being a Discovery 'Tragedy in the Kitchen' special."

Landry rips a sheet of paper off the notepad lying on the table and chucks it at Davis's head. It doesn't go very far.

"Oh, and did I mention Landry's a terrible shot? Never choose her in a game of pick-up basketball."

"Noted," I say and grin at Landry.

She smiles back and lust surges through me so powerfully that my knees nearly buckle. I force myself to turn away. In a curt voice, I say, "Holler when you're done. I'm going to take another look at the set list."

I leave knowing that there are four sets of bewildered eyes following me into the back. Scratch that. Three sets. Ian probably knows exactly why I'm pissed off. And it's not at anyone but myself.

11

LANDRY

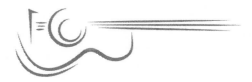

Tour Stop: Augusta

The bar in Augusta isn't a bar. It's a squat, drab gray building with a large parking lot and a fifties-style neon sign that says "Dance's Hall" with the word "Vacancy" in neon orange underneath.

"Are we even at the right place?" I ask. We're all in the front, watching as the driver makes a sharp turn into the parking lot. Our bus driver is a magician because I was sure we were going to hit the stop sign, but he manages to maneuver by it with an inch to spare.

It's Adam who answers. "There's a bar inside."

Davis presses his nose to the window. "How many people does it hold?"

"Three thousand at max capacity." There's a healthy dose of satisfaction in Adam's voice.

And why shouldn't there be? Three thousand people? Davis and I exchange surprised looks. Excitement simmers in his eyes. He's never played in front of a crowd so large. He bolts from the bus almost before the wheels roll to a stop. He can't wait to see the inside.

"You excited?" I nudge Rudd with my arm. His head has been buried in his phone for the last half hour.

"Yup," he says. But he doesn't sound excited. Not like Davis is.

"He's too busy making arrangements for after the show," Ian mocks. He taps out a cigarette and pops it into the corner of his mouth before passing the pack to Adam, who plucks one out and tucks it above his ear. The thin hoop threaded through the upper tip catches my eye. It's the second piercing I've seen. Not that I'm counting.

"I'm doing PR work," Rudd protests. His fingers fly over the screen's keyboard. "I'm inviting the local girls to the show."

"How's that PR?" Ian asks skeptically.

"Simple math. Guys go where the girls go. Get a lot of girls at the show and you'll have a lot of dicks there, too. You should be paying me for this."

"PR work. That's a new one," Ian scoffs. He hops out and lights his cigarette.

Adam is next, but he pauses at the bottom step and looks back. "Coming?" he asks.

I hesitate, looking around for a moment.

Adam's brown eyes darken. For a moment, apprehension quivers in my tummy at the prospect of seeing the first flare of his supposed temper. But then he reaches a hand toward me and says, "No one's going to hurt you while I'm around."

Heat rushes to my cheeks, partly from pleasure but mostly from embarrassment. I force myself to march down the three steps to the pavement. "You must think I'm ridiculous."

His arm swings by mine and I regret not taking his hand. "Nope. Smart. My dad had his share of stalkers. Why do you think the celebs all have bodyguards? Because they're ridiculous or because they're smart to be on guard against stupid people? But we're here and the ass-wipe is a day's drive away. You're safe."

From Marrow, but not from myself. I can't tell Adam that so I force a smile onto my lips. "Thanks."

It's better he thinks I'm scared of Marrow rather than the truth:

that I have a crush so strong that if I ease the lid off my control, I'm going to attack Adam.

We walk the rest of the way in silence. Inside we find Davis talking to Keith Dieter, the front man for Threat Alert. He's wearing tight black jeans, a white T-shirt strategically ripped around the torso and collar, and tan Timberlands.

"What do you think of TA?" Adam jerks his head in Keith's direction.

"They're okay."

Adam huffs a small laugh. "Not as good as we are, of course."

"Of course." We share a small smile and the quiver that snaked around my belly earlier reappears. I know what it's like to be on the receiving end of an unwanted fixation. I'm not pushing that on Adam.

But in some way, because I know he isn't attracted to me at all, the need feels good—healthy, even. Recklessly, I stoke that small fire and let it spread. Standing next to Adam, feeling the burn in my blood like a shot of good whiskey, I have the urge to throw myself at the poor man.

"You need to stop looking at me like that," Adam says sharply.

"Like what?"

He closes his eyes, as if seeking patience. I wonder if I'm going to be treated to my first exhibition of his temper, but he does nothing except shake his head before stomping off.

His reaction irritates me a smidge. Yes, I might have an inconvenient crush, but I'm not acting on it. And he can suffer through a few thirsty glances. From what I saw the other night, I'm not the only one who makes those eyes at him.

My smile dims a bit at that thought, because somehow being one of a crowd of girls who want to see Adam without his clothes doesn't feel good.

I rub a hand across my tummy and look around to find Rudd and Ian coming through the doorway, both with their arms full of instruments.

"How'd the PR go?" I call out to Rudd.

He lifts his chin. "Awesome, of course. Place is going to be packed."

"Of course. What can I bring in?"

"Nothing, sugar. It's bad luck to let a non-band member touch these babies before the show."

After a few aborted attempts to help, Davis finally sends me away, telling me that I'm being a hindrance and bothering everyone.

I end up at the bar, sipping water garnished with a lemon and talking to Bob, the bartender. He's wearing one of those mechanic's shirts with his name embroidered on it. We chat about his favorite restaurant which happens to be a barbecue spot. We end up spending the next fifteen minutes debating dry rubs over wet rubs. Bob is a wet rub enthusiast.

It ends up sounding dirty and weird talking about different types of rubs for a particular cut of meat so we shift topic to the crowd he expects tonight. It's a mix of college students and young professionals. He prefers the young professionals. College students don't tip worth shit. His words, not mine.

As the staff starts to trickle in, I see that everyone wears some version of the mechanic's shirt. A few of the waitresses have the shirt unbuttoned and tied under their boobs. Another bartender wears his open over a torn wifebeater.

Bob is a chatty guy, and while he does pre-opening prep he shares that the show is sold out and has been since last week. Lots of people want to hear Sid Rees's son play. Apparently Death to Dusk is strangely popular in Georgia. I assure Bob that the band is awesome, but inwardly worry that everyone will expect screeching guitar solos and screaming vocals, neither of which Adam or Davis deliver.

FMK is set to play the fourth hour. Starting at eight, each band will play a fifty-minute set separated by a thirty-minute break, which allows the various groups to break down the existing stage and set up for the next set. It's apparently bad luck to use someone else's instruments.

The space fills up quick once the doors open, and Bob has little time to chat with me after that. I leave him a hefty tip and find a quiet booth in the corner where I can see the stage and the door. I'm not looking for Marrow anymore. Detective Pressley kept a close eye on him while I was preparing to leave, and aside from her, my parents, and May, no one knows I left with Davis. Heck, I'm not even sure Davis's former coworkers know where he is.

Davis joins me when the first band, whose name is Jane Eyre Sucks so I automatically hate them, starts playing. Adam is close to the stage, surrounded by a swarm of girls. I don't know where the other two are.

"How're you doing?" my brother asks.

"I'm good. How about you? Nervous?"

"Nah. Excited," he admits. "This is wild."

He's wired and not from booze, because Davis doesn't drink before he plays. During? Yes. After? Hell, yes. But not before. I wish he'd give it up, but so far he appears to have it all under control.

His fingers drum against the tabletop. His knee bounces repeatedly. He stares at the crowd, too, but for different reasons. He can't believe how many people are going to see him play. I'm so happy for him. He's earned this.

I need to stop monitoring his liquor intake. He didn't invite me on to the tour to keep track of how many times he gets drunk. Even Davis deserves to lose control now and again.

He leans close so I can hear him over the music. "I know it was selfish of me to make you come with me, to give you the ultimatum, but I'm not sorry now. You still mad?"

"You know I'm not." I reach across to squeeze his hand. "What would I have done at home? Sat in front of the computer screen and pretended not to be incredibly lonely while you, May, and Mom and Dad were gone? This is an adventure."

"See, I was right," he says smugly.

"Don't make me come over this table," I threaten.

He gives me a return squeeze before sliding out of the seat. "I'm going to get a water and chat up the fans. Adam wants us to do some in-person marketing."

Is that what Adam is doing? Because it looks like he's flirting with dozens of different girls, flashing his beautiful smile in their direction, allowing them to touch his tats. One girl even sticks out her tongue and pretends to lick his arm. Gross. Thankfully, Adam backs away from her.

"Sounds miserable. I'm going to hide in the corner."

"We're watching out for you, Landry. Nothing's going to happen while you're on tour with us."

"Don't worry about me." Worry about Adam getting a disease from the arm-licker. "I'm fine. This is awesome." It's a good thing that noses don't grow when you lie or mine would be poking Davis in the arm.

He gives me another squeeze, probably to reassure himself as much as anything, and disappears into the crowd.

By the time FMK takes the stage, I'm close to better. A drink or three has helped, but I stay in the booth and for the most part, I'm left alone. A couple of girls wander over, wanting to find out why so many FMK members are talking to me, but they take off when the music starts. The stage is an inexorable draw. Davis's voice is so gorgeous, full-bodied and deep with a surprising dash of falsetto. And Adam? His music is exactly right for Davis's voice. In the back, Ian's arms flash in and out of view. I boost myself onto the back of the booth so I can see over the waving hands and jumping bodies. The crowd's in a frenzy, particularly the ladies. I swear a few of them are trying to haul the guys down off the stage.

A cute guy with Fabio hair wanders over shortly before the end of the set.

"You look lonely!" he yells. He waves a hand and a waitress appears almost immediately. "Corona and...?" He raises an eyebrow.

"Whatever's on tap is good for me."

"She'll have a Corona, too."

I open my mouth to object, but the guy speaks over me. "Bottles make more money, and as part of the band, spending some of the money on the house makes a good impression."

I shut up. I've got a lot to learn about this touring business. I should start taking notes.

"I'm Mike. Saw you rolled in on the grand deluxe."

"Landry Olsen." I shake his hand. "And if that's what you're calling the bus, then yes. Adam calls her Bessie."

"It's a girl?"

"I guess? I mean, we could change her name to Mike."

"That's just mean." He winks and lifts his hands behind his head, catching his hair in a pony and twisting it into a bun with more efficiency than I've ever seen a girl wield.

"Are you with a band?" I ask, guessing that he's connected somehow because of his ease and the way the waitress came over so quick.

"I'm Threat Alert's manager."

It's said with an air of importance, so I pretend to be impressed even though I have no idea what he does. "This seems really well put together. I thought everyone'd be playing at bars. This the biggest crowd they've had yet."

"Georgia's a great state for live music. Most places down here are. Plus, it helps that Rees is involved."

That's the same thing that Bob told me. "How so?" I ask. "FMK doesn't play heavy metal." I looked up Sid Rees' band, and while their wiki page said that they were one of the greatest metal bands in the last couple of decades, I couldn't make it through even one of their songs.

"A bunch of reasons. He's got a lot of connections, so places like this open their doors. He's a known name. People think they've heard of him before and so they come, thinking it's a sound that's familiar," he explains. "Plus, of course, Threat Alert just signed to a label, so they're big."

I don't tell him I've never heard of them before this tour. "That's awesome. They must be loving this crowd tonight."

He nods almost absently. His hands go up and the hair comes down. "So I hear you're the new front man's sister?"

I sip from my drink before nodding. "Yes. Davis is my brother."

"He's a good fit. Hopefully Rees won't drive him off."

"What do you mean?"

"Rees is a musical genius, but he's difficult as fuck to get along with, don't you think?"

"No, actually I don't think so. He's been nothing but good to"—I was going to say *me*, but I adjust—"to Davis and me."

Mike shrugs carelessly. "It's new. Wait a bit and he'll do something to piss you off. He always does. It's why this is his third band. He's a stubborn prick that always wants things his way." Mike slides a curious glance in my direction. "You don't see it?"

I fold my arms across my chest and give him a chilly stare. "No."

He meets my gaze for a moment before shifting his attention back to the stage. "Didn't mean to piss you off. Look, Davis is a talent. When Adam's done with him, send him my way." He slides a card across the table.

I let it lie there.

Mike shakes his head. "Don't be stubborn."

"Give the card to my brother directly." When Mike doesn't reply, it dawns on me. He already tried and that's why he's cozying up to me. I huff in irritation. "I make no decisions in the band. If you want to break up FMK, that's on you. I'm here to enjoy the tour before I go back home."

"Because of the stalker?" Mike asks with narrowed eyes.

I glare at him in dismay. "How do you know about that?"

He waves his hand. "Everyone does. I think I even bought drugs off that guy once. He lives over in Oak Park, right?"

"Right."

"I always thought he was weird." Mike taps his finger on the table before getting to his feet. "When the honeymoon is over, give me a holler. My door will always be open."

I still make no move to take it, eyeing the white card like it might turn into a snake and bite me.

12

ADAM

My mood doesn't improve. Not even after the righteous set.
The cheers grow as Davis holds the last note, and the longer he sings it, the louder the crowd gets. He holds the final syllable in the last lyric as Ian riffs heavily on the snare. Rudd and I lock eyes as we slash our strings, the pick digging into my thumb. I've played so hard tonight blood is trickling from the frets to my wrist.

Davis raises his fist, the sign to cut off all sound. Rudd and I slam our palms against our guitars. Ian catches his sticks.

And while the stage falls silent, the crowd yells the last line again and again and again. They don't want to let go.

From the back, Ian counts down from five, four, three, two. On one, we pick up the bridge again. The crowd screams in glee. Hands go up, bodies start jumping. Hair is swung around. Davis wraps one hand around the pole of the mic stand, one hand fisted around the mic itself, and then leans over the edge of the stage, dripping his sweat onto the front row.

Hands reach out to grab his jeans. He steadies himself, singing about how much he wants his girl's sweet taste on his tongue, all over his body, all over him.

He's getting laid tonight by at least one of those honeys, if not more. Hell, we all could. Even Rudd.

My fingers are sore, nearly cramping. When my dad was king of the scene, he always talked about how hard he'd get up here, looking out into the lust-filled faces of the girls who were so turned on by his music, they would strip down right in front of him and throw their clothes onto the stage.

This is what those old guys who sit at the top of my old man's bar, Gatsby's, reminisce about. It's a high that can't be re-created by any drug. No number of pills can light you up inside like this. And I should be enjoying the hell out of it, but I can't take my eyes off Landry, who's been chatting up some guy for the last thirty minutes.

Oh, she's nodded her head a few times with the beat, but mostly she's engaged in some intense conversation with a guy wearing one of those trendy-as-fuck man buns. He keeps taking it down and wrapping it back up. I'm going to tear it off, since it obviously bothers him so much.

The last note arrives, and Rob, the sound and light guy, douses the lights as we fall completely silent. Ian's sticks are up. My palm's flat on the strings. Davis is running a hand through his sweat-drenched hair. On stage, we're silent, but the bar is rocking. It's the crowd making the noise—screaming for us to play one more song, one more lyric, one more note.

The lights come up in the bar, signaling that our act is over. The crowd isn't happy. They boo for a bit. Davis grins down from his elevated perch. Rudd joins him and the two spend a long moment looking over the crowd, no doubt deciding which one of the eager honeys they're going to take back to the bus tonight.

A none-too-quiet shuffling sound offstage to the right grabs my attention. I look up to see Keith waiting impatiently for us to get our asses out of the way.

Ian spots the same thing and hops up from his seat. I drop my guitar into the stand and help Ian break down his kit. Even if Threat

Alert's drummer wouldn't mind using Ian's drum set, Ian would pimp out his sister and mother before anyone laid hands on his instruments. Musicians are like that. In all the years I've been around music, I've seen more fights break out over someone fingering the wrong guitar than someone fingering the wrong girl.

"You're supposed to warm them up, not give them a full-blown orgasm," Keith says as he toes his guitar case out of the way.

"They're wet and ready, dude. That's the best way to get a woman," Rudd proclaims as he drags Davis offstage.

"I'm not a fan of sloppy seconds," Keith's bassist, Albie, grouches. He's pissed that we played so well, because it means he'll have to be on the top of his game to maintain the same crowd response. Albie wants to play well enough to get a few free drinks after the gig and make his girl's pussy wet. He doesn't love the music enough to be inspired by someone else's play. Keith's going nowhere with this guy, but that's on Keith. Dude will have to figure it out for himself.

I set the bass drum by the door with the rest of Ian's kit. Rudd flings open the door to see if Ian's back from the bus with the cart. He's not, so I lean against the wall and lift the bottom of my T-shirt to swipe the sweat off my forehead. Across from me, Albie's pretty girlfriend runs into a mic stand. That boy is punching so far above his weight class, it's a miracle he hasn't torn a muscle. The way she's eating up the glimpse of my abs, though, suggests that the minute he unstraps his guitar, she'll be moving on. I drop my shirt and angle away from her.

"You ready, man?" Albie asks.

Keith adjusts the strap and shakes his head. "No. Give them a minute to come down off the high." He leans toward me. "Don't mind, Albie. He's bitter cuz his girl followed him down here. He was hoping for the night off, if you know what I mean."

Translation: Albie was hoping to get laid by some out-of-town strange, and his old lady is ruining it for him.

"That's unfortunate." For the girl, for him, for Keith's band. He'll need to get that sorted.

"He had his eye on Davis's girl, I think." Keith tips his head toward Davis, who's peering out the back, yelling for Ian to get his ass inside.

"You mean his sister," I correct sharply.

"Sister. Girl. Whatever," Keith rolls his eyes. "She's off-limits, right?"

"Right." The possessive urge I felt from the first moment I laid eyes on Landry rises up. If she belongs to anyone, it's me.

Threat Alert is good, but they're not FMK. The crowd never gets as loud, never gets as hyped. They still have fun, though. A couple of Threat Alert's girlfriends come to collect me again, and I end up a sweaty mess by the end of the night. After Threat Alert finishes its playlist, a DJ takes over.

Rudd's stumbling around while Ian smokes something that's not a cigarette in the booth I abandoned. Davis is in a deep conversation with a pretty blonde. She's so close to him, she's practically inside his T-shirt. I turn away from that scene, because there are things I don't need to see, especially when they involve my brother.

My eyes scan the large venue for Adam, but I don't find him. Even though I know I'm just having an affair with him in my head, I'm sad that he's already replaced me with a real girl.

"We're headed to the bus, dollface," Rudd says. "It's party time!" There's a girl on either side of him. They all look lit.

"What about the party in here?"

"Nah, we need some privacy, don't we, girls?" He squeezes them tight and, like Tickle Me Elmo dolls, they giggle on cue.

"Where's everyone else?" I ask.

"They're coming." He jerks his head. "Come on."

That wasn't a real answer, but when I look over at the booth I vacated, a new crowd has taken over. Ian and his smoking buddies are gone. Davis has disappeared, too. I spent way too much time searching for Adam, I conclude.

"All right."

Rudd gives me the thumbs-up, or as much of one as he can provide without taking his hands away from the girls' waists.

"Who are these lovely ladies?" I ask as we push our way through the crowd.

"I'm Lacey," the one closest to me says. "And this is Meg, my sister."

"Sisters!" Rudd exclaims in a theatrical whisper.

"I don't think they actually are, Rudd." Lacey has short, black hair and Meg is a half foot taller with dark, smooth skin I'd kill for.

"Shhh," he says in a voice that's way too loud. "You're ruining the fantasy."

The girls don't mind, though. And hell—if they don't, neither do I. The three are full of drunken confidence that's almost charming.

The bus is already crowded when we arrive. Several other band members are there. Some guy I don't know palms my ass. Rudd plants himself in the back, one girl on each side, making up his metaphorical sister sandwich. In the front, the blonde Davis was talking to is now straddling his lap. His hands are busily pulling her dress completely off. Ian's propped in the banquette watching it all. I avert my eyes and flee.

Outside, I see a pinpoint of red light flicker.

"Adam?" I call out.

"The one and only," he replies.

It's not quite an invitation, but I'll take it. I follow the flare to the rear of the bus to find Adam lounging on the bumper. A tall, thin, gangly man with a wispy goatee slouches across from him, using the back of a van as a rest.

"Oh, am I interrupting?"

Please say no.

"Nah, have a seat." Adam points to the side of the bumper next to him. "Landry, this is George Dance. He owns this joint."

"Dance? Really?" I ask. "That's amazing." The name of the place, Dance's Hall, takes on new meaning.

"It is now. Not so much when I was in school," he jokes. "Want some?" He offers me a hit off his joint.

I shake my head and lower myself next to Adam. "I thought the apostrophe on the sign was a mistake."

"Ha! I wish. Had to have the damn thing remade three times because the fucking signmaker thought he knew better. You have a good time tonight?"

"Yes, it was great. I couldn't believe how well your staff kept up with the crowd."

"They're a good group of kids." He inhales deeply before offering it again. Both Adam and I refuse. George pinches off the burnt end of his joint and sticks it in his shirt pocket. "Well, I'm going to take my old ass home. Thanks for playing. Your riffs had shades of your old man tonight."

Beside me, Adam's shoulders stiffen, but his tone is light as he replies, "Thanks for having us. We had a great time."

"Tell your dad hey for me next time you see him. We'd love to have him down for an event."

"I'll pass the word along."

Adam rises and gives the older man a hug, and then it's just the two of us. I rub my arms briskly. I didn't grab a jacket when I bolted from the bus, and now that there aren't a thousand people pressed against me, the early spring weather is making itself known.

"Here."

I look up to see a piece of fabric dangling in front of me. I realize it's a shirt. Specifically, Adam's shirt. He'd pulled off his long-sleeve oatmeal-colored Henley and is offering it to me.

"It's clean," he says, jiggling it slightly. "I changed after the set."

"I wasn't worried about that," I say, taking it. "I just don't want you to be cold."

"I can't feel it. Don't worry."

I slip my arms into the sleeves and let the big shirt fall around my shoulders. It smells like warm man and tobacco. It occurs to me that if I'm wearing Adam's shirt, then he's naked. Right? *RIGHT?*

"Better?" he asks as he settles back beside me.

Is he closer or is it my imagination? I peek to the side and am super disappointed to see he's wearing a wife-beater.

"Better," I confirm, slumping backward in disappointment. "You guys were amazing tonight."

"Yeah, although I think the transition from 'Flip Out' to 'You Kill Me' wasn't as smooth as it could've been."

"You sound like Davis, obsessing over the smallest detail that no one knows about but you." The sleeves of Adam's shirt are so long that my fingers stop before the cuff. I keep my hands tucked inside, enjoying the warmth.

"I guess Davis is a good fit for me, then."

It's funny how chemistry works. Earlier on the bus, I sat next to Rudd and felt nothing. Now, my heart beats faster and goosebumps are surfacing despite the fact I am fully covered head to toe. My skinny jeans feel tight, the lace on my bra strap feels extra scratchy. I want to throw all my clothes off and then rip Adam's off as well.

I allow a small smile to settle across my face. It's dark and I doubt that Adam can see it. And if he did, he'd just assume that I was happy, not that I was embracing the way he turns me on like a light bulb. When you've been in the dark for a long time, being lit up is a treasure.

"What are you doing out here?" I ask curiously. "Shouldn't you be inside, celebrating?"

"Tired of me already?" he teases. He bends forward, resting his bare forearms on his knees. Long, elegant fingers dangle between his legs. I wonder how he'd react if I started tracing his tattoos with my tongue.

"Hardly." The word comes out a little too hot, a little too eager, even for me. I bite my lip and wait to see if he notices.

But he doesn't move from his position. His tautly muscled arm and equally built leg rest next to me. I swear I can feel heat radiating off his big frame. I'd like to curl up like a cat beneath a ray of sunshine and sleep basking in his warmth. That's not weird, right? As long as I don't say it or do it, it's not weird. It's just my own private, safe fantasy. I take my glasses off and use Adam's shirt to wipe off the foggy lenses.

"Is Man Bun not on the bus?"

"Man Bun?" I'm confused.

Adam twirls his finger next to his head. "The guy with the long hair that was sitting with you during our set."

"Oh, you could see us?" When he gives me a curt nod, I continue with, "That was Mike. He's Threat Alert's manager. And anyway, my brother is currently putting on a public sex show. So, no—nothing and no one could entice me back on the bus right now." Thinking about Davis mauling that poor girl kind of puts a damper on my own lusty feelings.

"Not even Man Bun?" Adam's grinning now.

"Especially not Man Bun. I don't think he could love anyone more than he loves his hair."

Adam hoots. "True."

"How about you? Why aren't you inside partying?" There are many pretty girls more than willing to lavish attention on him.

He leans back, stretching his long legs out in front of him. His shoulder brushes mine, but despite all the available space, neither of us makes an effort to give the other one more room.

"Guys like George Dance are the backbone of the scene. Sure, a few bands make it to the top, although these days it's more about individual voices than actual bands. But for the most part, what makes the music world go around are people like George. If venues like his close, most bands couldn't afford to tour."

"Spending time with George is more important than Rudd's marketing?"

"Nah, Rudd's marketing is important, too." Adam cocks his head. "You bothered by Rudd's techniques? Because I can tell him to knock it off."

"Not at all. He comes off as harmless. I'm sure that if I returned any of his passes, he'd run away screaming. I've developed a pretty good radar when it comes to guys."

"Oh yeah? Where do I fall?"

"What's the Byronic saying? 'Mad, bad, and dangerous to know'?" I quip.

I sense his frown rather than see it.

"Is that how you view me?" There's almost a hint of hurt in his voice.

I hurry to assure him. "No. It was a stupid joke. There was this poet in London, and he was all the rage at the time—"

"I know who Byron is," he cuts in. "You afraid of me?"

"No. I wouldn't be sitting here if I was."

"Good. Good." He adds the last one almost as an aside.

In between the tall bus and the long van, almost no light creeps in, but the dark isn't scary. I tip my head back against the bus and stretch my legs out. They barely reach Adam's calves.

"Your legs are really long," I remark.

"Or yours are really short."

"I'm above average in height for women," I inform him. "You're the one who's freakishly tall."

"Six three is not freakishly tall."

"The average height for a man is five feet nine inches. At six three, you're eight percent taller than the average man."

"Are you just pulling these stats out of your ass?"

I snicker. "Nope. It's fact. I'm on the computer a lot, remember?"

"Right. Well, I don't think I qualify as freakishly tall. Like, no one is going to pay to come see the six-foot-three-inch man."

"If you were displayed in a community of Lilliputians, you would be freakishly tall."

"You've got me there." His shoulders shake again. He reaches up and grabs his cigarette. "Do you mind?"

"Not at all. It's your cancerous lung problem, not mine."

"I know. I keep trying to quit. I used electronic cigs for about six months, but it's not the same." He flips the cigarette in his hand. "Maybe after the tour is over."

We share a look and then say, "Nah," in unison.

I wish I could sit next to Adam in this dark, safe place forever. Or for another hour or so, at least.

"How long have you smoked?" I ask.

He digs in his pocket and pulls out a matchbook that says "Dance's Hall" on it. "Since I was a kid. I think I was nine or ten when I had my first one."

"That young?"

"My dad toured for most of my life." He jerks a thumb toward the bus. "Think what's going on inside the tin can is shocking? That was nothing compared to what Dad and his crew got up to."

"Um, do I say I'm sorry or that's awesome?"

He snorts. "Both and neither, I guess. I grew up fast, but I learned a lot."

"Did your mom tour, too?"

"The first time," he says with amusement. "She was a groupie. Seventeen when he knocked her up. He had to get permission from her parents to marry her."

"Wow." Adam's life is completely different than my sedate suburban one.

"Yeah, I don't know what was more surprising—that he married her or that her parents were okay with it."

"Are they still together?"

"No. They divorced a long time ago." He looks in my direction again. "Heard your parents are having a rough time of it."

I nod. Davis must've told him. "Dad is, or was, a workaholic and missed a lot of important events in my mom's life. She got sick of it and told him she was leaving. I guess it woke him up because he sold his business and booked a three-month trip around the world. I think they're in Turkey right now. That's why I'm here, you know? Otherwise, I could've just stayed home."

He pulls a match out. "Care to tell me about it? About this Marrow guy, I mean."

"Not really. It's weird and embarrassing."

"Why?"

"Because I didn't even know this guy."

"So his problem doesn't make it weird or embarrassing for *you*."

"In my head I know that, but it's still awkward to explain."

"Then we don't talk about it again." He doesn't press and I could kiss him for that. "At least you're feeling better."

"I am. And I'm so grateful to be here. I know it's a huge inconvenience, dragging my ass along. I'm probably cramping your style, and—"

He interrupts me by placing a warm palm over my hands. "Do I look like a person who does things he doesn't want to do?"

I consider the litany of flaws that Adam and his bandmates recited and none of them lend themselves to him doing an entirely selfless act. "No."

He nods to confirm my answer. "Is Davis getting laid?"

I make a face. "Probably, but I don't want to think about it."

"Is Rudd in the back, enjoying a swarm of girls?"

"Definitely."

"And Ian's sitting, taking it all in."

He was. "I'm guessing that watching is okay with Berry, but not participating?"

"Yeah, she's cool with that. It's their thing."

"Is it your thing?" I ask without thinking. Adam bursts out laughing. I can feel myself turning bright red. "Oh shit, don't answer that. I'm so sorry. I don't know why it came out."

He chuckles. "I'm not into that. And don't apologize. You can ask me whatever you want."

He squeezes my hand once before withdrawing. I want to grab his hand back and place it on my thigh. Or maybe higher.

"You're obviously not cramping a damn thing," he assures me. "Everyone's doing exactly what they want right now. Your being here hasn't affected anyone."

I sigh, a full sigh of contentment. I didn't want to come on this tour, but now that I'm here? I can't imagine another place I want to be. Right here with this man. This honest, gorgeous, *sexy* man—

"Did you just moan?"

I jolt in surprise. Did I? No, of course I didn't. "No," I say way too emphatically.

"Thinking about anyone in particular?" There's a slight edge to his tone now.

"One, I didn't moan—"

"You totally did." His lips curl slightly. "Thought you weren't into Man Bun."

My jaw falls open. "I'm not!"

"Then who are you all starry-eyed and moaning about?" The edge has become a bite, as if the thought of me fantasizing about anyone is absolutely *not* cool with him. "Rudd?"

"No way," I say instantly. "I told you, there's nothing there with Rudd."

"So then we're back to Man Bun," he says flatly, getting to his feet. He shifts so that his back is half turned to me. "Just so you know, a lot of managers have the rep for being sleazebags."

Oh, for Pete's sake. "I am *not* lusting over Threat Alert's manager!" I burst out. "Jeez, if you must know, I was thinking about *you!*"

I regret it the second the confession leaves my mouth. Damn it! Why did I have to go and say that? We were having a nice moment!

Adam pivots toward me. A shaft of light hits the top of his forehead, illuminating his face enough that I can see he's frowning. "What?"

"Nothing," I say quickly. Perfect. Maybe he didn't hear me. I was talking pretty fast, so there's a chance that he might have misheard—

"You were thinking about me?"

No, he heard me loud and clear.

"Maybe a little bit," I mumble under my breath.

"What was that?"

I peek up from under my lashes and see that he's no longer frowning. He just looks stunned.

I take a deep breath. "Oh, fine. In the interest of full disclosure, since we're getting along so well right now, you should know that I have this tiny crush on you."

"What?" he says again, and he sounds as if he's choking.

In for a penny, in for a pound, I suppose. "Look, it's not like I want to jump you. It's that there's this warm, fluttery feeling I get when you're around."

He gives a strangled laugh. "That sounds like a condition that I should take you to the hospital for, not a crush."

There's a crinkly sound. In the dim light, I see his hand crushing the matchbook. I pluck it from his grip and smooth it out. All but one match is broken. I pull it out and scrape it against the striking strip. When the flame flares, I hold it up to Adam's mouth. The flame highlights his gorgeous lips and cheekbones so sharp they could cut glass.

He stares at me, two pools of dark against his too-handsome face. Then, with a sigh, slides the cigarette between his lips.

"Don't worry," I tell him, cupping my hand around the flame. "Davis told me you're not a relationship type of guy, and I'm not looking for a relationship, either. I'm not going to act on the crush. I'm just enjoying how it feels. It's...safe. It's like..." I struggle to put the words to the emotions. "It's like evidence that I'm really over the fear that I felt after Marrow attacked me. The first time," I clarify. "God, I sound like a nutcase. It played out perfectly in my head. Listen, I'm harmless."

He shakes his head slightly before lighting his cigarette. I drop the match to the ground and he stamps his big boot on top of it. He inhales deeply and then pulls the cigarette out. "You know that I have a dick, right?"

"Yes?" I don't know what he means by that.

He sighs, sticks the cigarette in his mouth again and puffs on it heavily. "Let me get this straight. You have a crush on me because I'm...safe?"

"That's about right."

"That's a hell of a confession, Landry. What would happen if I told you that I wasn't safe? That I think you're gorgeous and I've spent my fair share of moments fantasizing about what you'd feel like underneath me?"

My jaw drops. Adam Rees has had fantasies about me? That can't be right. I haven't sensed any sort of interest on his part. He's glared at me. He's been kind. We had this nice moment before I went and ruined it, but not once did I feel lust on his part. Well, maybe I felt a bit of lust the first night at the bar, but it faded fast after he found out I was Davis's sister.

"Are you saying that to make me feel better?" I demand.

He sighs again and sits down next to me, covering my small hands with one of his big ones. "Yeah, I'm saying it to make you feel better. Crush away, baby. You're safe with me."

His tone is resigned, as if he can't believe he has to deal with me, but he's going to because I'm sharing a bus with him for the next two months.

"I promise to never speak of this again," I say helpfully.

Adam takes another drag, then releases a cloud of smoke into the dark night. "That's what I'm afraid of."

14

ADAM

Tour Stop: Tallahassee

She trusts me.

If there was one thing she could've said to put the brakes on my behavior, that was it. I can't violate her trust by making moves on her now. But knowing the girl you want would crawl into your bed at the snap of a finger is like your mom dangling your favorite dessert she just made in front of you and telling you it's for company only.

"Are your pancakes not cooked in the middle or something?"

I flick my eyes up to meet Landry's. They're green, like I first imagined, but light with flecks of gold. Right now, the early morning sun makes them glow.

It's not like I've lived a life of restraint. I've had money, girls, things for the taking. Now I'm supposed to sit on my hands and do nothing. Actually, worse than nothing. I'm supposed to sit across from her and return her seductive smiles with bland ones.

"No, my pancakes are just fine."

"Fine" is becoming the only word in my vocabulary. It stands for *this sucks, let's toss everything in the garbage and go fuck until the world burns down.* But Landry's not fluent in my language.

"I love dives where I know everything is full of fat and calories but it's all too delicious to resist."

Like you.

"Will we be at a place like this tonight?" she asks.

I struggle to pull myself together and answer her innocent question instead of hauling her across the table and kissing those cherry lips until every part of her is hot and flushed. "Not in Tallahassee. It's a smaller place, but has a long history of supporting new and undiscovered bands. Hollister's done a good job of picking places that aren't so large that it looks like we're a failure and that have enough capacity to make sure all the guys put a little money in their pocket." I allow a hint of a smile to surface. "Rudd really does do marketing for us. He's in charge of our electronic press kit. He runs the Facebook, Instagram, Twitter accounts. We give him hell, but he takes care of a lot of shit the rest of us can't stand."

She forks a little of her omelet between her lips, a flash of white teeth peeking out. Even her teeth are sexy—small and white and straight. Holy shit, I'm losing it. I'm getting hard watching her eat. That's a first. But then, everything Landry does turns me on.

When she smiles, when she flicks her hair out of the way, when she sticks the stupid fork between her lips. This is ridiculous. I force my attention away.

"I don't like interacting with people, either," she says. "When we sold our app, May handled everything. Her and a lawyer my dad hired. I like my basement setup." The last bit is said with a tinge of longing. "I couldn't do what you and Davis do. Maybe Ian. I could hide behind a few drums."

"Would we need to pile up a few more cymbals so no one could see your face?"

"Yes, that would be perfect. I prefer the booths in the corner. No one is running into me, and I get to see it all. My favorite bit is when you do the song 'Dark Riots' because everyone starts jumping up on their feet and screaming."

I could make you scream.

"That's one of my favorite parts, too."

"What's it like? Standing up there?"

Focus on the music and you won't make a fool of yourself here.

"It's great when you're locked in and finding the groove. It's terrible when the songs are flat and the crowd is booing you. One of my first gigs was up at State and the students started throwing their trash at us. We'd played a few times in the dorms and at one frat house and thought we were hot shit. Ben Tausch was my singer and he felt that rehearsing would make our sound stale and since our jam sessions were so lit, we should wing it. But he forgot the lyrics to the Radiohead song we were covering, and Ian broke his drumstick halfway through the set." I can't help but laugh at my own hubris and idiocy. "We're lucky they didn't throw the chairs at us."

"May and I wrote three apps that failed before we wrote Peep. And even then, we thought it was too similar to other stuff out there," Landry shares.

"What set it apart?"

"File compression. We reduced the file transfer size of a high-quality video so that it uses exponentially less data. Streaming videos are the future and any tech that can deliver it faster and cheaper is going to be popular. We stumbled on it almost by accident." She shrugs like her thing wasn't some huge deal.

But it is. I did my own share of googling. Her little app sold for eight figures. She might have more money than me.

"May took off about three months ago to tour the world," Landry adds. "She's currently in Asia."

"And you feel like you should've gone with her?" There's a wistful quality to her words.

"Maybe?" Her mouth twists into an uncertain curve. "I'm a bit of a homebody, and the idea of riding wild ponies through Mongolia is something I don't mind reading about, but I can't say I want to do it." She peeps at me under a set of long, pale lashes. "That probably sounds boring to you."

"I can't say I'm interested in riding ponies, either."

"But you're on tour," she points out.

"No one likes going on tour. It's a necessary evil. A musician likes to perform. He likes the feedback loop between him and an appreciative audience. He might even enjoy the different crowds, but touring itself is the devil. You're tired all the time. The cities start to blend together. By the time we reach Arizona, someone's going to think we're still in Texas."

"Is that why Davis has the name of the city inked on his palm?"

"That's right." I gave that tip to him after the second night. You never want to get caught thanking the wrong town. It's a surefire way to turn locals against you.

"Still, this is the most adventure I've had my entire life." She shoots me a rueful smile. "The one good thing Marrow did is push me out of my comfort zone. If it weren't for him and Davis—and you, I suppose—I'd still be in my parents' basement."

"That would've been a real shame."

We dig into our breakfasts after that, talking more. She shares a little more about her family and how she hopes her folks return with their relationship glued back together. I tell her about my mom, living out in LA, trying to win a contest on who can have the most plastic surgery done to her body.

I've never met another person so easy to talk to. I could sit here all morning, doing nothing but watching her smile and eat.

By the time breakfast is over, I'm throbbing with need, but I do the only thing I can—I get back on the bus, change into running gear, and sweat out my lust as best I can.

I run the next morning. And every morning after for the next two weeks. It's the only way I can cope. I don't allow myself time alone with Landry. It's too dangerous. During the day, I crash or jam with Davis or talk to Rudd about the marketing.

It's the early morning hours that are a problem.

Like me, she's up early. I don't know if she can't sleep or she just enjoys the time out of the bus. For me, it's getting my ass off the sardine can. The run tires me out.

She waltzes around innocently, blissfully ignorant of how she's tearing me up inside.

Only Ian guesses that my balls are bluer than a Smurf.

It's cold comfort that Landry's having fun. She doesn't hesitate to get out of the bus anymore. No dark shadows lurk behind her eyes. Her smile is ready and beautiful.

Objectively, I know I shouldn't be having breakfast with her each morning. I don't do this sort of thing with any other band member and I wouldn't be doing it if it weren't with her. But I can't give it up. These are the only times I have with her away from it all. In random cafes across the south, out in public so I won't be tempted to put my hands all over her.

So I suffer. It's exquisite torture.

We've fallen into a routine. We know each other well enough to order breakfast for each other. Large stack of blueberry pancakes for me, syrup on the side, accompanied by hash browns and an extra order of bacon. She never orders meat with breakfast but enjoys stealing two pieces from my plate. She only orders a Denver omelet.

"Mike told me you were a creative genius," Landry says during today's breakfast.

"Who's Mike?" I blink because she's so damned gorgeous. Idly I wonder what she'd do if I dragged her across the table and onto my lap, then kissed the daylights out of her.

"Mike, the Man Bun."

"Oh, him." I hate him. He joined us a few weeks ago and spends more time in Landry's company than I like.

"Yes." She leans forward. "Did you know that he and Keith are seeing each other? I think that's a recipe for disaster, don't you?"

"Keith? The lead singer for TA?" I lean back in surprise.

"Yup."

"No. I had no idea they were seeing each other." Thinking back, though, I guess I did see the two of them together. "Mike talks a lot of shit."

She bobs her head in agreement. "At first I didn't like him, but he's grown on me. I guess we're friends now. Like you and me. He told me you went to Juilliard."

Great. I've now been slotted into the gay best friend category. My dick presses urgently against my sweats to prove how hetero he is.

"Nah. I got accepted and turned it down."

She looks at me expectantly. "Why would you do that?"

"My dad had a stroke and I didn't want to leave him."

"Oh no. I'm so sorry. When did that happen? Because I didn't see it on his—" She breaks off with a guilty expression.

I grin. "Snooping?"

"A little."

"Find out anything?"

"That you don't have a lot of pictures out there. I tried to send one to May, but all I could find were band photos."

"Do you have a lot of pictures on the internet?"

She thinks hard. "I guess not. Too creepy."

It feels good that she's looked me up. A nice ego stroke.

"My dad's thing was kept quiet," I tell her. "It happened at home, and he has a doctor friend that I called. Medical stuff isn't supposed to get out anyway."

"But things get leaked all the time."

"Mostly by people who can't keep their shit locked down. Anyway, he's better now. "

"Do you regret not going to Juilliard? That seems like an amazing experience."

"Nah, I went to State, roomed with my friend, Finn. You remember him? He helped reno Bessie. I started my own band in college and that was better than going to Juilliard."

"How many bands have you had?" The question is asked lightly, but it sounds like Mike talked about more than my Juilliard past.

"This is my third. I had one in college. It broke up after we couldn't get any decent gigs in Chicago because of behind-the-scenes stuff." No way am I telling her what really went down. She'd think I was a dirty, rotten bastard. "I was in another band right out of college, but I broke my leg at a show. While I was recuperating, the singer took my music and played it with another band. I had to sue him to stop it."

"God, what a dick!" she exclaims.

"This is my third." And last, I think.

"Which one do you like best?"

I give her a look. "Landry," I say with exaggerated patience. "You always tell the girl you're with that she's the best you ever had."

"Even if you don't mean it?"

"Would you want to hear something else?"

"Yeah, I think I'd want the guy to be honest. If we were dating and he thought that his third girlfriend was his best girlfriend ever, then I'd want to know."

"And you'd do what with that information?"

"Well, I think I'd throw a pot at his head and storm off, telling him that he might as well be with his old girlfriend if she was so awesome."

I die laughing at her honesty.

"What do you think of the other bands?" she asks when I get my act together enough to wipe the tears out of my eyes.

"Besides TA, the other three bands are chaff. They're fine for filler, but no one's paying a fee to see them in the future. They're bar bands, at best. But TA isn't going anywhere, either."

Her eyebrows shoot up. "How can you say that? They have a hit single."

"Exactly. A single."

"So this is the beginning of great things for them."

I give her a pitying look. "Is that what Man Bun is telling you?"

"Sort of?"

I lean forward, elbows on the table. I know things about music. Maybe it's because I've been part of the scene since I was born. Since I was a twinkle in my dad's testicles, even. But I know music. I know it like I knew Juilliard would bore me to tears. Like how I knew my first two bands were duds. I have an ear or feel for what is going to be successful and what's not. The best A/R folks in the industry have it, too.

"Subconsciously, we all like familiar things." I point to our plates. "We order the same thing every morning. We have our favorite pair of shoes or favorite jeans. We, as a general rule, aren't fans of change. People want that feeling from their music. They want something that sounds familiar. Did you know that nearly all the songs that have been hits in the last few years have the same chord procession? C, G, A-minor and F. There's a YouTube video on it. Look it up."

"What does that have to do with TA? Their music sounds like what's played on the radio."

"Exactly. TA's writing music that's indistinguishable from what's already out there. They do a good job, and Keith's a good front man, but his music is uninspired. Have you heard of the band Outkast?"

"It sounds vaguely familiar." She makes an embarrassed face. "I'm pretty music dumb."

"That's okay." *Not why I like you, baby.* I hum a few lines from "Hey, Ya" for her.

"Okay, yes. I've heard that before."

"When that first came on the radio, it was a failure. A total dud. People were changing the station before the first verse was out of Andre 3000's mouth because it didn't sound like anything they'd heard before. Radio execs from Arista Records paid to have the single placed between songs from artists like Celine Dion and Smash Mouth to get people to actually listen. *Speakerboxx/The Love Below* is ranked one of the ten best albums of the 2000s. It changed the music scene. It changed what people wanted to hear."

"And you want to do that?"

I toy with my fork. My personal dreams sound fucking pretentious when I talk about them out loud, but Landry's inexperience with music makes me more comfortable. Landry has already had her own unbelievable success. Big dreams probably seem normal to her.

"The Beatles pretty much invented the modern band. They were one of the first who wrote their own music. The Rolling Stones melded blues and rock in a way people hadn't experienced before. Black Sabbath did for metal what the Stones did for rock. Grandmaster Flash blew them both up with his rhymes and swag." I point the fork at her. " Yeah, I could write a hit tomorrow for this band. Use my dad's connections to get it played on the radio, make a top hundred song, but then what?"

"I don't know? One-hit wonder?"

She takes me seriously in a way that no one really has before, not even my dad who wants me to drop this whole band nonsense and come back home and enjoy the fruits of *his* labor.

"One-hit wonder," I confirm.

"You aren't worried that all the best stuff's already been done?"

I shake my head. "No. The best songs have yet to be written. They're out there, waiting for someone to find them."

"And you're it?"

I study her face and find only earnest interest, not disdain or incredulity over my grand ambitions. "I don't know if I'm going to find a song like Hallelujah by Cohen or a classic by the Beatles or make a record as incredible as Outkast but I want to try. That's all I want to do."

"You want to change the collective consciousness of people when it comes to music," she muses thoughtfully. "You want to...Facebook Myspace."

See, pretentious but, holy fuck, she gets it. "Something like that. It's easy to make a hit, Landry. So much harder to last."

"And now?"

"I think it's going to last."

"Because you know things."

"I know things."

Like I know that Davis is a special kind of talent. Like I know you're a special kind of person.

"I know things," I repeat.

15

ADAM

Tour Stop: Austin

"Do you guys think those two were sisters?" Rudd asks, stumbling out of his bunk and down the aisle.

Ian looks up from his cards to stare at our bassist. "No. No one thinks they were sisters."

"But they said they were. Why would they lie about that?"

"Maybe because you said, 'Are you sisters? I've always wanted to have a threesome with sisters.'" I toss in a pack of gum and order Ian to deal me two more. We don't play for money. Money always has a way of fucking things up.

So when we do play cards it's for small shit like gum or mints or cigarettes. Currently the kitty holds two packs of Trident, a joint, and a small package of Oreos. I want those Oreos. The two cards Ian sends my way are perfect.

"I definitely didn't say that. Who wants to have a threesome with sisters?" Rudd scoffs, apparently not remembering what he said the other night while drunk. He rummages around the kitchen for something to eat. "That's incest-ish."

"Ish?" Ian asks.

That's the correct question. I eye the Oreos. What's the punishment for stealing from the kitty?

Ian lays down his four threes.

I toss my cards at him. "Motherfucker. I had an ace-high full house."

"You had your eye on these cookies, didn't you?" He gloats, pulling the kitty to his side of the table.

"You know I did. Where'd you get them, anyway?"

"Part of my goodie bag that Berry packed for me."

Ian can be such a fucking smug bastard at times. I pick up the cards and shuffle while Ian directs his attention back to Rudd.

"Yeah, as long as the sisters don't touch, there's no incest," Rudd explains. "It's in the dictionary, bros. Look it up."

I grin. "I didn't realize you knew what a dictionary was, let alone how to look anything up."

"Fuck you, man. I can use my phone as well as anyone." He pulls his mobile out of his pocket. "Siri, what's the definition of incest?"

"*Sexual relations between people classed as being too closely related to marry each other*," the mechanical voice recites.

Rudd frowns. "Does that mean cousins are out? Because I did cousins at Ian's family reunion last summer."

"What the fuck are you talking about?" Ian says, giving up any pretense that we're going to finish this hand. "I never had any family reunion."

"Sure you did," Rudd replies, sliding into the booth next to Ian. "Last summer at Festival Park, you were there with Berry and bunch of other folks. There was a shit ton of people and someone made this awesome lemon meringue pie." He rubs his belly. "Never thought I liked lemon until I had that shit. Anyway, these two brunettes invited me back to their room at the Holiday Inn. Your cousins."

"Dude, that wasn't my family. It was Founder's Day. Berry and I were just hanging out in the park." Ian's face is red with laughter.

"Well, who the fuck did I go to bed with then?"

Ian lays his head down on the table, howling. It might've been his laughter or Rudd beating Ian around the head with the now-empty muffin box that wakes Davis up from his nap.

The sound of the pocket door sliding open and heavy boots on the tile signal his arrival. I don't need to glance over my shoulder to know that his sister's still in the back. An electrical charge shoots up my spine every time she's within ten feet of me, and my Landry radar hasn't gone off all afternoon.

Surreptitiously, I flip over my phone to see if she's answered the text I sent an hour ago. Nothing.

Across from me, Ian tears up again. This time laughing at my expense instead of Rudd's.

"Asshole," I mutter under my breath, but the significance of my actions isn't lost on me. I can't remember the last time I was anxious to hear from a girl, particularly one I wasn't sleeping with.

"Landry sick?" I ask, giving up any pretense of not caring.

"Nah," Davis says without any more explanation. "I'm hungry. What're we eating?" He leans against the counter.

"Muffin," Rudd replies, only it comes out more like "mmmffnnn" because his mouth is full of the baked treat.

"There's another box of donuts in the cabinet above the sink," I tell Davis before repeating, "Landry sick?"

Davis doesn't answer because his mouth is stuffed with half a donut. I'm forced to wait impatiently, squeezing the cards in my hands so tightly that they begin to crease. Ian frowns as he pulls them out of my grip.

"Landry?" I prompt when Davis opens his mouth to shove the rest of the donut in.

He pauses. "May got access to the internet again, and they're working on some project. Dunno what it's all about. When she gets involved in that shit, she loses track of time."

"It's been four hours."

He cocks his head and studies me. "You keeping track?"

I resist the urge to fiddle with my phone. "Just making sure she's still happy to be with us. After all, didn't you say that if she bailed, you were gone, too?" Technically, the threat was that he'd leave if one of us laid our filthy hands on her.

He presses his lips together, as if slightly embarrassed I'm calling him out on the whole blackmail thing, and then gives an abrupt nod. "She's fine. If she needs something, she's a big girl and can use her mouth."

That conjures up all sorts of dirty thoughts. Like her mouth opening wide around my dick. Or her mouth running over my abs. Or her lips tugging on the piercing through my left nip. Fuck, I'd settle for just her mouth on mine.

Rudd opens his mouth to probably say the same damn things I'm thinking, but I don't want to hear it. I give him a *not today, fucker* look at he sits back, confused but silent.

I'm pathetic. I'm ready to throw down with my bandmate over a girl I haven't even laid a finger on. I flip my phone over. Still nothing.

Davis grabs a gallon of milk from the refrigerator. "Heard you have some of your crew coming to the Austin show tonight."

"Yep. A couple of my roommates are from Texas so they're flying down to see the show and then driving to see their families." I suspect, although no one has said it outright, that Noah wants to introduce his girlfriend, Grace, to his dad. Grace is the kind of girl who would want that before she walked down the aisle, and Noah's been trying to drag Grace to the altar since he first arrived in town.

Before, I didn't really get his devotion. Grace was some girl he wrote letters to while deployed in the Marines. When he separated from the military, he thought he had to make himself worthy of her before he parked his boots under her bed. He didn't come to her immediately, making her wait. When he finally did show his face, she was pissed off and this time, it was his turn to cool his heels until she came around.

I find myself understanding them both better now. Waiting sucks balls and so does wanting.

Three weeks of Landry laughing and flirting with me is slowly driving me mad. I've never jerked off so much in my entire life. I've never had to. Someone's always been around to do it for me. When I was thirteen, a groupie gave me my first blow job. Another groupie relieved me of my V-card a year later.

If my hand even strayed near my dick, there was a girl ready to address my needs. I took full advantage of it because why the hell not?

Since I started on this tour, though, I haven't touched one girl. And it's not like I'm lacking for attention. One thing about tours is that new pussy's always available. Every joint we've played has held a bevy of gorgeous women. Young ones, old ones, every shape and size. Girls pretending to be sisters and girls who probably are sisters.

But not one of them turned me on like Landry.

My phone pings. I nearly knock it off the table in my haste to grab it. It's Landry.

Her: I'm good. Got caught up w May. I have an idea for tonight after the show.

Please tell me it's you and me finding a private place and fucking until we're too exhausted to stand.

Me: Yeah?

Her: How about this?

Sadly, it's not a picture of her naked. Instead, it's a link to a site that offers neon mini-golf.

Her: Too hokey?

Me: No. Think the guys would like it.

Her: I'll set it up. How many do you think?

I look at my crew. *How about none of them and just you and me in the dark?*

Me: Reserve enough for all of us. If some don't show, they don't show. I'll cover any cancellation costs.

Her: Coolio. We stopping soon?

Me: Not until we get to Austin. Need something?

Her: Nah. I might nap, tho. The bus is making me sleepy.

Me: I'll wake you when we get there.

Her: K have a good jam session.

∼

"YOU KILLED IT TONIGHT," Bo yells as he hops onto the stage and gives a hard blow across my back.

"Austin loves its live music."

"Nah, they loved you. Yo, Ian, put that thing down, son. We're your roadies for tonight." Bo shoves me out of the way so he can get to Ian, and the two engage in a short tussle before Ian gives up. Bo's got about thirty pounds on my drummer.

"You're getting Bo's help whether you want it or not," Noah murmurs beside me.

I bend and unplug the mic cord from the amp. "I see that. How was the flight down? I heard Grace convinced you to fly first class." Noah is a notorious cheapskate, trying to save every penny so he can amass his first million before he turns thirty. He'll make it easily, but Grace comes from money so he has a hard time recognizing his own successes.

He grimaces. "She said it was a gift from her mother."

"And you believed that?"

"Couldn't really accuse my girl of lying." He looks over his shoulder where Bo's girlfriend and Grace are standing with Landry. "By the way, Landry's pretty great." He gives me a nudge. "You did good work there."

"Not mine yet."

"What's the holdup?"

I grab the amp and gesture with my head for Noah to grab the mic stand. "She had a bad run-in with a guy before."

"You need Bo and me to pay a visit?" the former Marine asks with a hard edge to his voice.

"No. She's safe here, and I already have Mal looking into it. Landry's stalker dropped by the week before we left on tour, but the guy had two witnesses. Mal says the two guys are the stalker's old frat brothers, and apparently junkies, too. Marrow might either be dealing to them or he has some good contacts. Mal figures he can peel them away from Marrow, but it's taking a little effort. In the meantime, he's a thousand miles away, and she's having a good time." I heft the amp onto my shoulder. "While you were waiting for Grace to come to her senses, what'd you do?"

Noah gives me a speculative look. "I lifted. A lot."

"I've been running five miles every morning," I confess.

"How's that working out for you?"

"Not well. How'd it work out for you?"

"Not well."

That isn't encouraging.

"So what's the holdup?" he asks again.

"She told me she trusted me."

Noah winces.

"Exactly. Maybe some girls would be thrilled to hear that my dick gets hard at the thought of her, but she's not one of them."

He hands the mic stand to Ian, who packs it away in the belly of the bus. In a low voice, Noah says, "I thought it might be the brother."

"If it were just him, I'd tell her exactly where I stood and let her make the decision."

"The band be damned?"

I look over his shoulder at Davis, who is mock boxing with Rudd while Ian lights up a joint and watches. "I don't think it'd come to that, but if it did?" I shrug. "Bands come and go. A girl like Landry is once in a lifetime."

"You should tell her that."

"And have her run screaming for the hills?"

"She doesn't act like someone who's scared of you. In fact, during your set, she couldn't take her eyes off you. Grace and AnnMarie tried to talk to her, but she was too focused on what was happening onstage to pay any attention."

I shove the amp at Ian and draw Noah to the side. "She say anything?"

Christ, I feel like I'm in middle school, trading notes on the way to class.

Noah doesn't give me shit, though. He knows what it's like to want and not have. "Before you got onstage, it was Adam this and Adam that. She believes the sun rises and sets on your ass. I don't think telling her how you feel is violating any trust she might have. If she tells you she's not interested, then you deal with that. I know you're not going to force yourself on her."

I hesitate. "I don't want to spook her." I need to handle her with care. The crush she once said she had doesn't seem to have materialized into anything concrete. I don't want to scare her off.

"Nothing ventured, nothing gained," Noah says.

I turn it over in my head. She's comfortable with me because she thinks I'm safe. If I don't make it weird for her if she turns me down, then, yeah, what do I have to lose? And she's only here for another few weeks. Although, *that* thought bothers me more than it should.

"Are we going to the bus tonight?" Rudd yells.

I shake my head. Noah and Bo won't want to sit around in a pot-fueled, post-gig orgy. Besides, if there was a time to talk to Landry, tonight would be a good one. Away from the party for one night, it'd give us both time to breathe. "Thought we'd do this."

I pull up the website of the golf place and show it around.

"Mini-golf? I'm out," Rudd declares. "No offense, dudes, but the only stick I want to handle tonight is my own."

"Good, because the ladies of Austin are too high class for you," Ian snarks.

"That's not what I meant!" Rudd protests.

I smirk. "Ian?"

"Nah, I think I'll sit this one out."

Davis is shaking his head, too. "I told a girl I'd meet her after the gig. But you take Landry, why don't you?"

Yes, why don't I take her?

In a million ways—999,999 of which you wouldn't like.

"No problem. Have fun and wrap it up tonight, boys."

I'm whistling as we leave.

"You sound way too happy for a mini-golf outing," Noah says quietly.

I fight hard to keep a big grin off my face. "Nothing ventured, nothing gained, right?"

16

LANDRY

The mini-golf place is fairly crowded despite it being midnight, but I guess if you're playing neon golf, it should actually be dark.

The three guys cause a minor commotion when they stroll up to the rental counter. A couple girls separate themselves from their own group to sidle up to Adam.

"Didn't you play over at the Centurion tonight?" one of them exclaims.

"I did." Adam gives them a cool smile but neither of the girls registers his social signal.

One drags a hand down his tatted arm. "You were so good up there. I love your song about the ride. What's the name of that?"

It sets my teeth on edge to see her touching him. I don't really get how people can just up and invade someone else's personal space like that. He peers down at her hand, then glances over his shoulder at me. Like he's expecting me to do something.

"You're not getting very far with a musician if you can't remember the name of his songs," mutters AnnMarie.

"No kidding," Grace chimes in. And, in a louder voice than her friend, she says, "I can't believe how rude people are these days."

Exactly. It's rude and annoying and...and...I don't give life to that other thought. The one that says if anyone should be touching Adam, it's me. Because I don't get to touch him, either. I told him about my crush weeks ago and he pretty much shrugged and walked away from me. What we have between us, the post-gig talks and the early morning breakfasts, is something friends do and I'm not ruining it by telling him this crush is becoming too big to deal with.

The girls throw us a few dirty glares, but the one with her hand on Adam's forearm doesn't back away. If anything, she steps closer, this time brushing her big boob against his biceps. "So what're you doing now?"

Adam steps to the side, putting a bit of distance between him and the fan. "Playing a round with my friends." As he's saying this, he gives me another unreadable look.

"As if it isn't obvious since we're here at a mini-golf place," Grace says with a sniff of obvious disdain.

"Well, if you need some help finding your way around in the dark, give me a holler." She holds up her phone and waves it back and forth. "If you gave me your number, it'd be even easier."

I don't know why my mouth opens and the words come out, but they do. "Sorry, honey, that's my man you're hitting on right in front of me."

The girl turns to give me a good onceover. "Her?" she says in barely concealed disbelief.

Adam grins, his white teeth flashing bright against his tanned skin. "Her."

She wrinkles her nose before pinning her attention back on Adam. Then, proving she has big balls to match her big boobs, she pulls out a pen and jots something down on a napkin. "If you get bored, here's my number."

"We're right here, bitch," AnnMarie calls out.

"Who you calling a bitch?" the handsy fan's friend snarls.

The three guys take a step back, as if they don't want to get in the way of this potential girl fight. I roll my eyes. *Men, honestly.*

Stepping forward, I take fangirl by the arm. "Trust me. I'm doing womanhood a favor by taking Adam off the market. He's got a huge ego. And he's super temperamental. Rock stars." I make a sad face. "You think they're going to be awesome, but then you get them home and they think they're above the little things, like picking up dirty socks and putting down the toilet seat."

As I'm holding back the fangirl, Grace and AnnMarie usher the boys to the first hole. Once the dark swallows them up, the fangirl's interest dims.

"It'd be Adam Rees in your house, though," she says, but her heart is no longer in it.

"No matter what they do, they're all the same in the end. Trust me on this. Besides, if you really want a rock star experience, you need to seek out Rudd."

"Chris Rudd? The bassist?" She chews on her lip. "I dunno."

"He's really in demand." This girl wants to sleep with a rock star? Rudd's her absolute best chance from everything I've seen. I build him up a bit more. "There's never been a night that hasn't ended with Rudd surrounded by girls, but you? You're exactly his type."

"Really?" She isn't quite convinced, but she's wavering. The uncertainty in her voice begs for a small push.

"Absolutely. Look at you. You're gorgeous." I'm not blowing smoke up her ass. She really is pretty. "You go up there with all the confidence you showed tonight, and he'll be putty in your hands. The band's playing at Eighth Street tomorrow."

We near the concession stand her group is hanging out when the fangirl unexpectedly throws her arms around me. "Thank you for the tip. You've been super nice. I'm sorry I hit on your man."

"Don't worry about it." I awkwardly pat her on the back. "Be safe tonight, ladies."

I give the two girls a jaunty wave and find my five friends hiding just beyond the concession stand.

I sense, more than see, Adam shaking his head.

"When I get big, you're in charge of all the fan interaction," he announces.

"No thanks."

"Why? That was a masterful performance. Rudd couldn't have done it better himself."

"You heard?" I ask in surprise.

"We were right behind you." Adam hands me a putter. "In case she turned and tried to jump you."

"They were still hoping for a fight," Grace chirps.

Of course they were.

"I only said it to protect you," I tell him.

"You should stick around. There are a lot of other women here. I'm afraid."

"Ha. You could crush them all with your mighty fist."

As I give my putter a practice swing, Adam calls out, "Hey Landry, it's not my fist that's mighty."

I nearly drop the club. Next to me, AnnMarie snickers. She knows exactly where my mind went which is in the gutter, where I'm on my knees checking out exactly how mighty Adam's dick is. I presume it's awesome. I wipe one sweaty palm against my leg and then the other.

"Are we talking sticks or balls," Bo jokes. "Because I've got the longest stick here." He lifts his golf club up and waves it in the air.

The three guys fold themselves in half laughing, thankfully not noticing that I'm engaging in a dirty fantasy in front of them. AnnMarie gives me a nudge. "Start playing, Landry. We'll leave these yahoos behind."

I gather myself and manage to hit the hole—golfing is dirty—in four strokes. The next hour or so is more of the same—the guys make dick jokes while we girls roll our eyes and proceed to kick their asses on the green.

On the fourth green, there's a series of ladders and slides that you have to get the ball up and over in order to complete the putt. Noah grows frustrated and slams his putter on the green. The head of the putter actually breaks, bounces off the green and strikes one of the miniature ladders.

"Here, have mine, tough guy," Adam extends his putter.

Noah starts forward, his hands raised as if to try to strangle Adam.

Grace jumps forward. "I'm hungry, honey. Let's go find some food and someone to fix this."

"I'm hungry, too," AnnMarie announces.

"Since when?" Bo asks.

"Since right now," she insists. She drags the big man off the green toward the concession stand. Grace and Noah follow, leaving Adam and I standing beside the broken apparatus.

"Guess it's just you and me," I remark dryly.

"Looks like it." There's a husky note to his voice.

Surreptitiously I wipe my hands against my skinny jeans again. "Should we play on?"

"If you want."

"Um, sure." I walk off to the next green before I do something I regret.

Being near Adam—in the dark and without Davis around—is making me think dangerous thoughts. As in, if I move slightly to my left, I could be the one rubbing my boob against Adam's perfectly muscled biceps. As in, if I lifted my hand, I could slide my fingers between his. As in, I could tuck myself under his arm, wrap my body around his and pull his gorgeous mouth against mine.

And no one would see. The tiny lights barely brighten the ground. The neon glow-in-the-dark balls emit no light. The only things on this course giving off any illumination are the targets.

Although I can't see him, I'm more aware of Adam now than I ever have been. His clean, male scent—some kind of woodsy fragrance that beckons me to stick my nose in his neck to fully decipher all of its notes—fills my lungs. The air is so thick between us that I swear it's almost as if he's caressing me. I can hear his breathing, even and strong.

By the ninth hole, I'm a mess. My legs are weak, my heartbeat is worryingly fast, and I'm wishing I'd worn a bra with more padding, because I'm so turned on that my nipples are standing at attention. Good thing no one can see a damn thing.

Others are taking advantage of the dark. It's nothing but scattered whispers, stolen kisses, and throaty purrs from people abandoning golf in favor of a different sort of game.

I wish I could snuff out all my senses, like midnight smothers the light to cut off my awkward feelings toward him. What had started out an enjoyable distraction has turned into annoying neediness.

"I don't think our friends are coming back," I note at the tenth hole.

"I think they probably found better things to do." His voice is dark and rough.

Maybe he's not so calm, either. There's a harshness in his tone, a winded quality as if he's back from his post-breakfast run. Sweaty, disheveled, and impossibly hot.

I find myself stepping off the faintly lit green to stand on a patch of AstroTurf. My sneakers sink into the ground. The denim of my jeans scrapes against my thighs, the seam of the crotch pressing against an ache between my legs.

My pulse points are alive. A flutter at my neck. Twin drums at my wrist. A reverberating echo in my center that thrums through my veins until my entire body feels lit up like a Christmas tree.

In this shadowed place, I'm more exposed than if I were on the beach at noon. I rub a shaky hand across my chest, my nipples straining in response to my own touch. My mind imagines Adam's touch. His hands would be larger, rougher. Calluses have built up from years of holding the neck of his guitar. The pads of his fingers would abrade my skin in a wonderful, stomach-clenching way. His palm is more than large enough to engulf my breast.

A moan escapes my lips.

"Landry," he say, the sound squeezed out of the back of his tight throat. He drops the putter and takes a step toward me.

I don't move. I can't. I remember what he first said when I stupidly confessed my crush.

"What would happen if I told you that I wasn't safe? That I think

you're gorgeous and I've spent my fair share of moments fantasizing about what you'd feel like underneath me?"

"Adam...I..."

"I promise never to speak of this again."

"Landry," he repeats. Takes another step, then hauls himself up short. His chest heaves. Beside his thighs, his marvelous, magical hands fist and unfist.

"That's what I'm afraid of."

He's waiting for me. He's *been* waiting for me. Because he doesn't want me to be afraid. He doesn't want to spoil my sanctuary. But my refuge feels more like an ivory tower, cutting me off from fully living.

If I stayed in my parents' basement, hugging my solitude close, wouldn't Marrow be beating me once again?

I gather my courage and close the gap between us. It takes three steps. Three long steps. I think he stops breathing. I hook a hand around the back of his neck and place the other on his chest for leverage. Rising on my tiptoes, I draw his mouth down to mine.

"Kiss me," I whisper.

With a groan, his mouth crashes against mine. He gathers me in his arms and pulls me hard against his frame. I feel the press of his erection against my belly as he pulls me off the ground. My legs have nowhere to go but around his waist, and he groans again as the maneuver presses the thick ridge of his cock against the hollow ache of my core.

His tongue slashes its way into my mouth, taking away my breath, my worry, my fear, trading it for desire and lust and *need*. There's a possession in his kiss that I've never felt before. A naked want that makes me tremble.

I clench my legs harder around him.

"Please," I beg, although I'm not certain what I'm pleading for. I don't want to stop kissing him or touching him or rubbing myself along the hard, seemingly endless column of his erection.

His answer is to grip me tighter and start moving. My hands are busy, caressing the skin at the base of his neck, running through the short strands of his soft hair. His mouth rubs against mine, never quite removing the contact.

We abandon our putters, our balls, our surroundings. I have no idea where we're going or how we're getting there. I simply hold on to Adam as he strides down, comes to a halt in a copse of trees.

"You've picked a hell of a time to be brave, Landry," he growls, pushing me back against a tree trunk.

The rough bark scratches my palms as I reach behind to brace myself. The stubble along his jaw abrades my cheek and then my neck as his hungry mouth forges a sensitive trail from my chin to my collarbone.

"I, uh, wanted to kiss you."

His teeth close over the throbbing vein in my neck. "Here? In the middle of the mini-golf park?"

"Why not here?" I ask.

His hands find the hem of my shirt and push upward, baring my skin to the cool breeze of the Austin night. I shiver, more from his greedy touch than the brisk air. He nips at my earlobe, traces his tongue around the upper shell.

I lose my train of thought—if I ever had one in the first place—as his hands come up to cover my lace-covered breasts. He tugs the cups down, replacing the delicate fabric with his coarse palms. My breasts feel heavier. I draw his head downward and am rewarded with a wolfish laugh.

My pussy throbs in response. At my whispered yes, he lifts me up until my boobs are on level with his mouth. His thumbs hold up my shirt while his mouth covers one aching nipple and his palm rubs against the other. I squeeze my legs together, wishing I'd pushed his head lower.

He must be able to read my mind—or my motions—because he slowly lowers me to the ground so he can press a hand between my legs. "You aching here?"

"Yes, right there." I gasp as the heel of his hand grinds against my pelvic bone. Greedily, I thrust my hips forward.

"Right here in the park?"

"Right here." Why would I want to be anywhere else but here, in the dark, with Adam's mouth on my breast, his fingers rubbing me through the jeans, pressing the thick seam into my damp, swollen lips?

"Right here," I repeat.

"Shit, baby." He rises in one smooth motion, his hand remaining hard against me. He braces a forearm against the tree above my head and bends to taste my lips. His fingers rub and stroke me until my body shudders and a small cry flies from my throat to be swallowed by his kiss. The orgasm races through me, throbbing in my blood, and I'm whimpering against Adam's lips as I shudder with pleasure.

"Shhh," he whispers until I cool down.

And as the heat fades away, my brain cells kick in. What do we do now? How awkward will this be on the bus? What am I going to tell Davis?

"I can hear you worrying." Adam murmurs. His chin rests on my head, bumping gently against me as he talks.

"This was...unexpected," I say.

"Was it?" He sounds amused. "What's unexpected is that I lasted this long. I've wanted you since the first moment I saw you."

He eases back far enough to bend down and kiss me again. It's a light peck, but it still sends a spike of electricity down my spine.

"I thought you were mad at me that night," I confess.

"What night?"

"When we first met. You saw my cuts and bruises and got all... pissed." I snug my arms close to my body and take advantage of the heat emanating from his. Now that we're not all wrapped up in each other, now that he's not warming me from the inside out, the cool Texas air is raising goosebumps.

He rubs his hands briskly down my arms. "Pissed you got hurt, yeah. At you? Never. Why would I be?"

"I dunno. You had this angry expression. And then Davis almost didn't go on this tour because of me—I figured you were labeling me Yoko Ono in your head. Thinking I was going to break up the band before it even got its feet planted."

"No, I never thought that. And yeah, I wanted to murder that Marrow guy. But, you—I definitely wanted you that night."

I can barely remember Marrow and tell Adam that. "He's a distant memory. I don't even worry about him anymore."

"Good." He kisses me again. This time, his lips linger and his hands on my arms slow until it's less about keeping me warm and more about enjoying the press of his flesh against mine. "Let's go, Landry," he says in a husky voice that promises more if I just follow him.

"Where we going?"

"Home."

I nod, my body vibrating with anticipation. We walk a few feet, then it hits me. He stops abruptly, too, and judging by his sigh, he's come to the same realization. Home is a bus full of drunk, rowdy people.

"How about a hotel?"

"What about Davis?" I counter. I hadn't fully thought this through, but I know that Davis isn't ready for the news that I'm hitting the sheets with Adam. This thing with Adam might only last for a hot second. I don't want to ruin Davis's band over that. The whole point of me coming on this tour was to make sure Davis's dreams could come true.

"What about him?"

"I'm not telling him about this."

"Why not?"

"Adam, come on."

He sighs again. "Fine. We don't have to say anything for now, but that doesn't mean we can't get a hotel room. I'll get one for everyone and say it's because of the success we had."

That sounds like a good plan for me. "I'm good for half."

I'm not used to throwing money at a problem to make it go away, but I can see the appeal.

He chuckles. "I'm good for it. It'll be my treat."

I reach for my phone to text Davis, but a message pops up. Before I can read it, I see Adam pulling his phone out of his pocket.

Davis: Where are you? You with Adam? He needs to haul ass to the bus. Amazing news.

I show the screen to Adam. He flips his around for me to read. He's got several missed messages, but the one showing on his screen is from Rudd.

Dude. Get back here. Hollister has something for you.

Adam texts back. Don't need a girl.

Rudd: It's not pussy. Better than.

Adam: Tell me tomorrow. Thought we'd get some hotel rooms. Sleep in a real bed.

Rudd: You're gonna be too excited to sleep.

Adam stares at his phone for a second, then at me. "I don't think they're going to stop bugging me. Why don't we go back, find out what they want to tell me, and then go to the hotel?"

Before I can answer, my phone buzzes again. Davis again.

Srsly grab his ass and drag him back here.

Adam drops his head in sad resignation.

Can you die from an erection? I'm currently testing the theory. At the green, we find Bo and Noah studying the chutes and ladders contraption. A young, gangly kid is standing to the side wearing a neon-green polo with the logo "Our sticks work in the dark" in black lettering over his left breast. He's glaring at the two former Marines. Ah, the precociousness of youth, given that my two roommates could snap his thin neck like a twig.

"I can't believe you're going to charge us two hundred bucks for this thing," Noah grouses, waving his broken putter around.

"Finn could've fixed it for five," Bo adds.

"Well, he's not here," says AnnMarie, exchanging an exasperated look with Grace.

I pull my wallet out and hand two hundred-dollar bills to the attendant. "Sorry about that." To Bo and Noah, who look peeved I've paid the guy off, I say, "I need to get back to the bus."

"That's a ripoff," Noah grumbles.

"Gosh, Adam, thanks so much for taking care of that for us. I'm sorry I suck so bad at mini-golf that I broke the putter," Grace chirps in a spot-on imitation of Noah.

"You're welcome," Landry says before I can respond, doing a spot-on imitation of *me*. "I'm happy to do it and I'm not going to rub it in or be an ass about it."

The girls dissolve into a fit of giggles.

"Very funny." Noah slaps Grace on the ass as she climbs into the rear of the Escalade.

"Thanks. I thought it was."

"Me, too." Landry joins Grace in the back and they exchange high-fives.

The humor helps to take the edge off. Concentrating on something other than the taste and touch of Landry works, too. But it's not enough. I'm acutely aware she's only a couple inches behind me and that if it were just the two of us, we'd still be in the parking lot, only we'd be horizontal and we'd both be wearing substantially fewer clothes.

Next to me, Bo is rambling about how we all need to play real golf. I hate golf, but I throw myself into the conversation because I don't need my mind wandering back to that patch of fake grass and trees where I kissed Landry until we were both too weak to stand.

It works, because my hard-on subsides by the time we roll into the parking lot where the bus is still stationed. It's lit up, but it appears the crowd has dispersed.

"Thanks for coming down," I tell my roommates and their girls.

"Wouldn't have missed it," Noah says. He gives me a back slap and hug. Bo does the same. The two girls throw themselves into my arms.

"I like her," Grace whispers. "She's perfect for you."

AnnMarie nods. "I agree. Don't mess this up, hotshot."

"Not planning to." I give them both a kiss on the cheek. Another time, I would've kissed them on the mouth, mostly to rile up their boyfriends. But now I feel that part of me belongs to Landry.

Landry also gets hugs from everyone before my roommates hop into their vehicle and speed off to their hotel. I watch the SUV with a little wistful longing.

Landry punches me lightly in the arm. "Come on," she says, "We have tomorrow."

I perk up immediately. So does my dick. "Tonight, you mean."

She glances at her phone. "So it is."

"Dude, my fucking God, did you walk from the joint or what?" An excited Rudd tumbles down the stairs. "Get in here." He motions with his arm.

Landry arches her eyebrows but says nothing as she follows Rudd inside. Davis is seated across from Hollister. Leaning against the counter is Ian, his tattooed arms crossed in front of his chest and an impassive expression plastered on his face.

Davis is vibrating with excitement. He explodes out of his seat when he spies Landry and me. "Fuck, why the hell did you two take so long?"

Because your sister and I were busy trying to rip each other's clothes off.

I rub a hand across my forehead. Landry averts her eyes.

"It doesn't matter." He waves a hand. "Come on, Hollister. Tell Rees the news."

Hollister gets to his feet. A genuine smile curves his lips upward. I've seen that shark smile before. It's the one Hollister's wallet generates when it senses an influx of cash.

"Yeah, tell me," I say, although I'm fairly sure I'm not going to like whatever it is he's going to try selling me. Ian's lack of emotion is not encouraging.

"A guy from InMotion was at the bar tonight with his girlfriend and he really liked your music. Said your sound was 'fresh and clean.'"

"Sounds like he's describing a mouthwash." I lean my hip against the edge of the banquette. At my back I can feel the warmth of Landry's body as she stands just over my right shoulder. She chuckles, but no one else does. In fact, I catch Ian wincing slightly.

"It's not a mouthwash," Rudd says. He's tired of waiting. He pushes by me, throws an arm around Hollister and says, "Our man Hollister is going to hook us up with a tech company. Some fruity company wants to use 'Classic' for their next commercial. Is that amazing or what? We're the new Fitz and The Tantrums!"

He raises his arms and forms devil's horns with his fingers.

"A commercial?"

"I told you he wouldn't go for it." Ian turns and heads for the back as if he doesn't want to hear any explanation or excuses.

"Come on, Rees." Rudd drops his arms. "Seriously? This is a big-time opportunity. Fitz didn't get big without all its pop culture creds."

"It's true," Hollister adds. "Commercials are one of the primary methods of discovery for new bands. These tech companies love using little known musicians and pushing them into the mainstream. It makes them look cool and hip. My guy says they'll pay well. You'll have national exposure, which means your band can headline instead of being backup."

"No." I push by a disappointed Rudd and a confused Davis to find an angry Ian in the back, shoving empty beer cans and red Solo cups into a trash bag. Behind me, I hear some cursing and Davis saying, "What just happened?"

"You said no, didn't you," Ian says.

I crouch on the floor to grab some trash. "Yeah, you mad?"

"Frustrated," he says tersely. "You fucking love that company. Every piece of tech you own has that damn brand on it, but you're turning it down because of some musical ideal that no one even cares about anymore."

"We're three weeks into this tour and we're already growing our audience." I stuff some gross wet napkins and a couple bottles into the bag. "Let's see where we are at the end of the tour. Growing our audience organically makes the most sense. We've both been around long enough to know that one hit makes zero difference." Fuck, everyone is so shortsighted. Threat Alert has no staying power and Ian knows it. "In a year, no one's going to remember TA beyond their single song. Even now, the audience doesn't care about their music. They only want to hear the hit on repeat."

Ian grits his teeth. "That's because their music sucks on the whole. We don't suck, Adam. With Davis, this is the real deal. You know it and so do I, but if we don't take every advantage offered to us, our chance will dissolve. In two months, this offer isn't going to be on the table anymore. Hell, it might not be on the table in two days. You can do stuff with this offer that other bands can't."

"He's right," Rudd says from the doorway. "The other guys on tour would kill for this opportunity."

Over my bandmates' heads, I spy Landry. Her face is filled with confusion. To a girl who didn't hesitate to sell her work, my attitude makes no sense. When I start talking, it's more for her sake than anyone else.

"We let ourselves be defined by one song, and we'll never be the band we can be. This is the only song our crowd will want to hear. I don't want that for us. Look at Threat Alert."

Davis's eyes soften in understanding. Landry looks thoughtful. We've been peeling away the other band's audience, one night after another. It's making everyone on the headliner's group testy.

They try to hide it, but the snarky remarks they shoot in our direction have more than a little truth to them.

I press my advantage. "I'll subsidize this band for however long it takes for us to gain the right audience that can keep us playing for years. If we take a shortcut, we're cutting ourselves off at the legs. We've got a great sound. Let's not sacrifice that for some quick money. If you need a loan, I'm good for it. Hell, it doesn't even need to be a loan. I'll just give you the money."

"It's not about the money for me," Davis says. "The idea of national exposure sounded good, but I've never done anything but play at a few local bars and fraternities. If you think turning this offer down is the best thing for us, then I'll back you."

Relief fills my chest. Feeling about a hundred pounds lighter, I turn to Ian. "You in, man?"

He shakes his head and snorts before holding out his fist. "I'm in."

"Rudd?"

My bassist makes a face but puts his hand in the middle. "I think we're stupid as fuck to turn it down, but I'm in."

Davis's hand lands on top. "No shortcuts."

"No shortcuts," we all yell.

It's not until I'm in my bunk that I remember Landry didn't stick her hand in.

And it bugs me. All night long.

~

THE NEXT MORNING, she's waiting for me. We go to breakfast. We talk about everything but last night. Not the almost sex we had at the mini-golf and not the offer from Hollister. I wait for her to bring it up, but she doesn't. Not once.

"We still on for tonight?" I ask as we walk from the IHOP back to the bus.

"I don't know, are we?" A pair of metallic aviators shield her eyes.

"It's all I can think about."

Her head swings in my direction. "Same."

I push away any feelings of unease. Or rather, my lust does. This morning, my phone was full of texts from my roommates.

Finn: Heard you've been bagged by the redhead. Nice.

Mal: Still working on our project. Keep in touch. Sounds like this one's a keeper. Thumbs up.

Bo: We like this one.

Noah: Don't fuck it up.

The challenge is, I'm not sure what fucking up entails. For a moment last night, I wondered if not selling my music to some ad company was the fuckup, but since Landry hasn't uttered a word about it, I chalk up my unease to an overactive imagination. There wasn't disapproval in her eyes, and she didn't chime in because she doesn't feel like she's part of the band.

"I'm not sure what I'm going to tell Davis," she says, breaking into my train of thought.

"Huh?" I must've missed something. "Tell Davis what?"

"About us. I don't want him to know."

"Why not?"

She shoots me a skeptical look. "You really think Davis is going to be okay with you and me hooking up?"

Oh, right. No touching his sister. But he's going to find out at some point, because she and I aren't a one-time deal. I'm not going to hide in dark, secret places every time I want to make her come. Landry's the one who I see my future with.

She's smart, honest, and doesn't only want to be with me because I'm a musician. I can talk with her for hours without a single awkward silence, and I can't see that ever changing. When I look at her, I see a future full of laughter and easy conversation. And yeah, sex. Lots and lots of sex.

"I don't think that lying to him and sneaking around behind his back is the right thing to do. I don't mind talking to him."

She grabs my arm, pulling me to a stop. "I don't want to lie to him, either, but there's no reason we have to rush out and plaster it all over the side of the bus. You said yourself that this band has something special. That's why you agreed to this tour, recruited Davis, and why you're turning down this big deal commercial thing."

And there it is. I hate when my arguments are used against me. I place my hand over hers. "Davis knows this band is special, too. He quit his job and he won't give up simply because you and me have gotten close."

Landry glances toward the bus and back to me, her beautiful features drawing tight. "Davis is a hothead. The minute he found out about Marrow, he went and beat the guy up. He didn't think about the consequences for a second."

"That's what you're basing your worry on? I'd have done the same thing."

She drops her hand from my arm. "Ugh, you guys. Violence is not the answer. It didn't stop Marrow from stalking me. Instead Davis got thrown in jail and Dad had to pay a lot of money in legal fees to get the charge reduced from a felony to a misdemeanor."

"I doubt Davis was sorry for standing up for you. I sure as hell wouldn't be."

"Does standing up always have to include your fists?"

"Sometimes it does."

She shakes her head in dismay. "You once told me that you know things. You know when songs will be hits. That Threat Alert is likely a one-hit wonder. That *this* band has magic and the potential to be great. I want that for you. I want that for Davis." As I absorb this, she adds, "I'm not going to be here in another month. Let's wait until I go and then we'll tell him. Four weeks. That's all I'm asking. Four weeks for you to build your connection to each other."

Four weeks? My mind balks at this. "There's no reason for you to leave the tour after two months."

"My parents will be back by then."

"So?"

"So the danger of me being alone will be gone."

"Again, so? You should stay with us the entire tour." She's part of the band now, in some strange way.

"You know I can't."

"I don't know a damn thing."

As we get closer to the bus, Davis waves us over. He has a guitar on his lap. "You two okay?" he calls out.

"Of course. Why wouldn't we be?" Landry laughs lightly. "Aren't we?" she asks, and she's not merely asking if we're all right, but whether I'm buying into her subterfuge.

"Is this an ultimatum?" I say quietly.

"No. It's a request."

I pull a cigarette out of my pocket and jam it into my mouth. At this rate, I'm going to be smoking a carton a day and dying of lung cancer before the end of the tour.

"We're fine," I say as we reach him.

"You guys looked like you were in an intense discussion."

Is that suspicion in his voice?

"I was telling Landry we should stay in a hotel tonight. Get out of the bus and get a decent night's sleep."

Davis perks up. "Hotel, huh? That'd be awesome. Not that the bus isn't great," he hurries to assure me. "Can we afford it?"

I look to Landry. "Don't think we can afford not to."

18

LANDRY

Tour Stop: Austin Night Two

Tonight's show drags. The first two bands get almost no attention, and what little crowd there is seems unenthused. Only a few diehards are on the dance floor. I gaze up at the lead singer and wonder how demoralizing it is to stand up there and sing when no one is interested. Adam is standing at the edge of the dance floor, a bottle in one hand, tapping his foot and nodding his head to the beat. I don't know if he really enjoys it or is putting on a good show.

Ian is watching Rudd hit on a very pretty blonde while Davis and I enjoy a moment alone.

"You holding up okay?" he asks.

"Yeah, it's not as bad as I thought it'd be."

"I know. I've heard horror stories about touring in a van. Usually, you crash on someone's floor—hopefully not someone with pets. Remember Pete Appleton?"

"Vaguely. You went to college with him?" Davis brought a lot of guys home over break, but I never paid much attention to them. I was too busy with my own stuff.

"Well, he was in a band and they'd drive five hours for one gig and turn around and drive back home so he could be at work the next day. So this," Davis waves around the room, "this is great." He drops his arm back on the table. "I wish Adam wasn't such a tight-ass about his music, though. Can you imagine me singing on a commercial?"

"No, that'd be amazing. I think we'd have to call Mom and Dad and make them come home for that."

He grins. "No kidding. Although, from what Hollister says, it'd be months before the ad would air. Rudd was telling me that Fitz and The Tantrums' songs are on video games and TV promo spots." He whistles a few bars.

"Oh shit. I recognize that!" I exclaim. "That was on The CW last fall."

Davis slaps a hand on the table. "Exactly. They had their own tour last summer and now they have a couple billboard hits. They're the next big thing." He shifts in his seat so that he can see Adam better. Or maybe so he can glare at Adam better. "I don't get him, Landry. He's obviously a musical genius. He's got more connections to this industry than most and not just because of his dad." He turns back to me. "Did you know he writes music for other artists? That he wrote four hits last year and three the year before that?"

I recoil in surprise. "No. I had no idea."

The information hits me like a brick. I don't know much about Adam other than what I've read on the internet and what little Davis has shared. Sure, we've had breakfast with each other every day for two weeks straight, but in all that time, he's not once mentioned his music writing career.

I've had this suspicion that our connection would last only as long as the tour. Heck, I sort of set the parameters myself because I knew, deep down, that this is where his head was. If he really wanted a lasting relationship, we'd be telling each other everything. But, we aren't. We're both holding back.

Why that thought depresses me, I'm not sure. It's not like we're in love. We're hot for each other. We'll enjoy each other and go our separate ways. He's gorgeous, and I haven't had sex in a long time. So long that I'm a little nervous about tonight. He has a lot of experience and I've had close to none. What if I'm terrible and he doesn't want to hook up again? Wouldn't that be humiliating?

"It's true. I mean, to some extent, I understand where he's coming from. We don't want to become known for only one song. But if he can write seven hits in two years, there's no reason he can't do the same for us, right?"

I shrug, because music isn't my thing. Davis makes a frustrated sound, either at my lack of understanding or Adam's stubbornness. To Davis, whose mantra is getting shit done, both are likely incredibly annoying. But he surprises me with a self-deprecating laugh. "Christ, I'm a shithead for complaining. I've got it so good compared to other people. Slap me upside the head the next time I bitch and moan about this band, okay?"

"That I can do," I say with a smile.

He stands up and reaches out to ruffle my hair. "Be good, little sis."

I bat his hand away. "Whenever am I not?"

"True," he says nonchalantly as he walks away, not realizing the sting of his words.

I've been good, closeted in the basement working away, ignoring the outside world and what did it get me? A nice bank account, a stalker, and a dusty vagina.

I peek over at Adam. He wants me. He turns me on. I mean, what more could I ask for? I don't need a love connection or a promise of forever. I like him. He's safe and he's experienced. Some girls might not like that, but I think I'll enjoy the benefit of his expertise. If we keep our hookup on the down low, there's no reason why we can't enjoy each other for the rest of the tour.

"You look happy, girl."

I glance up to see Mike sliding into Davis's abandoned chair.

"It's a great night in a great city with great music on tap."

He picks up my glass and sniffs it. "How much have you had to drink tonight?" he asks suspiciously.

I laugh. "One glass. And no, I'm not drunk."

"Then you're getting laid, because the band sucks, the crowds suck, and the tap beer is weaker than piss."

I avoid the first part of his statement. "You have a lot of experience tasting pee?"

Mike snorts into his bottle. "Not as much as the bartenders have if this is what they drink every night." He looks around the bar. "Why do you think it's so dead?"

I have no idea. "I write lines of code for a living. The social decisions people make are beyond me."

He turns slightly to look at the empty stage. "The natives are restless tonight. I don't know. Maybe FMK can get them out of their seats." He swivels back. "TA's falling apart and I wanted to offer Davis a job. I had that wrong, didn't I?"

Disarmed by his honesty, I can only blink in return. Mike doesn't require a response.

He taps his fingers. "Thank fuck Adam agreed to do the collaboration." The two bands are performing together at the end of FMK's set. "Wonder if we should change up the set list. Maybe start with 'Destiny's Here.' What do you think?"

Their hit single? Blowing out of the gate with the one song everyone wants to hear doesn't seem to be the best idea. Then again, like I told him before: I write code, not music sets. "You guys should just go with your gut."

He grimaces. "That's the problem. My gut is fucked up." Lines crease his perfect forehead. "Can I be straight with you, Landry?"

"Of course."

"This tour is killing me. Hollister expects Keith to be on social media, schmoozing all the girls. Back home in Central City, we have this solid crowd and Keith doesn't have to offer himself up like a piece of meat. Out on the road, he has to constantly be on—both in the club and every minute leading up to the show. He's got to be sending winky faces and compliments. Tweeting out pics of his abs and shit."

Mike rubs a hand across his chest, as if trying to soothe a bad ache. "I hate all this fucking hiding."

"Why can't you come out?"

He gives me a disdainful look. "Because the front man brings in the girls. If they find out he's gay, they can't imagine themselves with him. It ruins their fantasy."

"I dunno. I don't think you give women enough credit." Two attractive guys together? That's hot.

Mike doesn't agree. "Hollister would kill us. He told me that if I even hinted at Keith being in a relationship with me, that he'd drop us. He says we need to wait to get bigger and then we can go public."

"That sucks," I say, but I feel like a fraud.

Hiding is what I want to do. What I'm asking Adam to do. It's not that I'm ashamed of hooking up with him, but I don't want to make waves, and while my reasoning is not remotely the same as Hollister's, the result is the same. I'm asking Adam to be dishonest.

Glumly we both fall silent, brooding over our beers.

"Fuck. Now I've depressed both of us," Mike laments.

"Nah. I'm not depressed." I'm more confused, feeling both horny and guilty at the same time.

"Let's talk about something else. Word is that FMK might be the soundtrack to some commercial."

"I, ah, I..." I look around, unsure of what I should say. Is this band-only business? I don't want to leak something.

He clucks his tongue. "Honey, there's nothing in this industry that stays secret long. They going to do it?"

"I don't know." That seems like a safe answer.

"Adam probably said no."

"Why would you say that?" I ask, defensive on Adam's behalf.

"Because he's been asked before and always says no, that's why."

"He's been asked before?" I repeat dumbly.

"Yeah. Don't know how many times, but it's been a few. He's written a lot of pop hits, which is kind of funny if you think about it." At my look of confusion, he says, "Because his dad is the opposite. His dad shits on pop music."

"Oh, right." Sid Rees's music is heavy on the guitar and light on the melody. It sounded more like screeching to me. So, yes—a far cry from the peppy, upbeat, bubblegum tunes that populate the radio stations. "Is that why he doesn't sell his stuff?"

"Who knows? Rees is one of those musicians who has money, so he's a little off. I can't really read him."

Ditto, apparently. In fact, I'd like to go clear some things up with Adam. I don't need to know every single secret of his before we have sex, but I don't want to sleep with a mystery, either. But I don't have time, because FMK hits the stage. Mike leaves me in the middle of the set, but I barely notice. My eyes are glued to the band.

Davis is worked up, chatting with the crowd between songs, telling little stories which he must've cribbed from Adam and the rest of them since Davis wasn't around when these songs were written.

"Love Scars" was the song Adam wrote after Rudd admitted he was afraid of dogs because he'd been bitten by a Rottie when he'd delivered food as a teen. The story, as Rudd tells it, is that as he ran toward his car, the dog bit him. The bite in the ass caused him to stumble. The pie went flying and some landed on his bare arm, burning him. He said his love of pizza was forever ruined after that.

He does have a strange pepperoni-shaped scar on his forearm. Hence the lyric, "my love left a mark on me."

Davis regales the audience with the story and they are screaming their laughter.

He isn't the only one who draws the eyes. Plenty of thirsty girls are positioned on Adam's side of the stage, their faces upturned, their hands in the air. He walks to the edge, dips his shoulder low, making them scream with excitement. Davis is flirting with them and Adam's teasing them. Ian and Rudd provide the beat and the bass to anchor the sex that Davis and Adam are selling.

And it's working, because the once sleepy crowd is vibrating with excitement. I rub my hands between my legs, as if I can exorcise the heat Adam's performance is generating inside of me. He's too damn talented. My body doesn't care that he's a mystery. My body is just thrilled with the attention and the idea of all that muscle and sex appeal at its disposal.

"Austin, we love you. We'd play all night, but I know you're excited to hear Threat Alert," Davis shouts into the mic.

There's a chorus of noes but FMK drowns them out by barreling forward into "Destiny's Here," Threat Alert's hit song. As choreographed, Kevin strides out, playing his guitar. He stops next to Davis, who holds the mic out for Kev, and the two sing together, ensuring that the crowd is happy once again.

They jam together for two more songs—a cover of an old Fleetwood Mac song called "Landslide," then one of their originals that Mike suggested, "Those Aren't Tears," before announcing that the set is over.

I join the guys in the back. Adam is the first to reach me. His eyes are lit up and there's a fine sheen of sweat on his forehead. His T-shirt looks drenched, too. But that's hardly a turnoff. I lick my lips, wondering what he'd taste like.

His eyes darken knowingly. "Liked the show, did you?"

"A little bit."

His laugh is rough and sexy.

I take a deep breath, barely able to hear myself over the pounding of my excited heart. "How long do we have to stay?"

His eyes gleam. "Not long at all."

19

ADAM

Landry looks like she's ready to burst. I'm only a half step behind her and that's because I'm exerting phenomenal self-control over my dick right now. Otherwise, he'd be standing fully upright, flying his eager flag for everyone and their brothers to see. And since we're supposed to be keeping this from Davis, I'm thinking about amps and riffs and tour schedules. Basically, anything but how amazing she looks in her uniform of tight jeans and slouchy shirt, anything but how good she smells, clean and fresh.

Oh hell. My jeans get tight. Reluctantly, I turn away. The disappointed sound that sneaks out of her mouth makes me want to bend her over the nearest table and take her right there.

"If we ever want to get out of here without Davis knowing, I need to calm down," I mutter.

"Oh," she says, all wide-eyed and intrigued.

"Not helping." I turn my attention to the stage and take a long draw from my water bottle.

"Sorry," she says, but the quiet glee in that one word tells me she's not repentant at all.

Threat Alert runs off stage which means I need to get out there to help break down our equipment and make room for theirs. It's a much-needed distraction.

"Took you long enough," Albie grouses as we haul our shit off the stage.

"Sorry about that," Davis says. "Lost track of the time."

"Do better, dickhead. This is a group effort, not a one-band show."

"Albie, it's fine," Keith says. "No big deal."

"What's going on here?" Hollister steps up.

I exchange looks with Keith. *You take care of your act and I'll take care of mine.* No sense in making Hollister believe that his tour isn't running smoothly.

Keith gives me a terse nod of agreement. "Nothing, man. We're discussing the next set."

"A little loudly. I can hear you out there."

"Sorry."

Immediately we all look shamefaced. No need for anyone to hear the family fighting.

Davis sticks out his hand. "I'll do better next time."

Albie brushes his fingers against Davis, albeit reluctantly."

"We all right?" Hollister presses.

I nod. "Hunky dory."

Hollister draws me aside. "You need to do a little sucking up here. There's already some hard feelings developing because of the crowd response. Throw in the rolling hotel-on-wheels that you and your crew sleep in as opposed to crashing on floors or staying in motels that have more rats than maids, and you've a recipe for a lot of resentment. This tour is dependent on five bands, not one."

"How about we invite them to the hotel tonight," Davis suggests.

"What's this?" Hollister perks up.

"We were thinking of staying in a hotel tonight. Why not invite the guys to come over and crash. We have what? Five rooms? That'll house twenty guys."

Hollister looks in my direction.

I clench my teeth together. Christ, what a disaster. All I want to do is have sex with my girl. In relative privacy. Not in the dark against the bumper of a bus. Not against a fake tree in a mini-golf park. But in a bed. In a room with four walls.

I want to take her clothes off, worship every part of her beautiful body

"Rees?"

"Yeah, fine. We'll get more rooms, though."

"I'm not paying for this," Hollister warns.

"I'll pay."

"Great." Hollister claps his hands. "The tour is springing for hotel rooms tonight."

A cheer goes up.

"Thanks for taking credit," I grouse.

Hollister slaps me on the back. "Thanks for paying."

Threat Alert makes its way back onstage. The only salvageable thing about this whole situation is that Landry looks as miserable as I feel.

"I'm tired," she says. "Can we go to the hotel?"

I shake my head regretfully. "We better not. Threat Alert's on stage. We need to support them."

Davis throws an arm around her shoulder. "You love their song."

"But not more than ours, right?" Rudd says, taking up the spot on her other side.

I fall in behind them, content to stare at her ass.

"Your music is the best music in the entire world," she proclaims.

"That sounds sincere," Davis replies dryly.

"I'll take it," Rudd announces. "What other music do you like? You look like a goth chic."

"How so? I love color."

"You're serious, so I think you'd like mysterious, meaningful lyrics."

"Instead of ones about dogs?" she teases.

"That dog ruined my life. I can't have a pet now," Rudd complains.

We reach the booth, and when Davis turns to look for a waitress, I push Landry onto the bench and slide in next to her. Ignoring Ian's glare of exasperation, I ask Davis to get me a beer.

"Want anything?" Davis asks his sister.

"Whiskey sour." She turns to Rudd. "No goth chic likes whiskey sours."

"Not true. I knew a girl once who wore all black, even down to her underwear. All her drinks were green."

"Absinthe is often green."

"Oh. Didn't know that." Rudd sits back, momentarily nonplussed. "Think she lied about being goth like those two girls lied about being sisters?"

Ian puts his head in his arms while Landry presses her lips together to stifle a laugh. My chest tightens. Her kindness is one of the traits I find so attractive.

"Tell me the story behind the lyrics," she says to change the subject.

"Sure." He's always happiest talking about himself. "When I was a wee lad of fifteen, I got a pizza delivery job. At the end of Mulberry Street was this big white house with a ginormous lawn—" He spreads his arms wide, almost knocking the drink glasses out of Davis's grasp.

I get up and help Davis distribute the drinks while Rudd regales Landry.

"They always ordered ham pizza with extra pineapple. Anyway, Paulette Conrad lived there and would mow the lawn wearing a teensy tiny white bikini." Rudd bites his fist. "Fifteen years later, and I still can't look at white on a girl without thinking of her big—"

"Rudd," Davis threatens.

"—lawn mower," Rudd finishes with feigned innocence.

He winks at Landry, who giggles.

"And she had a dog?" Landry guesses.

"Nah, the neighbor did, but Paulette loved that little shit. Only he wasn't little. He was huge and ugly and wore a studded collar. I practically soiled myself every time I had to get out of the car. I could've let some other delivery guy take the order, but—"

"Then you wouldn't see Paulette," she finishes.

"Exactly. So I'm there, delivering the same ham with extra pine when I hear this growling right behind me. I tell myself that the dog is still tied up and force myself to keep walking. But then I hear it again." Rudd growls in a bad imitation of the Rottie.

Landry's caught up in his story, though. Her elbows are on the table and her eyes are sparkling with humor.

The shirt she's wearing has pulled out from her jeans and a small portion of her spine is showing. The jeans slide low and I swear if I lean back I can see the top of a pair of lacy panties. I grab my Shiner Bock and pour it down my throat until the urge to slide my hand inside the back of her jeans is drowned.

"What happened then?" Davis hasn't heard the whole story, only the highlights. He embellished a few details up on stage, but Rudd didn't care. Davis's ease with the crowd is a major reason why everyone in the club is engaged while we play.

"My foot is on the bottom step, but instead of going up, I look back. And then I see him. He's pulled the motherfucking chain out of the ground. It's trailing behind him like a big silver snake. He jumps forward and I just start running, pizza out in front of me. He's barking like a rabid dog, chasing after me, that big-ass chain weighing him down. I almost make it to safety when my foot catches on the edge of a sidewalk. The pizza falls to the ground and then I land face-first into the steaming hot pie. A piece of pineapple flew off and burnt me" He points to his upper arm where there's the tiniest white scar.

"And the dog? What happened to the dog?"

Rudd shakes his head mournfully. "That's the worst part of the story. The Rottie started licking my face, eating the cheese and sauce and ham. I'm lying there with pizza guts all over my face, being strad-dled by a hundred-pound dog when Paulette strolls out of her house, holding hands with Brent Fuckface."

"Love does hurt," Landry says dryly.

"I know, right?" They trade high-fives.

She tilts her head to the side. "Are all your songs so inspired?"

"Tell her about the slushie one," Rudd urges.

But before I can say another word, a group of girls appears at the end of our booth. They're pretty enough, I suppose. By the expressions on Davis and Rudd's faces, you'd think they walked off a runway.

"Want to dance?" a tall, thin brunette asks.

"Yes," Rudd says immediately. He pushes at Ian's shoulder, and our drummer gets up with a sigh. "Come on, Davis. Let's go."

Davis holds up one finger and downs his drink. He gets up and points to Landry. "Coming?"

"Nah, you go ahead. You don't want your *sister* to cramp your style."

The girls grab Davis and Rudd and drag them away before anyone else can form an objection. Although, I wasn't planning on it. In fact, I give Ian a hard look. "I think I hear your wife calling."

He snorts. "Doubtful."

"Then leave," I say bluntly.

"Adam!" Landry protests.

Ian rises. "Nah. I figure I can leave you two alone since we're in public. What could you get up to?"

He wanders off, maybe to call his wife, but more likely to watch the dancers.

"I feel like that was a challenge," I say, only halfway joking. I place a hand on her jean-clad thigh because it's been far too long since I've touched her. "You should think about wearing skirts. "

A hand lands on my leg, not high enough to be in the same zip code as my dick, but her touch is enough to short out all my circuits.

"Maybe you should," she teases.

"Move your hand a little higher, baby. I could be convinced." Hell, I'd work a skirt into the wardrobe if that meant I could have her hands up it anytime we were sitting down. "I'm in a band. I can get away with that shit. So what's on the table?"

Her fingers dance a little higher. She leans in, her mouth now barely a hand's width away. "I heard you have a piercing," she whispers, almost soundlessly.

I arch a brow. What did Bo's and Noah's girlfriends tell her? I tug on my eyebrow ring. "Like I said, move your hand a little higher."

She does. Her thumb swipes across the ridge in my jeans, a touch so light I almost wonder if I imagine it. I reach down and place her finger directly over the ball of the half-moon ring that loops through the head of my cock.

"You don't have to be careful," I tell her, helping her stroke me.

"It doesn't hurt?" Her touch is still gentle. I press down, showing her that she can go harder and rougher.

Her fingers close around me, as best as they can through the denim. Which is not even close to how I want it, but I don't dare risk unzipping my jeans. While I have few inhibitions, I don't think Landry's the type to enjoy so public a display of my affection. Plus her brother's here, and me throwing Landry on her back and taking her in this booth would not be keeping this thing between us quiet.

I tuck a strand of loose hair behind her ear, my fingers lingering around the delicate arch. "No. Not anymore. Now it just feels good. More importantly, it's going to make you feel good."

The petting continues. It's pure, wonderful torture. I flatten my feet on the ground, take a few deep breaths and try to control myself.

"Will it hurt?" she asks softly.

"No one's ever—" I halt. I was going to say no one's ever complained before, but I don't want to reference past women. "The brochures say it can help a woman get off."

She bursts out laughing. "The brochures say that, do they?"

I grin back. "That's what I read in my tattoo artist's office."

She continues to laugh. "That's sweet, but you don't have to make up stories for my benefit. I know you've had sex before."

"Really? I could be a virgin."

Her eyes grow wide with shock. "You are?"

"No." I can't lie to her. "But I don't want to talk about past partners. They aren't important. I don't want to hear about your past, either."

"I don't have much of a past. I haven't had sex in years."

"Was everyone at your college dead?"

"I was in the computer lab a lot."

"Jesus." Their loss, my gain.

"So back to your dick," she says.

Said dick swells to unheard-of girth. "We'd better not," I choke out.

She smiles impishly and I brace myself for whatever torture she wants to inflict. Having her hand on me is better than not.

Unfortunately, Davis returns too soon and Landry immediately pulls her hand away.

This sucks. I'm going to have to have a sit down with Davis.

Sooner rather than later.

20

LANDRY

I nearly fall asleep waiting for him. In that time, I have second and third thoughts. I wonder if he will show up. If he's found someone less complicated. With fewer strings and no conditions. I bite down on a nail and message May five times, but given that she's not responding, I'm guessing she's out of reach.

Probably falling in love with one of her guides and getting dicked so hard she can't ride her pony, while I'm pacing a hotel room and drinking every minibar bottle. I brush my teeth twice and take off my robe, wearing a little nighty that I bought.

I catch a glimpse of myself in the mirror. In the mall, surrounded by a volcano of lace and fake silk, this looked great. Now it looks ridiculous. I take off my glasses, but it's the clothes, not my frames that are the problem. I shove my glasses back on and wrap the robe around me again. The robe makes me look like a belted marshmallow. That's the furthest thing from sexy.

I toss the robe on the bed and decide to get comfortable. Adam wants to have sex with me. My clothes aren't going to make a difference. If I have to wait, I might as well wait in clothes that don't make me feel like I'm playing dress-up in a bad porn movie.

I throw on my sleep shirt with a Grumpy Cat picture on it. As I'm stepping into my boxers, my phone buzzes. I reach for it, forgetting that the boxers are around my ankles.

"Gah," I yell as I fall forward. I try to brace myself on the coffee table, but I misjudge the distance. My hand hits the side and slides off. I plow face-first into the carpet, knocking my frames askew. At least I was able to grab my phone.

Head throbbing, I roll over onto my back, resettle my glasses, and read the text.

Adam: On my way

I kick off the boxers and gingerly get to my feet. A quick inventory tells me that nothing's broken. I stagger over to the dresser and inspect my face in the mirror above it. I have a little rug burn on my cheek.

Sighing, I take the T-shirt off and rummage through my bag until I find the sexiest pair of panties I own—a fire-engine red thong that's too uncomfortable to wear for more than a half hour. Hopefully, it comes off before then. I slip the robe on and leave it untied.

I position myself on the edge of the bed. Then move to the sofa. I toss back my hair and lean back on one arm until I catch a glimpse of myself in the mirror. Ugh. I look like a bad catalog model.

Finally, there's a knock on the door. I start to say "Come in" and realize like a dolt that he can't open the door. It's locked. I'm in a freaking hotel room. He needs a key.

Okay, I might be letting my nerves get the best of me.

Taking a deep breath, I get to my feet, carefully skirt around the coffee table, and make my way to the door. I peek through the peephole to confirm that the knock was from Adam.

He's standing there with his hands in his pockets. His dark hair looks wet and he's wearing a different T-shirt than the one he had on earlier. My heartbeat kicks up. He took the time to clean up for me. Seeing that settles my own nerves a bit.

I throw open the door.

"Hey," I say, giving him a small smile.

He takes one look at me and kicks the door shut behind him. "I'm sorry," he says, grabbing the robe ties and pulling until I'm flush against his rock hard frame. With a wave of his hand, my glasses are off and my tongue is being devoured by his as it sweeps inside my mouth. I moan and give myself over to his dominating, possessive kiss.

My head is full of cotton and clouds. The sexy underwear feels too tight. The plush, thick robe is too heavy and too coarse.

His leg slips between my thighs, lifting me off the ground. Delicious pressure is placed against my needy core. The barely-there thong protects nothing from the abrasion of his jeans, but even that feels good.

I curve my fingers around his broad shoulders. God, it's been a long time and I don't have much experience, but I don't remember any guy feeling like this: big, strong, powerful.

One of his hands tangles in my hair, angling my head into just the right position for his passionate assault on my mouth while the other palms my butt. I let the robe fall off, leaving me in nothing more than the thin scrap of red.

Adam's fingers dig into my skin. The pain only heightens my arousal. I grind against him, wishing that his jeans and shirt were gone and we were skin to skin. I can't do anything about the jeans, so I attack his shirt, pulling it up until his hard chest is exposed, but because I'm hanging on to him and he's holding me, I can't get it fully off.

I pull back and try to wriggle out of his grasp.

"Oh no, you're not getting away from me," he rasps, walking quickly toward the bed.

"I'm trying to take your clothes off."

"Good plan. Poor execution." He dumps me on the bed. As I bounce lightly on the mattress, Adam reaches behind him with one hand and whips the shirt over his head. He toes off his boots and reaches down to pull off his socks. His jeans finally come off.

Through the fabric of his boxer briefs, he cups himself. The outline of his dick looks enormous, and I don't think it's my fuzzy vision to blame. He really is that big. I lick my lips in anticipation. I can't wait to feel it inside me.

"Jesus, baby, you are so beautiful." His voice is reverent, erasing any ounce of discomfort I had been feeling lying naked under his gaze. He draws a hand down the middle of my sternum, almost as if he's laying claim to my body.

He gives me the confidence to crook my finger at him. "I'm in a hurry here. It's been a long drought."

"Want this?" he says cockily as he strokes himself.

"Yes, definitely." There's no point in pretending. I'm splayed on the bed, wearing a very damp thong. I don't remember ever wanting anything more in my life.

"Good, because I'm fucking dying for you." He pushes his boxers off, and his dick sticks straight out from his body, a silver piercing adorning the ruddy head.

I back up and close my legs. Alarm and arousal shoot through me in dueling forms. Alarm, because I don't think he's going to fit—and arousal because, holy hell, what if he does? He'd fill every inch of me.

"It'll fit perfect," he says, reading my mind. Then he grabs my ankles and drags me down to the edge of the bed.

He pushes my thighs apart and draws his fingers up my wet channel, spreading my arousal. Then his mouth replaces his fingers and all my fear and apprehension die a quick death under his erotic assault.

He tongues me deep, making an incredible noise of hunger in the back of his throat as if he's never had anything so delicious before. I clutch him to me, swiveling my hips upward, wanting more of everything he seems so willing to give.

"That's right," he murmurs, drawing back enough to give me a graphic, dirty command. "Fuck my mouth."

He shoves me back and works at me until my toes curl and my

thighs tremble. I stuff a fist in my mouth to keep from shouting out as I come in a rush.

"Goddamn, that was beautiful." He rises to his feet. His dick looks even bigger, but I want him so bad, I don't even care that he might split me in two. What a way to go.

He reaches down and plucks a condom out of his discarded jeans. As he rolls it on, I notice that the piercing is gone.

"Are you taking the piercing out?" I ask.

"Yeah, condoms and piercings don't mix. I'll tear the condom and then, well, that wouldn't be good, would it?" He smooths a hand over the latex-sheathed erection, giving himself one last squeeze before climbing between my legs.

"I have an implant," I tell him, tapping my arm.

"Yeah?" His eyes light up.

"Yeah. And I've only ever slept with one guy before. I was tested back when..." I pause, not wanting to bring up any of the details of my past. "Back before."

"I'm clean," Adam says. His eyes are glowing now and his face has taken on an expression of pained anticipation, as if he can't believe what I'm suggesting. "I get tested after every tat." He points to his left biceps. "Had this work done before we started planning the tour."

I reach between us and pull the latex off. "Go put the piercing back in."

His eyes flutter shut for a second, then flip open to reveal intense, vibrant desire. "No. Can't wait. Next time."

He takes himself in hand and guides himself to my opening. The thick head parts my lips. He glides in slowly, letting me feel every inch of his thick shaft.

I gasp at the intrusion. He halts immediately.

"Too much?"

I suck my lower lip in between my teeth. "No. It's...I haven't had this for so long. I forgot what it felt like."

He brushes a shaky hand against my forehead. The control he's exerting makes his hand tremble. I love that I make him so crazy.

"I'll go slow. We're in no hurry," he whispers.

True to his word, his motion is unhurried. He pulls out slowly, his cockhead dragging against my receptive nerves. The deliberate stroke of him inside of me is more erotic than anything I've felt before.

I arch underneath him, pushing my hips upward to feel him deeper, to capture as much contact between his body and mine that I can.

His mouth finds the bend of my neck, the curve of my shoulder, the hollow above my collarbone. With each kiss, he creates a constellation of pleasure, marking spots on my skin that I didn't even realize were sensitive.

"You feel amazing," he says, his lips caressing my cheek. "Tight. Hot. So wet. Everything I imagined."

He grips my hip to pull me up against him. It's as if we can't get close enough. There's no clothes between us. No condom. Nothing, but still our arms and legs and bodies strain for more contact, closer contact.

I tug on his hair. "Kiss me, Adam."

He obeys immediately. His tongue plunges into my mouth, mimicking the action of his cock between my legs. I close my eyes and allow myself to fall into the magic he's creating.

And it *is* magic because I never allow myself to be this open and this exposed—and not just in a physical way. It's scary and exhilarating, a spellI don't ever want to end.

I clench my legs around him. He responds by driving his hips harder, delving his tongue deeper until my body is no longer my own.

It's his to command. He pulls from it the strongest, longest, hardest orgasm that it has ever felt. My body shudders. My lips part and a cry—a plea, really—spills out. I don't know what I say. Whether I scream his name or God's name or whether I order him to go faster, slower, harder, hotter. It's all a dark, beautiful blur.

My limbs stiffen and then shatter, the ecstasy exploding through my veins, taking me apart and leaving me a wonderful, replete, utterly satisfied wreck.

∾

"WHAT TOOK YOU SO LONG?" I ask as we lie in a sweaty heap in the middle of the bed. The comforter is on the floor and the sheets are pulled away from the mattress, but I don't care. I'm too exhausted to care. I have only enough energy to trail my fingers across his chest.

"Your brother cornered me about a song he's written. I couldn't brush him off."

"Was it crazy down there?" There seemed to be an endless stream of people in and out of Davis's room.

"There were a lot of folks. Too many. I was glad to escape." His arm curls, pulling me close enough for him to drop a kiss on the top of my head.

"Do you need to go back down?"

"No. Besides, I can't. You destroyed me," he teases.

"That bad?" It's a joke. I mean it as one, but a kernel of uncertainty creeps in.

"Hardly. This is my smug-as-fuck voice. I knew we would be combustible the moment I laid eyes on you."

"Yeah?"

Adam runs one of his big palms over my back. He, too, can't keep his hands to himself. That's encouraging. "Couldn't you tell? I stared at you for the last three songs."

"I didn't have my glasses on," I admit with a pleased smile. "I was looking at the stage."

He slaps his free hand against his chest in a sign of exaggerated hurt. "Don't tell me that. I thought we were having a moment. I planned to write a song about it."

I'm glad I can tuck my face into the side of his chest, because the idea of him writing a song about me melts every bone in my body, and I don't want him to know that his joke is something I'd like way too much.

"Maybe I will anyway," he murmurs.

"Sure," I say with burning cheeks.

His body shakes as he chuckles. He knows. God, he knows how I'd like that. Of course he knows. He's a musician. He's gotten women into his bed all his life because they love his music, because they want him to immortalize them like John Legend did Chrissy Teigen.

"You know if I write a song about how amazing you are, I'm allowed to do anything I want."

My smile immediately turns to a frown. I shoot upright. "Like what? Cheating?"

He looks dismayed. "No. No. I meant like leaving my wet towels on the bathroom floor or drinking milk out of the carton."

"That's barbaric." My heart rate slowly returns to normal. "Drinking milk from the carton," I clarify.

"I know. I was an only child and grew up spoiled rotten." He sits up and slides an arm around my waist. "I have bad habits." He rubs his nose against my cheek. "I always like to get my way. I don't like sharing." He draws me down to the bed. "I'm not interested in any other women, Landry. Just you. Let me love you."

I open my arms and my body and let him. I know he doesn't mean *love* love. He means sex. *Fucking*. He's a musician, after all. They live in the moment. They hook up on tour, because that's just what they do.

Still, even if I only have him for a short time, it'll be worth it.

21

LANDRY

Tour Stop: San Antonio

"How long do we have until the bus leaves today?"

"About an hour," Adam calls from the bathroom. Through the open door, I can see his tight butt as he uses his towel to scrub water from his hair.

I bite my lip. There's not enough naked Adam in my life.

"And we get in when?" I tear my eyes away from his ass, pulling my hair back into a ponytail and double-checking for any signs of last night's activities. I found a couple marks while I was showering: bruises on my hip bones where his fingers held me tight as he thrust inside of me, and a red mark on the inside of my left breast. I'm wearing one of Davis's old band T-shirts that says "Pluck Me Good" on it, so the likelihood of anyone seeing those marks is low.

Anyone but Adam, that is. But I like our secret.

"We're supposed to meet there at four."

That gives me time to catch an Uber and do a little shopping. From the Google results, there's a mall not too far from the venue. I have plans for tonight. Just because Davis lurks around doesn't mean Adam and I can't enjoy ourselves. After last night's taste, the only thing I want to do is jump him again.

Adam comes out from the bathroom, drops his towel, and bends over to swipe his boxer briefs off the floor. He chucks them onto the bed and grabs his jeans.

"Going commando?" I tease.

He smirks at me over his shoulder. "My dick got a good workout last night. I think he needs to be rewarded with a little freedom today."

"I'll remember that." I wiggle my eyebrows.

He shakes his head in mock dismay. "Haven't you had enough of me?"

I run my eyes over the strong plane of his back and all the lines and curls of ink that I haven't even begun to map. "Not even close."

He throws his shirt over his shoulder like a towel and hooks a hand around my ankle.

"Wait! Stop!" I laugh as he drags me to the edge of the bed.

He sweeps a hand up my outer thigh. "What're you going to do today?"

"Shopping."

His hand ducks under the hem of my T-shirt and pushes my panties out of the way. "What're you planning on buying?"

I fall back on the bed as his fingertips glide against my tender flesh. "It's a surprise."

"I'm a big fan of red," he says. His fingers push inside me.

"Yeah?" I gasp.

"Yup. It makes your freckles stand out." He bends to place a kiss on my shoulder.

"I don't have freckles!" I use copious amounts of sunscreen to avoid those spots.

"What's this then?" he teases, moving downward to tease one taut nipple and then the other.

"So I have a few freckles." I arch into his caress.

"They're perfect. You're perfect." He moves lower, pressing his lips against my pelvic bone, nuzzling the trimmed hair between my legs, then lower still. All the while, his fingers pet and tease me.

My thighs fall open in anticipation. I wait and—

Ring! Ring!

He falls back onto his heels. "Fuck." Withdrawing, he wipes his fingers on his discarded boxer briefs and grabs his phone. "What?" he barks into the phone. "No, I'm not in my room. I had to run an errand."

Our playtime is over. I roll off the bed and grab my clothes. Adam gives me a pained, unhappy look but makes no move to stop me from getting ready.

"I'll be down in five," he says with a sigh.

"You look happy," Davis comments as he joins me in the back of the bus. "You have some code breakthrough?"

I look up from the measly five lines of code I'd written in the last hour and carefully close my laptop. "Yeah. Something like that."

He slides into the seat next to me. "Great."

Uh oh. His flat tone doesn't match the word. "What's wrong?"

He tips his head back to stare at the LED fixtures in the ceiling of the bus. "I wrote some lyrics and Ian laid down a sick beat, but I need someone to write the melody."

"Someone named Adam," I guess.

"Right on, but he likes the set the way it is. Doesn't want to mess with it."

"Your audience does seem to love your music," I tentatively point out. Sitting with my brother and listening to him complain about the guy I just slept with is highly uncomfortable. I want to be supportive of both.

"Sure, but his argument about turning down the commercial is all about not wanting to get stuck in a rut or be branded with a certain kind of sound before we discover exactly what we all want."

The emphasis is on *all*. Wasn't this what Mike, Threat Alert's manager, warned me of? That Adam liked to do things only one way? He wasn't that way in the bedroom. He didn't order me around or dictate how I should act. We responded to each other, perfectly in sync. Perhaps Davis just needs to talk it out with Adam.

I suggest that. "Maybe you should tell Adam how you feel."

Davis tips his head down to give me a slightly offended look. "You think I haven't already?"

"I'm guessing that you have and he hasn't listened."

Davis makes a fake gun with his thumb and forefinger. "Got it in one." He blows out a frustrated breath. "I didn't quit my job to just sing for this damn band. I want to be part of it. Adam's not letting me."

I rub the side of my neck and search for something diplomatic to say. "What do the other guys say?"

"None of them will say a word against Adam. We're on his bus, playing his music, singing his lyrics. He owns us."

Davis wants more control—over his life, over this band. Any thoughts of sharing the newfound connection I have with Adam are wiped away. Davis would see it as a complete betrayal.

And then what? Would he quit the band? Would he fall back into bad habits? He's been so good that I've stopped watching him like a hawk. Hasn't he proven, in the months since his jail time, that he'd put the past behind him? I needed to do the same.

"I think you need to bring it up to him again," I encourage.

Davis isn't convinced. "Maybe. It's not as if I don't get where Adam's coming from. TA's audience is dying off and ours is growing, but this commercial could push us places TA can only dream of."

"And you want to feel a real part of the band, not just an add-on component that can be replaced," I guess. It comes down to control again. Adam views this as *his* band and Davis wants it to be *their* band.

My brother gives me a wry smile. "Exactly." His smile turns speculative. "Maybe you should talk to him."

"Me?" I yelp in surprise.

"Yeah, you two seem to be getting along. You went to that golf thing the other night. What'd you talk about?"

I bite my inner cheek hard to keep the embarrassment off my face. A blush would give everything away at this point. "Nothing much. Nothing about the band. We talked about his roommates. They were Marines, you know. His friends are super nice. Did you know that Grace wrote to Noah for almost four years while he was deployed?," I babble. "Isn't that romantic? And AnnMarie and Bo have been together for a couple years. They plan to move to Chicago."

Davis's eyes begin to glaze over. I rattle off a few more facts I picked up until Davis's attention is completely gone.

"Is this a private party or can anyone join?"

My heart leaps at the sound of Adam's voice. "No. Come on in," I gesture in relief.

Davis is much less welcoming. He doesn't even move his legs, requiring Adam to climb over them to take the seat opposite.

"We were talking about the song I just wrote," my brother says. His chin is out and his tone is challenging.

Adam doesn't take the bait. "I like the lyrics."

"I'm excited to hear it," I pipe up.

Adam cocks his head and studies the two of us. "Davis should play it for you."

There's an almost audible grinding of teeth before Davis says, "Wish I could but I don't have the melody."

Adam shrugs. "It's there. You should tease it out."

Davis's frame stiffens until he's rigid as a board. "I'm going to get something to eat." He stomps out, no doubt wishing he could slam the door behind him.

I wait until the door shuts before turning to Adam. "What's that all about?"

"Davis wrote some lyrics and now it's time for him to write the music."

"He's never written music before. Not real stuff he's played in public."

"Then it's probably time."

I furrow my brow. "What game are you playing here? You could whip out a melody in a heartbeat. I know you write hit songs."

"So?"

"So. Write one for Davis."

"Then it wouldn't be Davis's song anymore," Adam says. "It'd be mine."

"Why isn't it the band's song?"

Adam bends forward, reaching across to grab one of my cold hands in his. "Because that's not how it works. Davis wrote this song because he wants to hear his music on television, not because it means something to him. If it moved him, he'd hear the melody, too."

"That's a pompous thing to say." I pull my fingers away and tuck them under my legs.

He slowly withdraws. "It's the truth."

We sit in complete silence for a long, awkward moment. Finally he says, "Is this going to be a problem? Because for me, the band thing is separate from what you and I are doing."

I'm too chicken to ask what that is and too weak to tell him that I'm not interested in him any longer.

"No. It's not a problem," I say.

I don't know whether that's the truth or a lie.

"Good." He gives me a heart melting smile. "Because last night was the best night of my life. I can't wait to repeat it."

I rub my lips together and squeeze my thighs tight. "Me, too."

22

ADAM

"Are you kidding me with that?" I growl under my breath as I follow Landry down the hall.

"I distinctly remember you saying I should wear skirts more," she teases.

Good Christ, it's a miracle I can even walk. I avert my gaze from the long legs on full display underneath the way-too-short skirt. My eyes spot a staff-only door. Instantly I come to a halt and grab her arm.

"What is it—" she begins to say.

I jam the door open and pull her into the room. In the next second, I have her up against the closed door, my mouth all over hers, desperate and rough. She reaches between us and tugs her glasses off.

My hands find her ass and hoist her upward. The skirt slides up easily, and my hands tunnel under a scrap of lace to find her wet and hot.

I groan against her mouth. She holds me tight against her, her thighs bracketing my waist, her arms gripping me firmly around the neck. I dip my fingers into her sex.

"This is perfect. You should wear these all the time."

"I'm confused," she pants. "You seemed angry when you first saw me."

I press the heel of my hand against her clit, and she gives an answering moan. "All the blood in my head drained to my dick. That wasn't anger. It was lust."

She rotates her hips as I fuck her with my fingers. I'm dying for a taste of her, but I'm afraid if I put my tongue between her legs, I'll have to fuck her with my cock and I've got to be onstage in five minutes.

"You need to come right now," I tell her.

"Make me," she demands.

Oh fuck. She's so damn hot. My dick grows even harder.

"Like this?" I drag my thumb between her ass cheeks until it catches on that perfect, private hole.

Her breath catches, but she doesn't move away. I push my thumb in past that tight ring of muscles and that's all she needs. Two fingers in her cunt and one in her asshole. She cries out and turns her face against the door so her moans are muffled against the wood.

I keep stroking her until the shaking subsides into tiny tremors.

"Fuck, baby, that was beautiful." I lean forward and kiss her neck. Regretfully I pull my fingers out of her body. She shudders again, her nerves so sensitive.

I spot a stack of paper towels on a shelf. I rip open the package and clean myself off. "Don't sit with Mike during the set, okay? Come stand in front of the stage."

"I can't." She sighs. "Davis will take one look at me and know what I'm thinking."

"And what's that?" I fold a towel and place it between her thighs. I don't give a damn what her brother thinks, but she does. Unfortunately.

She catches my hand and presses it to her. "That you're the hottest man to have ever walked the planet Earth."

Nothing wrong with that.

"All right," I say, slightly appeased, "but stay away from any penises. You look deliciously fucked right now and I'm the only one who gets a taste, right?"

"Definitely yes."

I want to flip up her skirt again, but I know if I do, I won't get on that stage tonight. I settle for stroking her hair back from her face and kissing her sweaty forehead. I wrench open the door and leave before my already weak resolve disappears.

"Where the hell were you?" Davis shouts when I reach the stage. "I thought I was going to have to send out an all-points bulletin."

I throw the strap of the guitar over my neck. "Stomach problems," I lie.

His brows crash together. "Hope it's nothing serious."

"Nope." *Nah, just me fucking your sister in some shitty-ass bar storage room.*

I swipe my fingers over all six strings, drowning out any further questions because the only answers I have are ones he doesn't want to hear.

I PLAY LIKE A GOD. The riffs fly off my piece. Even though he's pissed at me, Davis stops singing in the middle of one of our songs and makes a bowing motion in my direction. The crowd is so hyped that the waves of energy never stop crashing the stage.

My eyes are pinned on Landry, who has found a place in the back, away from TA's manager. Men are sniffing around her, though, like hungry wolves circling a rare piece of meat. I growl into the mic that she's mine, all mine, that her kissing, her loving, her touching is mine, all mine.

They don't move off. My play gets harder, more frenetic, and the set break can't come soon enough.

"I gotta hit the head," I inform Ian and shove my guitar in his face.

He nearly drops it, and I barely care that my two-thousand-dollar instrument almost cracked on the stage floor.

I jump off the stage and arrow straight for Landry. She sees me coming. Her eyes widen and she takes off. I chase her, catching her outside the men's bathroom.

"Inside," I order.

She squeaks in surprise, but obeys the command. Fortunately, the bathroom is empty, and a second later, I'm backing her into a stall and locking the door behind us.

"You like your panties?" I ask, working my belt buckle open.

She looks confused. "Um, yes. They're new."

"You better have them off in the next five seconds or I'm going to tear them off." I unzip and pull out my aching cock. Pre-cum coats the head. I squeeze my dick hard, trying to beat back some of my anticipation. I'm so hungry for her that I'm ready to spill all over the floor. "Also, lose the glasses."

The glasses get tucked into my back pocket. She hastily reaches under that scrap of fabric called a skirt. I take the panties from her and toss them aside. Then I spin her around, pushing the skirt up to reveal her bare, naked ass.

"Fuck, this ass is so beautiful. It's enough to make you believe in God." I smack my hand across it.

She yelps excitedly and then wiggles her ass for another. Christ Almighty. My knees go weak. I spin her around so we're face-to-face and reach between her legs to find her wet and ready.

"Hold on, baby. I can't wait another minute." I rub the metal ball of my piercing against her clit.

She moans softly. "Oh shit, that feels good."

"About to feel better," I promise and slide home, so deep and fast that she cries out.

"Quiet," I whisper, angling my head to mouth the nape of her neck. I give her a second to get used to the invasion, then I'm moving again, thrusting into her while she grips my neck with both hands and holds on for the wild ride.

"Right there," she gasps.

I hitch her leg up higher and piston forward. The entire unit shakes. She slaps her hand against the wall.

"Adam," she moans.

"Want me to stop?"

"Don't you dare."

I give her the best approximation of a smile that I can, but in my current state, it's only a feral baring of my teeth.

This position isn't the best. I can't dig my knee into a mattress for leverage. The jeans around my thighs are about to cut off my circulation, and the stupid bathroom stall feels like it's made from poster board. Worse, I'm so out of my mind with lust for her that I can't maintain any control. My dick's about to explode. The need to come is so palpable, I can taste it.

My hips jerk forward, and against the metal wall my fingers curl into a fist. I can feel her thighs tremble, her spine stiffen.

"Come on, baby," I beg. "You look so fucking beautiful when you come."

She wriggles against me, trying to find the perfect spot where the friction of my cock against her flesh makes her explode. If we were horizontal, I'd help, but I've got to keep one hand under her ass and the other hand against the wall so we both stay upright. I ease back, using the metal ball to rub places my dick can't.

I'm a second away from pulling out entirely and going down on her when her wet heat convulses around me. Under my hand, her thigh tightens. I fight the urge to go faster, to drive into her until my own release barrels from my spine right out of my dick. I bite my tongue and hammer inside, steady, sure and strong.

"That's my girl. Come for me."

"Adam, Adam, Adam," she chants. Her legs lock around me. Her arms crush my ears as she clenches my head tight against her, trying to hold on while she's losing control.

It's a beautiful thing.

A goddamned glorious thing.

I let go myself, pummeling her soft frame with my hard one. Her voice hits a high, thin note as she comes again on my dick. Her sweet, sticky essence coats my shaft. I fuck her hard until the last drop of come jets out of me. I drop my forehead against the wall next to her head and try to catch my breath.

"That was—"

"You okay in there, *Adam*?" A hard bang on the door jolts us both upright.

Landry nearly breaks my dick in her scramble to get off me and out of my arms.

"*Oh my God.*" Her mouth forms the words, but no sound comes out.

Davis. That boy has the fucking worst timing.

"Get out," Landry hisses.

I grab some toilet paper and hand it to her. She grimaces as the rough paper scrapes against her delicate, swollen parts.

"Sorry," I mouth, grabbing my own wad of toilet paper, which I use to wipe myself off. I toss the trash into the toilet while Landry scrambles around for her panties.

"Someone missing these?" Davis toes a scrap of red silk under the stall door. Any other time, I'd be laughing, too, but I value my dick too much to allow even an upward tilt to my lips. A quick peek at Landry's red cheeks tells me I made the right choice.

An expression of horror across her face, she leans down and swipes the panties up, balling the sexy underwear in her hand. Too bad. I was thinking of pocketing those.

"Go," she mouths again and points a finger at the door.

I tuck my dick away, pull up my jeans, and slide out, careful not to open the door too far. It doesn't matter, though, because Davis is at the urinal wall, pissing.

He looks over his shoulder. "Wondered why you were in such a hurry. Thought you had the runs or something."

"Or something," I mutter as I wash my hands.

How long is he going to take? Landry'd kill me if I abandon her in the bathroom while her brother is still here. Davis finally finishes and comes over to wash his hands beside me.

"So fucking some chick is more important than starting our set on time?" he grouches.

I rub my hands a little harder. "I was two minutes late and no one noticed or cared."

"I noticed. So did Hollister."

Christ. How much longer is he going to wash his hands? Our hands are so clean, we could be readying for surgery.

"I hope your groupie was worth risking pissing off the crowd." A low, angry sound emanates from the stall. Davis freezes, shoots a questioning look over his shoulder, then laughs. "Sounds like you had a live one."

He rips off a length of paper towel, dries his hands, then tosses it in the trash. On his way out of the bathroom, he bangs on the stall door. "I'm the one wearing the blue T-shirt, sweetheart, if you're interested in another go-around."

Inside the stall, there's a gagging noise.

He turns and frowns. "You bring a drunk girl back and fuck her, Adam? Dude, that's not right."

I run a hand wearily across my forehead. "She wasn't drunk. She's probably getting sick on toilet fumes. Come on, she's shy." I drag Davis out of the bathroom and shove him toward the front. "Get your own damn girl. This one's mine."

He cranes his head backward. "Really? I wanna meet her then. You haven't hooked up once since we went on tour and this one you were in such a hurry to fuck, you had to do her in the men's room?"

"I had no idea you were so interested in my sex life. I'll be sure to run all my potentials past you first." Not so gently, I drag him toward Ian and Rudd, who are leaning against the bar.

"That's not a bad idea."

"What's not a bad idea?" Rudd asks, handing Davis a bottle of Bud.

I gesture for the bartender, who gives a chin nod of acknowledgement but does not hustle over. I stick my hands into my pockets and sigh. One release is not enough. I want to go back to the bathroom, bend Landry over the sink, and take her again.

"Adam had a honey in the bathroom, but he was too embarrassed to introduce me to her," Davis says.

Rudd pats me on the back. "Doesn't matter what she looks like. No judgment here."

The bartender comes over and saves me, although I'm sure that Landry would prefer everyone thought I fucked a dog in the bathroom rather than her. "I'll have a Macallan, and make it a double."

The scruffy-chinned guy wrinkles his forehead. "Don't know what that is, brother."

"Of course not," I sigh. "Whiskey. Best you got. Fill it to the top."

"Must not have been very good sex if you gotta drink to forget it seconds after finishing," Rudd tsks.

"It sounded like he was enjoying himself," Davis says. "Thought the walls of the stall were going to fall down."

To Davis's chagrin, Rudd doesn't give a shit I was late. He's much more interested in hazing me. "Maybe she didn't finish and he's trying to drown his embarrassment in the bottom of a glass." Rudd pats me on the back again. "Don't worry, old man. Happens to the best of us."

"Not to me," Davis says.

"Not me, either," Ian chirps.

"Now you decide to chime in?" The fucking traitor has been watching me squirm like a pinned bug.

"Hey, I'm throwing you a life jacket. Don't shit all over it."

"If I was in the ocean, how would I shit on the life jacket?"

"Agreed. I think you'd be more likely to piss on it," Davis says.

"Why aren't we just using it to save ourselves?" Rudd asks in complete puzzlement.

Ian and Davis break down, folding themselves in half while Rudd keeps asking "What? What did I say?"

At least the attention's off me and Davis is no longer shooting darts my way, but I can't stop wishing I was still balls-deep inside Landry's sweet pussy. As Davis laughs gleefully, I plot ways to dispose of his body—temporarily.

23

ADAM

"Would you stop looking at me like that?" I grumble under my breath. I'm a sweaty mess from finishing the second half of our set. I need a shower, a beer, and Landry underneath me—not necessarily in that order.

"Like what?" She bats her eyelashes at me.

"Like you want me to fuck you."

"Is that what my expression says?" She holds out her phone. "Take a picture. I'm curious what that looks like."

I whip the phone out of her hand and toss it on the table. "I'm serious. My dick is so hard that it's got the rail marks of my zipper on it."

A saucy smile spreads across her face. "We can't have that. I like my property well taken care of."

I shoot out of my chair.

"Where you going?" Davis says, arriving from the bar three bottles of beer in his hand.

"Bathroom," she says.

Davis looks to me, and I pause, not good at this secret thing. Not good at hiding. I've never once in my life had to slink around. Women were proud of fucking me. They bragged about it. My first lay announced to the entire bus that she'd just finished popping my cherry. I barely had time to tuck my dick away before my dad and the rest of the band found their way back to the bunk to congratulate me.

"Me, too," I announce.

Davis's eyes dart from Landry to me and then back to his sister. "Okay, well, hurry back. I just bought these."

Landry sinks back into her chair. Her lusty expression is replaced with apprehension. "I don't need to go." She eyes the beers. "And I'm not thirsty."

"Well, I am. And a beer's not killing me." He thrusts out his chin.

And they arguing over beer? With a sigh, I join them.

"That set was good," Davis says, setting down the beers. He grabs one and downs half of it, staring defiantly at his sister.

There's a weird vibe here and it doesn't seem at all related to the fact that Landry and I were fucking in the bathroom not so long ago.

"It was terrific," Landry agrees. Her eyes are glued to the bottle in Davis' hand.

"One of my favorite sets ever." I can't keep the smugness out of my voice.

Landry kicks me under the table. I reach underneath and catch her foot, slipping off her shoe and pressing my thumb into her arch. She slides down in her chair even farther, until the heel of her foot presses against my crotch. Davis, ever the dim, doesn't notice.

"You excited, Landry?" He says, setting the beer down and pushing it slightly away.

I can see her tension recede.

"About what?" she asks.

"The 'rents are coming home in a week."

She jerks upright and pats at her hair, as if her parents had walked in on us fooling around on the couch. "I forgot."

Now it's my turn to start chugging my beer. I have one more week with her and then it's over? No. I don't accept that. It's time that Landry and I had a talk about this.

"I think we should stay at a hotel tonight," I announce. I get to my feet and reach for my wallet.

"Can't. Rudd invited the manager to the bus for a party tonight," Davis informs me.

I pause in the process of throwing down a few bills. "When did that happen?"

"When you were fucking in the bathroom. Pay attention to the band and you might keep up." Davis reaches for his half-empty beer. "Come on. Let's go support TA and then get lit."

Landry's mouth presses into a tight line. "No. I'm not getting drunk with you. In fact, I think you've had plenty."

"Whatever," he says and pushes away from the table.

I wait until the crowd swallows him up before pointing at Landry. "Bus. Now."

I TAKE her on the table. The lights are off. Ed, our driver, is outside smoking a joint with TA's driver, and we have a blessed moment of privacy.

"Anyone could walk in here right now," I growl in her ear. Her hair is fisted in my hand and I tug it back. "Rudd, Ian. Anyone. They'd see your sweet ass and how well you take my cock."

She whimpers, a reedy and wanton sound. I'd like to record it, play it on a track, layer over her sighs, the sounds of my flesh slapping into hers, and finish it with a smooth rendition of 50 Cent's promise that he's going to unbutton, lick, and touch just a little bit.

Of course, I want to do more than a little. I want to own her. I want to carve my name into her heart so that every time it beats, she hears the echo of my name in her ears. My feelings are barbaric and more than a little frightening, so I clench my teeth to keep them in, allowing only my body to show her how much I want her, how desperate I am for her.

"You like that, babe? You want more?" I tug on her hair a little harder.

"Yes, give it to me," she demands, pushing her hips back against me.

Outside the bus, I hear noise in the parking lot. "TA's done. They're leaving the club. They're going to be here any minute now."

"Oh, Adam, hurry," she squeaks.

I reach around and find her clit. She releases another one of those throaty moans.

"Fuck me, you're beautiful. Come for me, babe."

She does, convulsing and squeezing me until I let go, too. She's so responsive. We're in sync, making beautiful, lust-filled music.

Reluctantly, I withdraw. My come coats her lips, her thighs. It's an erotic sight that I'd like to preserve forever. I dip a finger in the creamy mixture, drag it upward, painting her ass with my mark. "I don't suppose you would let me take a picture."

"No. Don't you dare." She reaches behind to bat at me.

I sigh and grab a towel from the sink. The one good thing about close quarters is that everything's within reach. I wipe her up, towel myself off, and toss the used terrycloth in the drawer where I keep all my dirty clothes and shit.

By the time I get back to the table, Landry's sitting primly with her legs crossed and her hands folded in front of her.

"You look like you just robbed a bank," I tell her.

She raises a hand to her forehead. There's a slight tremble to it that fills me with a sense of satisfaction "Really? I was going for inno-cent victim."

I pull a beer out of the fridge. "Want one?" She shakes her head. "Victim of what?"

"Victim of a big dicking," she says wickedly.

I spit out my beer in surprise. "Nice, champ. Real nice."

She laughs. "I can be saucy when I want to."

"I know it, babe." I lean forward to kiss her just as Ian pops his head inside the bus. I pretend like I'm brushing something off her forehead and mutter, "I hate this."

"I know," she whispers back. But even as she says it, she scoots out of my reach. "Hey, Ian."

He shakes his head. "One of these days you two are going to get caught. In the bathroom, really?"

"Shut the fuck up," I reply, grabbing a beer and tossing it to him. "You and Berry had sex everywhere, twice."

"Yeah, but that's our thing," he says. "Didn't know it was yours."

Landry shakes her head vehemently side to side. "Not my thing, particularly when it's Davis walking in."

"You sure?" I give her an appraising glance.

Anyone could walk in here right now. She'd clenched so tight around me that she nearly cut off my blood circulation.

"Very sure," she says firmly.

I guess she liked the thought of it, which is fine. Exhibitionism has never been my thing.

"How was TA?" I ask Ian.

"They're losing their crowd. They ended up playing 'Destiny's Here again."

"Again?" They played it with us as the opener.

He nods in confirmation. "The second time it was slower, more ballad-like."

"Damn." When you resort to playing a song twice in a fifty-minute set, you know things are bad.

"Albie had a pissed-off look throughout the entire thing. I left before the set was over." He lifts a pack of cigarettes from his shirt pocket. "Want a smoke?"

"Nah, you go on."

He shrugs. "I'll leave one for you on the bumper."

The minute he's gone, I turn to Landry. "Let's tell Davis tonight."

Her expression instantly goes serious. "Why? I'll only be here for another week."

"Right, about that." I run a hand through my hair, trying to find the right words. "What if you stay?"

She blinks. "For what?"

"For the tour."

Her eyes grow wide and I don't know if it's astonishment or excitement.

"The rest of your tour?" she squeaks.

I nod.

"You want me to go with you for the rest of the tour?"

I rub my hands together. The idea had been percolating in my head for a while, but it didn't really coalesce until Davis brought up her parents' return to the States. "Yeah, for the entire tour. You've been with us for almost two months now. Three more will seem like a breeze. What's the downside?"

She studies me for a moment, longer than I like. I want her immediate agreement. Instead, she seems to be weighing things, and from her non-reaction, the cons are stronger than the pros.

"Even if we told Davis," she starts slowly, "I wouldn't want to have sex with him around."

"I'm not asking you to stay because of the sex," I protest. I mean, yes, I want to fuck her every five seconds, but I enjoy her company, too. "Besides, if we told him, we wouldn't be sneaking around."

"So anytime you wanted to have sex, you'd just kick Davis off the bus?"

"Why does he have to leave the bus? We'd go to the back." I point toward the end of the bus. "And he'd stay here." I tap the table.

"But he'd know." She scrunches up her nose.

"You're twenty-four, Landry. He thinks you're having sex."

"I don't care. Now's not the right time. Plus, there's the whole..." she waves her hand.

"Whole what?"

"You know. The stuff with the song. You not writing the melody. You refusing to allow the song to be used in a commercial. That sort of stuff."

"So what? Unless I give in to Davis's demands, you're out?" Anger rises. Why is she fighting this so damned hard?

"I never said that."

"But Davis wants those things, doesn't he?"

"I think everyone in the band except you wants those things." Ice coats her words.

"You think I don't want the band to be a success?" I ask incredulously.

Her face softens. "I just don't understand your argument that you're going to lose your sound if you sell one song to someone else. You write songs for other people all the time. You make hits for others, but you won't make one for yourself? Are you afraid of success?"

"Of course not." I get up from the table. I thought she knew me, that she understood where I was coming from.

Frustrated, I jerk open the refrigerator and take out another beer. She gives me a worried look, like I can't handle myself without a beer in my hand, so I shove it back in the refrigerator.

"Look, you write code, so you don't understand what it's like to be attached to your music. You're not building toward something bigger."

I know the words are a mistake before they even come out.

She stands up stiffly, ice in her voice and her eyes. "Just because I write code doesn't mean I'm not attached to it or that I don't care that the program I devoted four years of my life to so that girls could connect with their friends is now best known for porn. I may not make music, but I still do important things."

Shit. Shit. Shit. "Landry, I'm sorry," I apologize, but she's already down the stairs and off the bus before my words can register. Then the coach starts filling up with people, and the opportunity is lost.

Hollister shoves through the crowd to get to me. "I've got a radio spot for you guys when we get to Phoenix. You gonna do it or are you too good for that?"

I grit my teeth, but manage a mocking response. "Still mad about the commercial, huh?"

"Still being the *artiste*, huh?" he shoots back.

"Some of us create shit and some just peddle it," I retort, then regret it immediately when I spot Landry's head right behind Hollister. She presses her lips together in disappointment. "Fuck, I'm sorry," I say, feeling miserable. "Of course, we're going to do your radio spot."

Hollister glares at me. "You better. There's an A/R woman coming from WriteWorld Records. Try to be charming, or are you too good for albums now, too?"

I swallow another retort.

Davis pops into view, pushing Hollister aside. "You hear about the A/R person?" he says excitedly.

I force a smile on my face. "I did."

"You're cool with that, right?"

His anxiousness spears me. Have I been such an uptight asshole about the music that the entire band thinks I'm not interested in cutting an album?

"Very cool. We should bring our gear and see if we can play an acoustic set for them."

Davis slaps his hand across mine and leans out of the bus. "Hey, Rudd, grab my guitar, will ya? Let's jam."

SOMEONE MAKES a pit of castoff clothes and garbage and starts burning it in the back of Rack-n-Ruin, the venue we just played. A few other people grab brush from the side of the road. We sit on seats pulled from someone's van. They were meant to be removed, a guy promised me.

I look around for Landry and spot her standing next to Mike. Fuck, I hate that guy. I hate everything right now.

I want to throw the guitar on the ground, punch out Hollister, throw Landry over my shoulder and run out into the night.

I start off playing the A chord, then to G, D, and A again. It takes two more lines before Rudd catches on. I play the song fast, almost rapping it.

Secret lover. That's. Who. You. Are.

Davis joins in at the pre-chorus, caught up in the mood. We're all singing, pissed off for different reasons. Rudd and Davis are mad at me for not selling the song. Ian's banging his hands hard against the electronic drum set because he's worried that I'm going to fuck up this magical creation called FMK because my dick's too attached to Landry. And me? I'm pissed off at everything right now.

At Landry for not understanding where I'm coming from. At Rudd and Davis for being shortsighted. At Ian for not trusting me. At myself, most of all. I'm the real asshole here.

I love my dad, but I've learned lessons from him that I don't want to repeat. But in my stubbornness, am I on the verge of ruining a really great thing? I can't get Landry's hurt look out of my head. I should've never yelled at her.

I was frustrated because, yeah, I did want to fuck her whenever the urge came upon me without her worrying what Davis would say. But my feelings for her are so much more than physical. I love her.

I stop playing.

Davis and Rudd halt, too.

"What is it?" Rudd asks. "Too fast, wasn't it?"

I've only known Landry for a short time. It's only been a couple months since I first laid eyes on her, but didn't I have that gut feeling way back then that she was my destiny? That I was done with all other women? I write songs about love at first sight all the time, but I never really believed in that shit until the night I met Landry.

And my feelings for her only grew stronger the more I got to know her. She's smart as a whip. I mean, hell, I look at that computer code she writes. Gibberish to me, but she makes magic—and money—with it. She's gorgeous, adventurous in bed, and sometimes out of it when she lets her guard down. She's loyal to her brother, her friends, even strangers.

She's just...amazing. And yeah. I love her.

"Adam?" Ian prompts.

"No. It wasn't too fast. It was just right."

I pick up my guitar and change the tune. I pluck out a few notes, dropping in a G chord followed by E minor, fingering the E root note with my right thumb. I love those minor triads with the perfect fifth. Davis isn't sure what I'm playing but is game. He sets his thumb against the bass and starts moving the rest of his fingers along the treble strings.

Can he hear what I'm hearing? That this is the melody for his song. The one he wrote about second chances and feeling hope again, how he was going to bust open the cracks until all he saw was light. And I play it slow, with feeling.

"Is this..." Davis trails off. He recognizes the words, but I think the notes are speaking to him, too. He starts cutting the third note short, a little Ed Sheeren-esque, but I like it. Rudd joins in, pulling on the bass.

But it's Ian understands completely. I'm not just playing this song for Davis. I'm playing it for Landry. I'm inviting her and everything she loves into all parts of my life. Because you can't be an island of one when you have a band—or a family. Ian shakes his head in rueful acceptance. He has Berry, so he knows that once you're caught, you're caught. There's nothing to do but enjoy the ride.

24

ADAM

"Can I talk to you?" I ask quietly.

Landry hesitates, and I fucking hate that. Before our fight, she would've been on her feet immediately.

"I'm chatting with Mike."

I cast a quick glare in the direction of Threat Attack's manager. While I know he's gay, he's got a dick and it spends way too much time in close quarters with Landry. I keep my crazy-headed jealousy to myself, though. For the most part.

"Please?" I'm not too proud to beg. At least, I shouldn't be. That's my big problem. That I'm too arrogant. I know this. That's where my temper comes from—this feeling that I always know what's right and good for everyone. I press her again. "I need to apologize to you, and I want to do it right."

"All right." She leans over and gives Mike a kiss. "Talk to you later."

"Holler if you need me," he says.

Fuck that. She doesn't need protection from me. I open my

mouth, but Landry slaps a hand against my chest before I can make an ass of myself.

"Down, boy," she mutters.

I follow her as she weaves her way through the crowd. The fire's died off; we didn't have much kindling in the first place. She settles her ass on the bumper and waits. I pace back and forth for a moment, trying to gather my thoughts. On my return, a cigarette appears in front of me.

"I think Ian left it for you. And you need it."

"I'm trying to quit," I tell her, looking at the cancer stick with longing.

"Maybe not tonight."

Sighing, I pluck it from her fingers and pull a lighter out of my pocket. "Tomorrow, then."

"Okay. I'll hold you to it."

I take a long drag and let the tobacco fill my lungs. I think about all the tomorrows I want to have with Landry. The cigarette doesn't taste as good as I thought it would, so I drop it to the ground and grind my heel on it. "Actually, let's start today."

She gives me a brilliant smile. Quitting smoking is a bitch, but it'll be worth it if I can keep making her smile like that.

"My old man's band got to tour with a bigger band, Hell Magic."

Sheepishly, she shrugs. "I've never heard of them."

"Most people our age haven't, but back in the eighties they were playing small auditoriums and booking major summer festivals. They had a gimmick, though. They would dress up in Grim Reaper costumes, then halfway through they'd rip off their robes and play the rest of the gig in their underwear and boots."

Her jaw drops. "They were popular for that?"

"It was the eighties. There was a lot of booze and drugs going on. Anyway, my dad's band was struggling. As do most bands. Hell Magic's manager convinced my dad to wear headpieces for a show."

"Oh, I saw those on your dad's wiki page. He had a crow's head."

I nod. "Basil, the bassist, wore a hawk. Moet, the drummer, wore the vulture. It was a huge hit."

"The wiki entry said that Moet never took his headpiece off, even during sex. Is that true?" Her eyes are wide.

"Sadly, yes. There were feathers everywhere." I remember one time a

"I think that would scare the shit out of me."

I give her a hard look. "You don't think some girls were into that? What kind of groupies do you think hang around bands called Hell Magic and Death to Dusk?"

"So you're saying there isn't a big crossover between your dad's band and, say, the My Little Pony faction."

I shout out a laugh. "That's one way to put it." I chuckle for another moment before continuing, "After that one awesome response, Dad donned the costume again. Soon they were wearing them all the time. It fit for the tour with Hell Magic. That's what the fans were coming to see, anyway—a spectacle."

"So they never did another concert without them?"

"No. They did. The following year, Death to Dusk cut a rock album, less heavy on the steel guitar, more melody. They went on tour right away to promote the album and it was a big fucking flop. They got heckled nonstop. Every gig they did, the fans wanted to hear the headbanging metal stuff and they wanted to see the damn bird heads."

"Oh shit." Understanding starts to dawn in her eyes, her mouth forming a little circle. "That was their commercial. Or, at least in your head, that was their commercial."

"It's not in my head, babe. You become famous for one thing and that's all you're known for. You can see it happening to TA. My dad was miserable. He wanted to make different music. Sing a ballad or two. Do some harmonies. But all the fans wanted were bird heads and death music. So that's what he did for two decades. Now, he doesn't even like listening to his own music."

"Oh, Adam, that's so sad."

Thinking about Dad and his near hate for the music industry makes me wish I hadn't crushed out the cigarette. "He was so angry when I skipped out on Juilliard. He wanted me to be a concert pianist or some shit. Said my music talent was wasted on a band."

"Does he hate your band?"

"No. He's proud of me, but worried. He doesn't want what happened to him to happen to me. Just like any parent."

"What about your mom?"

Now I really need that cigarette. "Too busy chasing the dream of being famous herself. I suppose if I get big, she'll come around and drag a camera with her."

Landry winces. "That sucks."

I shrug. "It is what it is. I don't let that ruin my life." I sweep a hand over the top of her head, enjoying the silky feel of her long hair against my palm. "I've never judged other women by my mom."

Landry catches my arm and presses a kiss to the side of it. "For the record, I think TA sucks, too. That's why they've only got the one hit."

"Maybe so. Keith's a good front man, but the other guys don't carry their own weight."

"Like Albie?"

"Like all of them. Keith would be better off going solo, but it's hard to tour as a solo artist. You need a band behind you, and if you're a one-man singer, you can't afford to pay session musicians."

She wrinkles her nose. "The music business is complicated."

"That's the truth. Which is why we should tell Davis what's going on. There's no sense in putting up false barriers. We're a family, Landry. We don't keep secrets from family or we're going to end up like TA."

"Every argument in your arsenal is that you're going to end up like TA. Or your dad's band."

I drag a hand through my hair. The pieces aren't all fitting together for me. There's a discordant measure here. I think back and try to unravel the strings. Is it Marrow? She hasn't seemed jumpy at all lately. So what exactly is her hang-up regarding her brother knowing about us? It's not like I plan to use her and discard her. I want her to be part of my life.

Since I can't figure it out on my own, I flat-out ask her, "What's the real problem here? I don't believe it's the sex, so what is it?"

She twists around the side of the bus to make sure we're alone, then returns her gaze to me. "Did Davis tell you about his first band?"

"A few things. He said he played in college with some buddies and that after they graduated, they tried to keep the group together but everyone splintered. Some got jobs and others lost the hunger for it."

Her green eyes dull as sadness fills them. "Davis got a job at CloudDox, but the reason that he quit the band was because of me. Marrow had been stalking me for about six months before I reported it. He'd leave notes by my computer and sometimes in my backpack. I wasn't really afraid of him until I found a note in my bedroom."

"In your bedroom?"

She nods. "On my dresser, between my phone charger and my hairbrush. I lived with May and she wouldn't have let anyone up, so we didn't know how he got in. Anyway, I reported it to the building manager and then I let it go. No more notes for a while. One of the lawyers who worked on the sale of Peep asked me out. Davis had been bugging me about getting out more, and I figured, why not? He seemed nice but ended up being a jerk."

"I don't want any details," I tell her.

"Nothing to tell." She pulls her legs up. "Anyway, we'd been going out for a couple of months when I got this knock on the door one night. I thought it was Carl."

"Wait." I hold up a hand. "You dated a lawyer named Carl? There's no way a lawyer named Carl knows the first thing about making a woman like you happy."

She smirks. "I thought you didn't want to know the details."

"Good point." I wave my hand for her to continue. "So there's a knock on the door and it's Marrow, right?"

Her smile fades immediately. "He pushed his way inside. He ranted about how I was betraying him and how he'd been so patient with me and that he was tired of all these low-energy guys getting attention when he had put so much effort into me."

"What happened?"

"He tried to drag me out of the apartment, but I wasn't having it." The corner of her mouth lifts. "I fought him. He grabbed a coffee mug on the table and swung it at me, I guess trying to knock me out. It hit me here." She strokes a finger down the side of her face where a small white line snakes down along her right ear.

"But you got away."

"Yeah, I did. A neighbor heard me cry out and banged on the door. Marrow panicked and tried to run out. He wasn't real bright." She grimaces, as if she feels bad for insulting the pencil dick who attacked her. "Anyway, when Davis heard about it, he went over and beat Marrow up." She flexes her left hand, the one that Davis uses to work the fret. "He broke three bones and got an Oxy prescription. It was weird. Both he and Marrow were going through the same legal process. Arraignment, decisions to plead, sentencing. Marrow went to prison supposedly for eighteen months and Davis went to county jail for three. The whole process ate at Davis, but I couldn't see past the end of my own nose. I was in therapy. My parents were freaking out. We forgot about Davis. *I* forgot about him."

Guilt drips from every word. She was caught up in her own trauma and kicks herself for not seeing Davis's spiral.

"When did you figure it out?"

"He took my ATM card and withdrew the max limit for an entire week. I didn't notice, but my accountant did." She reaches up to rub the sides of her neck, as if the memory still causes her pain. "I didn't care about the money. Like, I would've given it to him if he'd asked."

"Only not for drugs," I guess.

"Right. Not for drugs." Sad eyed, she tilts her head. "It's kind of ironic, but the jail time saved him. He couldn't get oxy in jail and he dried out. Don't say anything," she hurries to add. "He's not proud of what happened and he obviously doesn't want you to know." She gives me a worried look. "He turned his life around. Got a job."

I smooth a hand over her hair in what I hope is a reassuring manner. "Not saying a word." The awkward tension that would spring up between the two suddenly made sense. She was watching

Davis for signs of relapse, and he was tired of repeatedly proving himself to her.

She nods miserably. "I don't want to see Davis like that again. It was awful when he got out of jail. He was a shadow of himself, but Nothing would be worth it." She meets my eyes. "Not even us."

Her words are a punch in the gut. I want to understand and, in some part of my brain, I get it. But the selfish part wants me to shake her until she admits that without me she's lost. Because that's where I am—lost without her.

Tour Stop: Phoenix

"Good morning, Phoenix! This is KPRX, your home for all the top hits. Today we have in studio FMK. We can't say their full name on the radio because our producer told us we have to stop"—*bleep*, goes the censor—"on air."

Everyone laughs. We've moved on from Texas, but the air is still dry. I'm drinking at least two liters of water a day and still feel parched.

Adam and I are trying to stay away from each other, but it's not easy. The few times we've been together have only whetted our appetite for each other, but there's no privacy on the tour bus. Davis would know the minute that Adam and I slipped off together. I'm not ready to break the news.

"So which one of you is picked first the most?"

Rudd points to his chest. "Me, of course."

Ian shoves Rudd's head to the side and points to Adam. "That one."

"You, Adam Rees? You're the F of the FMK?"

Adam waves a hand in front of his face. "Not me. I think Davis is the one whose pants all the ladies are trying to get into."

"Not Rudd here? He's hot. I'd be all over him if it weren't the for the ring on my finger."

"Those are artificial barriers," Rudd says into the mic. "Love sees no boundaries."

The female personality—Nicole, I think her name is—smiles. "I like your way of thinking, but my husband might not agree."

She's sitting so close to Adam he barely has space for his guitar. Granted, the room is small, but she doesn't have to be rubbing her married tit against Adam's arm.

"Speaking of husbands," the male radio host jumps in, "we heard that you, Ian, just got married."

"Yeah, I figured I'd better wife up my girlfriend before someone else did. Like Rudd here." He nudges Rudd in the side.

"Berry's smoking hot. If you had to wife someone up, definitely her. But for all the ladies out there, there are still three of us single guys. You should come and see us at the festival. We'll be waiting."

"Is that right? No other significant others for the rest of you?"

"I'm concentrating on the music," Davis says.

Adam stares through the window separating us. Without taking his eyes off me, he says, "Same."

I look away because that hurts. And I've no right to be hurt since I'm the one asking for his silence.

"There's one reason to get yourself out to the Sand Festival today," chortles Nicole with one hand curled around Adam's biceps. "I, for one, will be angling for a front row seat."

I hate her. I really hate her.

"So, Adam, rumor has it that you're using your dad's old bus from *The Crows* tour."

"Yeah, but it's been gutted and renoed so other than the shell, it doesn't resemble the old Death to Dusk bus much."

"I've seen pictures of this sweet ride," the male host pipes up.

"And we're going to post a few of them on our Facebook page later. Your dad give you any tips for touring?"

The side of Adam's mouth tilts upward. "Yeah, sleep when you can and never shit on the bus."

Bleep!

"Fair enough. You've brought your instruments today. What're you going to play for us?"

"'I Wasn't Ready,'" Adam says. "It's a new song Davis and I have been working on during the tour. It's been a favorite of mine since we put the lyrics to music, but this is the first time we'll be playing it for anyone outside of the band."

"And who doesn't like being the first." The male host winks at the guys. "PRX listeners, you're in for a real treat—get ready for the debut of 'I Wasn't Ready' by FMK!"

Ian counts off the beat. "One and two and three and four and—"

Rudd starts first, laying down the bass line. Two measures and Adam joins in. Two more measures and Davis begins to sing. And then it's full on harmony—beautiful and pure. Adam's voice lower, more gravelly, providing the anchor for Davis's falsetto.

The hosts are into it. The male host is mouthing the chorus after the second verse. Nicole licks her lips as if she's imagining tasting one of the band members.

If this is how these jaded radio hosts are reacting, then the song is going to be a huge hit.

"Whew!" Nicole wipes fake sweat off her forehead. "Is it hot in here or what? I want you all to promise that you'll remember us when you get big, because I can tell you right now, this is a hit!"

Her co-host leans into the mic. "If you haven't bought your tickets for Sand Festival, start calling to win one of ten tickets to hear FMK and four other bands play tonight. We'll be back after the break!"

The sound in my room goes dead as the feed from the studio is cut off while a commercial plays. I watch as everyone slaps each other on the back and Adam thanks the producer for having them. By the two thumbs-up the headphones-wearing producer gives, the telephone response must be positive.

Davis is the first one to come bursting through the door. "What'd you think?"

"You guys were great."

"They're getting so many calls!" he says excitedly. "Higher volume after our segment than they've had all morning."

I offer a genuine smile. "I'm so happy for you."

Davis lifts me up and swings me around. "This is it, Landry."

"You deserve it," I tell him.

He grins happily and sets me down. "Let's get to the festival!"

"We gotta make the airport run," Ian reminds him. Berry's flying in.

Davis slaps him on the back. "Then let's go to the airport, pick up the wifey, and get to the festival."

"Davis is excited," Adam murmurs in my ear.

"What gave you that idea?" I say dryly.

THE OUTDOOR FESTIVAL IS A BIGGER, rowdier crowd than I'm used to. There's no table in the back of the bar that I can barricade myself behind. It's nothing but a sea of people. Even behind the stage, it's a mass of humanity, moving frenetically from one end to the other while readying things for the next act.

"This crowd is insane tonight," Berry yells in my ear. We have to yell. It's the only way to communicate.

She has little Jack strapped to her chest with a huge pair of earmuffs around his head. He's sleeping peacefully against her chest. I eye his ear protection with envy. I could use a pair of those.

"I've never been to a music festival," I confess. "Is it always like this?"

"Not even the Summer Festival in Central City?" she asks in astonishment.

"No. I always meant to go." But the local music scene bummed Davis out. I think he'd go and be resentful that he was in the audience and not onstage.

"Well, that's nothing like this. You can bring a blanket and hear the person next to you talk without shouting."

I give her a thumbs-up, because I'm tired of screaming our conversation. That and my attention keeps getting diverted to Adam. He's got so many girls around him, and they're so brazen, tucking their numbers into his front pocket, asking him to sign their tits and asses and tummies. And he has to pretend like he's interested because I've insisted on keeping our relationship a secret.

It makes me a little crazy. The noise, the smoke in the air, and the girls are all giving me a huge headache. I decide to retreat inside the bus.

Berry follows me. She unhooks her baby papoose thingy and carefully lays Jack in the portable carrier. One thing about having Berry on the bus, it's too crowded with baby things to accommodate many people.

"I need a set of those headphones." Inside the bus, with the door closed, it's like we're in the eye of a noise hurricane.

"I know, right?" She tucks a blanket around him and comes to take a seat at the banquette. "Fuck, I'd give anything to have a beer right now."

"You can't?" I know nothing about babies.

"No." She pats her boob. "He drinks from the tap. I could pump and dump, but that's a pain in the ass. Don't have a baby, Landry. They're so much work."

I look at Jack's sweet face. "But they're so adorable."

"That's the kicker. You're mad about a dozen things like not sleeping, having to use three diapers during one change, getting pissed on during said change, but he can smile at you and everything's forgiven."

I wink. "Kind of like Ian."

She laughs. "Yeah, just like Ian, but usually his smile has to come from between my legs before the forgiveness comes."

"Nice. I like that."

"So, you and Adam, huh?" She arches her eyebrows as if daring me to deny it.

"Ian told you?" I guess.

"I'm his wife. There are no secrets between us."

Her smile is inviting, but I'm not ready to share my feelings with Berry. I can't admit that I fell in love with him when she expressly warned me away. "You told me not to catch feelings for him because he wasn't going to settle down."

"Maybe I was wrong." Her voice softens. "Adam's careful. He's friendly with tons of people. Loves the women, but he doesn't open up to many. People want to take advantage of him—of his money, his connections, his talents. That's why I gave you the warning. Not because I don't think he can't settle down but because I haven't seen him want to."

I look out the window. Adam's now talking to some woman wearing a badge. The girls are hanging back, waiting for the opportunity to pounce. He's not paying them any attention. "You see something different now?"

I can't keep the hope out of my voice.

"Ian does."

My heart swells. "I want to believe," I find myself telling her. "But there's Davis. I don't think he'd like it if I was dating Adam."

"Has he said that or are you using him as an excuse so you can pretend that Adam's going to break your heart."

My jaw drops open at her blunt words. She makes a face. "Too harsh? I just love Adam to pieces and Ian says he's gone over you. I feel like I gave the warning to the wrong person."

"No." I shake my head. "No. You didn't. I'm—" I break off and then restart, forcing myself to admit the truth. "You're right." Those words are hard to say. "I've been hiding. I let Davis talk me into coming on this tour instead of facing Marrow down. I crushed on Adam because it was safe. And then when it wasn't safe anymore, I threw Davis in between us as a roadblock."

I swallow but it hurts because there's a big lump in my throat.

Berry's eyes hold no judgment. "So what do you do now?"

What can I do? Adam's already set up camp in my heart, and

short of clawing that thing out, he's there for good. Sitting on my ass and not grabbing the opportunity that's *right there* is idiotic.

"I guess I need to talk to Davis and tell him that I love Adam."

"Maybe tell Adam first." She winks.

"Probably."

"Go out and make a big show of it. Adam will love it."

"How do you know?"

"It's my motherly intuition." She taps the side of her head.

"Your baby's three months old," I laughingly protest.

"Hey, I was cooking that boy for nine months before he popped out. My intuition was being developed at the same time my belly got bigger."

"Is that how it works?" I say. The lump in my throat is gone and my tummy is filled with nervous excitement.

"Damn straight."

The door to the bus whooshes open and Rudd's head pops inside. He's wearing a "Pluck Me" T-shirt in forest green.

"Nice T-shirt," I tell him.

"Davis gave it to me. We're going to take the stage. You coming out or is Jack asleep?"

Berry groans but pushes out of the booth. "He's asleep, but I'll pop those headphones on and it'll be fine."

Rudd gives us a thumbs-up. "Cool beans. You coming too, Landry?"

"Wouldn't miss it. We'll be out in a few."

"'Kay."

"Wait for me, would you, Berry?" I say as I jog toward the back. "I want to put on some makeup and change."

"You look fine," she calls.

"I don't want to look fine. I want to look drop dead gorgeous. This is a big moment." I rummage in my makeup bag and reach for my contacts container. I rarely wear them, but if I have to fight for Adam, I might as well be battle ready. And it's hard to wear glasses in battle.

"Point taken. Do you need help?"

"Nah." After I pop the contacts in, I swipe red lipstick over my lips and dab on mascara. I pull out the short velvet miniskirt that made Adam lose control before and pair that with a white loose-fitting top that laces down the front. Tucking that in, I shove my feet into a pair of military-style ankle boots. Finally, I spray a sample of floral perfume that I found in the bottom of my purse, smack my lips together, and go out to meet Berry.

The makeup and outfit is more for my benefit than Adam's. I want to claim him in front of everyone which means I need to look the part.

"What do you think?" I ask, one hand on my hip.

"He won't stand a chance," she promises. Jack is already tucked in his little papoose, his sweet head listing to the side. "Let's go out and lay our claims on our men."

"Done." I slap her hand and lead the way.

Outside, a couple of roadies are helping Ian set up his drums while Rudd and Davis huddle around Adam, who's holding their set list, one hand cradled around a mic stand. Berry goes to give Ian a good luck kiss as I saunter over to Adam and the others.

I'm only a couple of steps away when I hear a commotion. A scuffle of feet, a curse or two, a girl's cry. I turn to see what the problem is and that's when I spot him.

Marrow.

26

LANDRY

My heart jams in my throat as Marrow runs at me. Fear races through my veins. His thin frame parts the crowd like a scythe. His hand is extended, holding something dark and shiny. A shove against my shoulder sends the whole scene spinning sideways. Everything is a blur. Someone shouts. My heart gallops uncontrollably as I try to regain my balance.

Adam lunges forward, but then I see a flash of green and Rudd drops to the ground in front of me. Marrow stumbles back, his hand empty. There's a loud, sustained screeching. I clamp my hands over my ears but I still hear it. Worse, the shiny thing is now in Rudd's gut.

His blue eyes stare at me in shock.

"Sweetheart, I think someone stabbed me," he gasps.

"Rudd! Rudd!" I scramble over to him, moving my hands helplessly over his frame.

Another pair of hands pulls me out of the way.

"You're just fine, Rudd. If you wanted more attention, though, you should've said something. I would've written you a solo," Adam jokes. He shoots a fierce glare in Ian's direction. "Call 9-1-1."

"Already on it, bro," Ian says with a phone in his hand. Davis drops down next to Rudd, pressing a t-shirt onto the wound.

I'm not needed here. Not that I can do anything. I raise my head and spot Marrow pushing through the crowd, and a fierce anger wells up inside of me.

For far too long, I've been afraid. Well, I'm done with that shit. A flash of silver catches my eye. I grab it and lunge forward. Damn, these mic stands are heavy. But adrenaline is driving me.

"Marrow!" I yell.

He hesitates and then turns around. The crowd pushes him toward me. I don't give him time to talk, to explain, to spout his poison. I heave up that stupid mic stand and swing it. The heavy base's momentum carries it all the way around, faster than I anticipated, faster than Marrow can react.

A loud, awful crack fills the air. His head jerks back as the base catches him across the cheek. He staggers, careening sideways. Blood lust surges through me. I charge forward, grabbing the next thing I can get my hands on, and bring that down on his head. Splinters of wood spray to the side. A discordant chord plays.

"Dammit, that's my fucking guitar!" someone screams.

I turn feral teeth on the complainer. "I'll buy you a new one."

Whatever he sees on my face scares the shit out of him, because he backs off. I bring the broken guitar back down on Marrow's bloody face again and again and—

"That's enough, slugger."

I'm suddenly hauled backwards, courtesy of Adam.

I glance at my hand to see that I'm holding only the neck and the guitar strings. The drum broke away and I didn't even notice. I rub a palm across my face and look down to find that it's speckled in blood.

"Shit," Adam curses. "Are you hurt?"

"I don't think so."

His face is as white as flour.

"It's not mine," I inform him.

He lifts the bottom of his T-shirt to wipe my face. His hands are trembling slightly. "I didn't think it was. The ambulance is here."

"Already?" It seems like only seconds have passed. I start to shake myself. We're both in a state. His fingers flex around the shirt. One hand bites into my upper arm as he holds me steady. I've never seen his jaw tighter.

"They have one on-site for a gig as big as this one. They're loading Rudd into it. You ready?"

I nod and let the last of the guitar drop from my hand.

"Is Rudd okay?"

"He will be."

"I owe that guy a new guitar," I say absently.

"I'll send him one of my dad's."

"Okay." I finally allow myself to lean into him.

He heaves one deep sigh and then another as he tries to get control of his emotions. I bury the side of my face into his chest and try not to think of all the terrible things that could've happened.

Two police officers and a handful of black-shirted guys with white letters spelling out SECURITY muscle their way toward us. One of them drops to his knees beside Marrow who is still out cold.

"You do this?" A police officer takes a threatening step toward Adam.

No way does he get to take credit for this. I wave my hand. "It was me."

"Maybe dial back the cheerfulness," Adam murmurs from behind me.

I ignore him and approach the officer. "I'm Landry Olsen and this is Christopher Paul Marrow. I have a restraining order that prohibits him from getting within two miles of me. Further, he's on probation and is not supposed to leave Central City."

The officer pulls out a smartphone. "What's his name again?"

I recite it and every other detail I know about Marrow. With each word, the bands of fear that have been constricting my chest since Marrow's first attack begin to loosen. By the end, when the Phoenix officers are loading Marrow onto the stretcher, I take the first free breath I've experienced in far too long.

27

ADAM

The metallic taste of fear lingers on the back of my tongue. When I heard Landry shout Marrow's name, my heart stopped. I didn't feel better when I saw it was Rudd on the ground, blood pooling around a nasty blade in his gut.

Now that we're here at the hospital, I can't seem to let go of her. Davis keeps glaring at me.

"Landry, come on. I want you to get that hand looked at," Davis says, crouching in front of her.

She shakes her head. "No. I'm fine."

"Seriously. You could have a cut." He reaches for her but she jerks away.

"I'm fine. All the blood was his. Marrow's, I mean," she explains unnecessarily.

"All right." Davis straightens, gives me another pointed look, then jerks his head to the side.

He wants to talk to me, and while the hospital where our band-mate is currently being treated isn't the optimal site, there's no point in putting off this confrontation.

Reluctantly, I release Landry and gesture toward the door. "After you."

He gives a sharp nod and stomps toward the exit door.

"Where're you going?" Landry calls out.

"Stay here," I say.

She doesn't listen.

"What's going on here?"

Davis whirls on us. "That's my question. What the hell is going on between the two of you?"

Landry stumbles back from the fierceness of his tone. I steady her with a hand at her back.

"Don't talk to your sister like that." Not even her brother gets to treat her like shit. Not while I'm around.

Davis doesn't want to hear from me. "How long have you been fucking him?"

She flinches at the coarse talk, but doesn't back down. "I've been sleeping with him since Texas."

He slams his hand against the wall. "And you've been hiding this the entire time?"

"That's enough, Davis. Not here." Out of the corner of my eye, I see Ian get to his feet.

He cocks his head. "Then let's take it outside."

"Fine." This fight between Davis and me has been a long time in coming. He's been pissed off at me ever since I turned the commercial down.

"Stop it, you guys." Landry pops between us. "Rudd's in surgery. You cannot be having a fistfight while your bandmate is fighting for his life."

Davis and I ignore her. He brushes by her and I follow.

"Ian," Landry hisses.

Ian stays in the corner with his baby and his wife. His silence is agreement. Davis and I need to have this out.

Davis slams the palm of his hand against the waiting room doors. Two more sets of doors and we're out in the parking lot.

"I can't believe you're doing this," Landry yells. "Seriously, you guys are both idiots."

"You've been lying to me for a month. Tossing aside my ideas. Refusing to allow the band to move forward. You scared, bro? A real man would've told me."

I clench my jaw. A direct hit. A real man would've told him. I've been hiding behind Landry's skirts, but not anymore. "Fine. You want to know? Your sister and I are a couple. Deal with it."

"Why don't you deal with this." He charges forward, driving his shoulder into my gut. I let him take me to the ground and give him one good shot at my face. Because every brother deserves that. But he only gets the one. I block his next blow and roll out from underneath him. Blood drips from the corner of my mouth.

"Nice shot." I raise my hands. "Let's see what else you got."

"Would you two just fucking stop it! You're making fools out of yourselves!" Landry yells.

Davis ignores her and charges at me like a bull. He gets in a good punch to my side because I'm expecting one in my face but I swing out of the way to avoid the uppercut headed for my chin.

"Would you two stop it!" Landry screams. "I beat Marrow and I swear to God, I'm taking a mic stand to your heads, too! This isn't even about me. It's about the music!"

Davis pauses, her accusation sinking in. She's right. It's not about her. It's about Davis wanting more control of the band.

He jabs and I feint. I'm not going to hit him while his sister is watching, but I'm not about to get my face beat in because he wants more control. All my front men wanted to be in charge. They thought they knew best one hundred percent of the time.

"This is my band," I say unwisely.

"Then you can sing your own songs, because I'm done." Davis straightens. He turns to Landry. "I'm going home. You can come with me or stay with Adam."

She gives an anguished cry. He's a dick for making her choose, but I'm the asshole who put them both in that position.

"Fuck. Wait." I hold out a hand. "I'm sorry. Look, it's been a while since I've had a band. I've been dicked over in the past, so I'm super protective of my shit. That's wrong. I don't want you to leave."

I'm saying this stuff to Davis, but it's meant for Landry, too. But she needs the words as well. "Don't go, Landry. I love you, and I'll be fucking miserable without you if you leave."

Her face grows pale with shock and...is that horror?

"You...love me?" she stammers.

Fuck, is there a worse way for me to confess this? But it'd be stupid and lying to deny it. Besides, I don't want to deny it, even if it loses me Davis. I raise my chin. *Hit me with your best shot.* "Yeah, I love you."

She stares at me. "Since when?"

"Since...I don't know. San Antiono."

"San Antiono?" She yelps.

"Christ, yeah. Maybe before. How can you not know? I haven't even looked at another woman since you showed up. Every song I sing, I'm singing it to you. Every time I'm up on stage, it's to make you want me more." I can't believe I'm arguing with her about this. Out of the corner of my eye, I see Davis cross his arms and lean back on his heels as if he's enjoying seeing me pour out my guts on the asphalt.

"You didn't even tell me you wrote songs for other people." She throws up her arms. "I thought you thought we were hooking up."

"Well, we're not," I say tersely. This isn't how I thought my declaration of love was going to go. A knot of tension balls up at the base of my neck.

She starts blinking and then tears start flowing. "I was going to tell you that I loved you and Marrow ruined it all," she cries. Her telltale blush quickly engulfs her entire face. She throws herself at me, digging her face into my chest.

I nearly collapse with relief. I dig my hands into her hair and force her face up so I can kiss that beautiful mouth of hers.

Before I can make contact, she jerks back. "Oh my God. I can't believe we did this in front of my brother."

I glance over and Davis is still standing there. I glare at him. He glares right back.

"I don't care who the fuck hears," I say for both the benefit of both the Olsens. "I think you have something to say, right?"

"I love you, too," she mumbles.

I pull back and tip her chin up. "Again, for the kids in the back."

She twists around to face Davis, who's standing there looking bemused. "I love him. Don't leave the band because of me. Talk to each other and work it out."

She wriggles out of my embrace, but doesn't run off right away. Instead, she pushes up on her tiptoes to plant a hard, tongue-filled kiss against my mouth. A kiss that rouses the beast in my jeans. He has no appreciation for time and place.

I draw back and swipe my thumb across her wet lip. "I can't handle anything more," I tell her ruefully.

"I'd appreciate it if you didn't do any more than that, too," Davis chimes in.

Landry lifts her finger to flick her brother off.

"If you two are done acting like five-year-olds, Rudd's out of surgery," Ian calls from the doorway.

"This isn't finished." Davis stomps forward.

Landry hears him. "Oh yes, it is. This is my life and I get to decide who I sleep with."

"There you go," I say.

"But, Adam, if you want Davis to be part of the band, then we all have to get along."

"Ha," Davis exclaims.

"You both need to shut up and focus on Rudd," she admonishes.

I drag a hand over my mouth and mumble, "Sorry."

Davis mutters something under his breath that may have been sorry or may have been fuck you.

"What'd the doctor say," I ask when I reach Ian. I give Jack a pat on the ass. He makes no sound. Little dude can apparently sleep through a tornado.

"It's good news. Nothing vital was hit. They had to remove his spleen and he has some ligament and muscle damage in his torso but they stitched it up and said that he shouldn't have too many problems in the future."

"What does too many problems mean?"

"He'll have some tightness, maybe won't be able to do as many crunches in the gym but Rudd's convinced that his scar is going to attract the ladies."

A surprised laugh bursts out of me. "Of course he does. He must be feeling better, then."

INSIDE THE HOSPITAL ROOM, a very pretty nurse is tucking the blanket around Rudd.

"Have I told you how gorgeous you are?" Rudd is saying as we walk in.

"Yes, a couple of times."

"It needs to be said a couple of times," he drawls. "Maybe a hundred times so that whatever deity made you understands we appreciate her good work."

"You're cute," the nurse says, patting him on the shoulder.

"I'll take the compliment and your number."

She waves as she walks out.

"I'm serious," he calls out, sitting up. He groans and clutches his waist.

I rush forward. "Lie down, you fool."

"I'm the fool?" he says but does as I order. "Heard you and Davis were out in the parking lot doing a little WWE."

"We were just messing around," I lie.

Davis crosses to the other side of the room. Rudd rolls his head in Davis's direction. "Found out about your sister and Adam, huh?"

Davis throws up his arms. "You knew, too?"

"Duh," Rudd says, lying back. "Everyone did."

"Everyone?" The two Olsens chorus together.

Rudd grins. "You can tell you two are related. You're both clueless as fuck." He rolls his head on the pillow until he can face me. "Hey, man, I'm sorry about this. I know this is going screw up your plans. You should get a session guitarist to fill in for me."

A chorus of protests erupt. I gape at Rudd. "A session guitarist? I'm not filling your position. What would make you think that?"

He shrugs. "You've got your plans for the band."

The band. Not our band. Rudd has played with me for over five years. I find a chair to settle my ass onto.

"This is your band, too," I say. "It belongs to all of us. Even Davis. While you're recovering, D and I will kiss and make up."

"I hope I get to watch that," Berry chimes in from the corner. Next to her, Ian smirks.

"But Hollister mentioned Burning Man. That's a big fucking deal," Rudd moans.

"We'd have to take a break anyway," I inform him. "Because WWR has offered us an album deal."

"WWR?" He shoots upright. "Are you kidding me? What'd you say?"

"That I had to talk to you all about it."

He flops back on the pillows. "Shit. I wish I could drink. We should be toasting this moment."

"I'll write a new song. One about how the best things take you by surprise," I joke.

"Or Davis could write the lyrics while you write the melody and Ian and Rudd can lay down the beat," Landry suggests.

My lips curve up. I reach out and grab her hand, pulling her to me. "That's perfect. See, this is why you need to stay with the band."

"Landry's joining the band?" Rudd asks. "What's her instrument?"

"The horn," she smirks.

Davis groans but everyone else, including me, laughs for a good five minutes.

The nurse kicks us out and I draw Landry aside.

"How are you doing?"

"I'm good."

"Well, I'm not. I was scared shitless." I draw her into my arms. I don't know if I can hold her enough. I bury my nose in her hair and take deep long draws until my lungs are filled with her scent.

"I was scared, too."

"Really? You didn't seem like it." The vision of her running after Marrow will live in my head for a long time.

"I was scared and then I was mad and then I was scared again," she says, leaning in to me.

I shift slightly, taking the welcome weight on my heels. "Adrenaline."

I bend down and seek out her mouth. She tastes like life and hope and all my tomorrows. My arms tighten around her when I think of how close I was to losing her.

Her tongue slides against mine, and we spend countless seconds, minutes, kissing each other deeply. My hands drop to her hips.

"We need to find some place private," I murmur against her mouth.

"Not another bathroom," she replies. I feel her smile against my lips.

"Stairwell?"

"We'll have to keep our clothes on."

"Can I put my hand down your skirt?" I'll take anything. I rock my growing erection against her.

Her small hand creeps around my hip to squeeze my ass. "Only if I can do the same."

"Done." I grab her hand and drag her down the hall, stopping at the first exit sign I see.

I sit down on a step and pull her on top of me. She straddles me, a knee on either side of my hip. Her mini skirt rides up. I might've helped it a little bit, just to make her more comfortable.

"I thought you said over the clothes." she scolds, but there's a smile on her face.

I squeeze her ass. "No, I specifically bargained for under the clothes touching."

She leans back to place her palms on my knees. The laces of her shirt have loosened and the fabric gapes invitingly. Beneath her eyelashes, she shoots me a wicked look. "Then lets make the most of it."

28

LANDRY

"Are you okay with Adam and me?" I ask. Davis and I snuck out to get something to eat in the hospital cafeteria.

Davis runs a hand through his hair. "Does it matter what I think?"

I jam my fists against my hips. "Of course it does," I reply indignantly.

"If it mattered so much, why keep it a secret?"

I exhale heavily. "Because I was worried about how you'd take it. You and Adam were mad at each other and I didn't want to add to that."

"Because you were afraid I was going to lose it and start abusing oxy again." It's not a question, but a matter-of-fact statement.

"Yes. That." I peer up into his green eyes, so like my own, and see understanding tinged with frustration.

"You gotta stop worrying about me. I know you count my beers and are afraid that I'm going to trip during a party and accidentally snort up a line of coke, but I know my limits."

"If it makes you feel any better, I stopped counting a while back. Besides, you worry about me, too. If you recall, I'm here"—I stretch out my arms—"because you were afraid that Marrow would come after me."

"And I was right to be afraid because he did," Davis replies smugly.

"Can you not with the 'I told you so?'" I say. "Anyway, I'm sorry."

"Why? Because you fell in love? I'm sorry you felt like you had to hide it from me. I didn't want you to get hurt, you know?" He swings an arm around my neck and pulls me close.

"I know. You were watching out for me, like you always do. I appreciate that."

"See, the problem is now I wonder if Adam's making decisions he's going to regret later because of you. Like selling the song."

"I don't see Adam doing anything with his music that he doesn't want to do."

"True."

"Besides, this is your band, too. You're a family, as he likes to say. You're going to be making decisions together." He scrubs his knuckles across the top of my head. I kick him in the shin to make him release me.

He laughs as I try to press my staticky hair into some semblance of order. Stupid big brothers.

"So where do we go from here?" he says.

"Are you okay with Adam and me as a couple?" My hope is tinged with worry. Part of me can't believe all that has happened—not just the Marrow thing, but Adam saying he loves me. If Davis said he wasn't okay with all of this, I wouldn't be able to give Adam up. Not at this point so I really need him to be on board.

"Is that what you are?"

"I think so." Davis arches an eyebrow. Okay, that's stupid. We confessed we loved each other right in front of him. I take a deep breath. "Yes. We are. He wants me to stay for the rest of the tour. So even if you're not okay with it, will you please try to work through this because I'm not giving Adam up."

"What if I demand it?"

"Why would you do that?" I cry. "And, no. Even if you demanded it."

"Even if I started using again?"

I punch him in the arm. He yelps.

"Stop being a smart ass," I glower.

He smirks. "Sorry. Couldn't help it. Look, I don't care if you're with Adam. I want you to be happy. All I ask is that you keep your sex stuff to yourself and no cooking."

"I don't want you to know about my sex stuff. Gross." The thought of having sex with Davis a few feet away is never going to sit right with me. I nearly died in the bathroom when he came in. Talk about a lady boner killer. "But I am going to learn to cook."

"Really?" Both eyebrows shoot up.

"Okay, maybe not," I concede. I have no burning desire to do that, but it's something I can tease Davis about.

"If you do, I'm voting you off the island. I'm going to get a cup of coffee. What do you want?" He reaches over to give me another irritating pat on the head, but I duck out of the way.

"Ham or turkey and a Coke."

He gives me a thumbs-up and ambles off to get us some food.

My purse buzzes. I pull out my phone and see that Detective Pressley is calling. Her name sends a shiver of unease down my spine, but I answer instead of avoiding her.

"Hello, Detective Pressley."

"Landry, how are you?"

"I'm fine."

"Good. No injuries?"

"Do you already know about Marrow?"

"Indeed, I do." She sounds immensely cheerful. "I even have pictures of your handiwork."

I grimace. "Am I going to jail for that?" I ask, thinking about Davis's stint in the slammer.

"No. It's a clear case of self-defense. No one will be charging you with anything, although an officer will be coming by to take your statement at some point. Where are you?"

"At the hospital."

"And how's your friend?"

"Good. The knife didn't hit anything serious so he's going to have a painful recovery but he should be fine. He's very excited about the dope scar he's going to have."

Pressley laughs merrily. I pull the phone away from my head and stare at it. This is wildly out of character for her.

"Who's that?" Davis asks, joining me with a tray full of food and drink.

"It's Pressley," I mouth and put the phone back to my ear.

Davis sets the tray and crosses his arms. A frown creases his forehead. I'm sure I look exactly that befuddled.

"I like his attitude," she's saying. "In any event, I wanted to let you know that Marrow is being booked for attempted homicide, violating his probation, and felony assault. Because he's across state lines in violation of his probation, he'll be sent back to jail immediately. He will await trial inside and will have to serve out his original sentence, in full, as well as any other time for the attempted homicide. It sounds like the defense lawyer is already trying to get him to agree to a plea deal which could carry a ten-year sentence."

"He shouldn't even be out," I growl.

She immediately grows serious. "I know, Landry. The laws around stalking are terrible, but the good thing is that he's going away for a long time."

"I hope he gets some treatment inside. Some therapy so that when he gets out, he doesn't do the same thing."

Pressley is silent a bit too long before she sighs. "The system isn't perfect."

"Sorry. None of this is your fault. Thank you for calling me."

She sighs. "Be well, Landry. I think this chapter of your life is over. Anyway, I called to let you know that a review of Marrow's cellphone reveals that he had contact with someone in your band and informed Marrow of your whereabouts."

"In my band? In FMK?" I can't believe it. No one in FMK would do that to me. My mind skips back to the first conversation I had with Berry. She warned me about Hollister. How he didn't like women with the band. Had he heard that Adam wanted me to continue to travel with them?

"A male named Albert Buchourd. He's five feet ten inches tall. Has a full sleeve of SpongeBob tattoos on the right arm."

"I know him." I cut her off. The Fat Albert makes sense now. "Everyone calls him Albie."

"Well, Good. I wanted you to know. Forewarned is forearmed. I've got to run. Call me if you need anything," she says.

"Thanks," I manage to say as I lower the phone to the table.

"What'd she say?" Davis asks impatiently.

"She says that Marrow's being sent back to prison for violating his parole and he'll have to serve out the rest of his sentence as well as whatever term he gets for stabbing Rudd."

Davis grunts in satisfaction. "Finally."

"He'll be out in ten years or something like that."

"But you know how to fight him off now. That was badass, Landry. Proud of you."

When I don't immediately join in his laughter, his grin falters. "What's wrong?"

"Pressley said that a male named Albert Bouchard contacted Marrow. Told him where I was."

"What?" he shouts. A few people clear their throats. Loud voices are apparently looked down on in the hospital cafeteria. He abandons the tray and drags me out into the hall. "Is that Albie?"

"Yup."

His eyes narrow. "What exactly did she say?"

"That he had contact with Marrow and let him know where I was."

"Oh, that fucker is dead."

"Why would he do that?"

"Pissant was jealous of our success." He strides down the hall. I have to jog to keep up with him.

"Where are we going?"

"To get Adam. He's smoking outside with Ian. Then we're going over to TA and beat the shit out of Albie."

"You can't do that."

"Why the hell not?" he asks as we near the exterior doors.

"Because you might break your hand again."

"Then I'll beat him with the mic stand."

29

ADAM

"Oh, he's a dead man," I declare the second after Davis finishes telling me how Marrow found us in Phoenix.

"Can we just shelve the beating for now? Haven't you both got it out of your system?" Landry asks.

"No," both Davis and I say at the same time.

I pull out my phone and dial Hollister's number. "Yo, Holly. Where is Threat Alert right now?"

"Right now?" he asks. "I have no idea. They finished their set about forty minutes ago."

"But they're at the venue, right?"

"I suppose. The bus is. Why? And how's Rudd, anyway?"

"He's going to be fine. You need to find Albie and make sure he doesn't leave."

"Why's that?"

"Because Albie is the one who ran his mouth to Marrow."

"Oh shit," he curses. "Adam, you cannot beat him up. I've got three months left on this tour. We can't lose the headliner."

"Guess what? We're not playing either."

"Why? You can get a session guitarist to fill in for Rudd. You just said he was fine."

"No, I said he was going to be fine." I hang up. There's no point in talking with Hollister any longer. "Albie's at the venue. They finished about an hour ago, but the bus is still there."

"Let's go." Davis has a car service app pulled up on his phone.

Landry snatches the phone away. "Both of you have to promise that you're not going to beat him up, threaten him, or do anything other than make sure he stays in one place until the police arrive."

"What exact crime do you think Albie is going to be arrested for?" I ask, trying not to let my frustration out.

"I don't know. I'm not a cop." She clasps her hands together. "But I do know that dumbass over here served fourteen days in jail because of assault. You guys go rushing over there to beat him up in front of thousands of people and you're going to get more time than that. Plus, it'll be Davis's second charge. Let's do something nonviolent, huh?"

Davis grabs the back of his neck and stalks off. She's gotten to him. He wants to do something, but it's hard to deny the truth of Landry's words.

I stick my phone in my back pocket.

"All right. I don't like not getting at least one punch in, but I'll settle for ruining this dude's life."

"That's the spirit," she encourages, then frowns when she realizes what I just said. "How exactly are you going to ruin his life?"

"Make sure that he doesn't play another note again. The music business is a small, small world, and this is one time I don't mind using my connections to get some guy blackballed."

"You should tell Keith first," she advises.

"You okay with this?" I ask Davis. Landry's his sister and I'm trying to be more open to others giving their opinions.

Jaw tight, he says, "It's not my first choice, but if you can get him blackballed, I'm in."

"It's done." I reach for my phone again and this time, I call my dad. "Hey, Dad. Adam here."

～

WE'RE a tired group by the time Rudd gets discharged. We rent an Escalade to take him back to the bus. I wanted to fly him back to Central City, but the doctors thought it would be okay for him to ride in the bus, once they had a look at it.

"You going to be okay back here, buddy?" I ask.

"Keep the drugs coming and I'll be great." He tries to raise his thumbs, but in his drugged state, all his fingers wave in the air.

"But not too much," Davis interjects.

"It'll be the goldilocks of drug dosages," I promise.

Rudd makes a big circular motion in Landry's direction. "I know you're taken but you're still a girl. Come over here and hold my hand."

Gingerly she crawls onto the big bed. Rudd settles his head on her lap immediately.

"Ahh," he croons. "This is a hundred times better."

She strokes his hair. I prop a shoulder against the doorframe and watch as the band all settles in around Rudd. Ian plops his ass on the end near Rudd's feet. Davis takes up space against the wall opposite of me.

"How drugged up are you?" Davis asks.

Rudd makes a measurement with his thumb and forefinger. Squinting, he says, "Five?"

A round of chuckles ensue at this nonsense remark.

"What was Hollister shouting about back there?" Rudd asks, tipping his head to the side so Landry will scratch a different area. She obliges.

"Threat Alert broke up. Albie's developed a bad coke habit. They're shipping him off to a treatment center. With us gone and them broken up, Hollister doesn't have a tour anymore."

"Poor Holly," Rudd says in a sing-song voice.

"He'll be alright," Landry soothes. "Guys like him always land on their feet."

Isn't that the truth.

"When we get home, can I meet May," Rudd asks. "She sounds fun."

"Eating snakes is fun?" I ask. Landry has been telling Rudd tales of her friend's adventures to entertain him and now Rudd has a full-blown crush on this mystery woman.

"Yeah. And all those weeks riding ponies. Her thighs must be strong enough to crush steel." He tries to waggle his eyebrows but fails miserably. He groans. "Give me another dose."

"Not yet, sweetheart."

Davis holds up a finger. "I've an idea. Be right back. Don't move."

"We're on the bus, Davis. We can't move," I say.

"Technically, we're in motion because the bus is," Landry chirps.

God, I love her. I push away from the door. "Technically, I'm going to kiss—"

"Not in front of the brother," Davis yells from down the hall.

Rudd taps Landry's hand.

"Yes?" she says, peering down at him.

"You can kiss me. Davis said so."

I burst out laughing. Rudd starts chuckling, too, but cuts himself off immediately.

"Oh, that hurts," he says.

Davis soon reappears with two guitars—his and mine.

"Let's play my song. I have an idea for the harmonies."

I take my guitar and fit the drum against my stomach. "Lead the way."

Davis perches on the side of the bed and starts strumming. I catch on immediately, and soon, we're finding music magic.

Over Davis's shoulder, I meet Landry's eyes. They're full of love and in them I see all the songs I have yet to write, the ones about our joys, our inevitable sorrows—but most importantly, the ones where we're together.

EPILOGUE

LANDRY

Six Months Later

An hour out from the J's Truck Plaza where we gassed up and stretched our legs, Ed pulls the bus over to the side of the road.

"What's wrong?" Davis yells.

"We're out of gas," Ed yells back in disbelief.

"Out of gas?" Adam echoes.

I stare down at my cards because just the sound of his voice is enough to make me squeeze my legs together. It's been far too long since I've had my hands on him and sitting so close is killing me.

Sex is out of the question so long as Davis is within hearing distance. I just can't do it. It's like listening to your parents have sex. I wouldn't want that, and I'm not going to subject my poor brother to that kind of familial torture. But my self-imposed rules have left me anxious. It's probably best that Adam's not within ten feet of me.

I keep wanting to launch myself into his arms.

Ed heaves himself out of the driver's seat and ambles toward us.

"Best I can figure out, but I've popped the hood. I'll check it out and let you know."

Adam tosses his cards face down. "I'll go with you."

"Me, too," Davis declares.

Ian shrugs but follows silently behind. I send an inquiring glance in Rudd's direction.

"I don't know shit about vehicles," he says in answer to my unstated question. He discards a six and gestures for me to deal him a new card. I flip over a jack.

"Nineteen." He holds up his hand. "I'll stay."

I look down at my own cards. An ace and a five. Shit. I'm going to have to take a hit. I flip over the next card and sigh when I see it's an eight.

"Bust," he crows and rakes in the kitty.

I eye the bag of Reese's Peanut Butter Cups with envy. "I'll give you ten dollars for the Reese's."

Since I haven't been able to have more than a furtive, unfulfilling, over-the-clothes groping session with Adam since I met up with the band four hours ago, I'm in a desperate state that only sex or chocolate will appease.

Rudd waggles a finger at me. "You know the rules. No money. What else you have to offer?"

I mentally review my carryon. I'm traveling light because we leave for Edinburgh from Houston—if we ever get to Houston. "I have a mini bag of Doritos from the airport."

For a moment, I think I've struck a bargain, but his excited expression quickly transforms into one of suspicion. "Oh no. The last time I bargained with you, I got a half empty bag of M&Ms. How many chips are left?"

I blink rapidly, attempting to convey innocence. "I have no idea what you're talking about."

"The hell you don't—"

"We're out of gas. Ed thinks that there might be a hole in the tank," Davis interrupts. "I volunteered to hitch to the nearest gas station. Want to come?"

"Where's Adam?"

"He's calling to see if an Uber can come out here."

I sigh. Of course he is. "I think I'll nap."

"Rudd?"

"Why not?" he shrugs. "But only flag down Kias, Jeeps, and Passats."

"Why?"

"Because those are cars driven by cute girls."

"I drive a Passat," Davis says.

"I know. I've always said you're the cutest pussy I know."

"Fuck you," Davis says, but he's laughing as they exit the bus.

Ian stops by his bunk to pull out a packet of cigarettes and his phone. "Ed and I are taking a smoke break."

"Um, okay. I think I'm going to go lie down. I didn't get too sleep much on the plane."

"Uh huh," he says.

I can't quite make out the weird tone in his voice and he's down the stairs before I can ask. Shrugging, I decide to go to the back room.

Back at the rest stop, Adam converted it from the U-shaped seating arrangement into the bed when I mentioned that I'd only gotten about two hours of sleep on the two plane rides to catch up with the guys in Baton Rouge. There was so much turbulence on the flight from Central City to Charlotte that I ended up spending most of my time hunched over, praying for the flight to end. The second leg, from Charlotte to Baton Rouge, wasn't so bad, but it was such a quick flight we barely had time for beverage service.

The bus is quiet without the engine running and with the guys all gone, it's strangely silent. I know Adam's busy trying to fix the bus. They need to be in Houston in a few hours, but I can't prevent myself from imagining him appearing in the doorway, stripping his clothes off, and ravishing me.

I haven't seen Adam in nearly two months—and since the new tour started, that's the longest we've been apart. Unfortunately, due to the delayed flights, I wasn't able to meet the band until right before they had to take off for Houston, which meant that Adam and I had to settle unsatisfactory dry-humping.

Once we reach Houston, we'll check into a hotel and while everyone else naps before the show, I'm going to assault my boyfriend. Which is why I need to rest up now.

I pull off my hoodie and yoga pants, folding both on the edge of the mattress, and crawl under the lightweight down comforter. Closing my eyes, I try to will my hyperactive body into a more restful state.

After Rudd healed up, the band spent six weeks closeted in a studio. Adam and Davis wrote what seemed like a hundred songs before settling on fourteen. Some of the best songs were ones they wrote on the back of napkins or, in one instance, in Sharpie on a beach towel.

Two of the songs were sold to tech companies for commercials that aired a month before the album's release. The singles hit the Billboard top twenty and that was that. FMK was a success.

I went on the East Coast leg of their tour, but had to return home to help take care of Dad, who supposedly broke his leg taking salsa lessons with Mom. I suspect, based on the grins they keep exchanging, that it happened while they were horizontal. Dad blames it on a slippery floor. Mom can't stop giggling when he brings it up. Mortified, I've stopped asking questions.

I sigh and roll over, pulling the blanket up over my head. It will be easier when we get to Europe. It's all private jets and hotel rooms. No buses.

A solid *thunk* has me sitting up.

Adam walks in and presses the button to close the door. I watch with wide eyes as he toes off his boots and pulls off his T-shirt. His gorgeous tattoos, a veritable garden of delight, shift and contract as he moves around.

He nods toward my pile of tidily folded clothes. "You got anything else on?"

I pluck at my T-shirt. "This?"

"Take it off," he orders. His hands busily undo his jeans.

I tuck one arm through a sleeve and then the other, but can't bring myself to pull it over my head lest I miss even a second of this delicious striptease Adam is performing.

"Get busy, babe. We've only got"—he glances behind him —"twenty minutes at the most."

He shoves his jeans down and his thick, heavy erection falls out. I lick my lips with greedy anticipation. I cup his shaft, holding the back of it so that I can run my tongue along the entire length, from tip to base and back again. The first taste of him inside my mouth is delicious. I can't keep the moan from escaping.

I close my lips around the broad head and then take him in as far as I can. He stares at me with lust-drunk eyes. His right hand reaches around to pull my hair away from my face while he strokes my cheek with the fingers of his left.

The rough calluses abrade my delicate skin, but his touch is so tender, so loving. I love him in return, fluttering my tongue against he thrusts lightly inside my mouth. His cock is a beautiful weight in my mouth. His flavor rich and deep. I don't want to let go.

I whimper my disapproval when he pulls away.

"Baby, it's my turn. You have to let me taste you."

How can I refuse that. His broad shoulders muscle between my thighs and then it's *his* tongue licking *me* from one end to the other. It's my hands gripping his hair tight as he delivers stinging bites followed by sweet caresses.

My heart races and the air in my lungs empties out. He leaves me gasping, full of longing and want and need.

I claw at his shoulders until he rears up, warrior strong. His lips are wet with my desire. With one thrust, he's inside of me, his piercing dragging along my sensitive tissues. My body stretches to accept him. He's big and hot and fills me until I don't know anything but him. I grip him so tight that he'll have marks for a week.

He bends down and kisses me. I taste myself on him, tangy and erotic.

"Harder," I urge.

Above me, he growls. A hand slams against the leather cushion and a knee digs in between my legs. He wastes no time in giving me exactly what I asked for. His hips jack forward, his pelvic bone providing delicious friction against my clit. I grind upward, searching and then finding that perfect release.

He's not far behind me. Neither of us can hold out. We both miss each other so much. He shakes as he comes. It's so magical with him. I hug his broad shoulders close as he collapses on me.

"I love you."

"Same. Love you so much, baby." He dots tired kisses along my forehead and cheekbones.

I tighten my Kegels. "Round two?"

A smile stretches from ear to ear. "Give me--

"Yo, ETA's about five minutes," Ian interrupts with a knock on the door. "You might want to pull the coil off the fuel line."

Adam groans and starts to roll away, his delicious shaft slipping out of me.

"Wait a sec," I grab his arm. "Did you disable the bus for the sole purpose of having sex with me?"

He grins. "Baby, I haven't seen you in two months. I would've fire-bombed the bus to have sex with you."

"Oh, Adam. I love you, but that's crazy."

"Yeah, well, as the song goes: that's love." And he winks at me.

And I guess that's the truest story that's ever been written. Love is a crazy little thing, but I get to share it with the best man in the world.

I caught feelings for Adam Rees. He caught them back.

ACKNOWLEDGMENTS

First, I have to say thank you to the awesome readers who waited so patiently for this book. I know it can be frustrating to want a book and see the author move in other directions. I really appreciate your patience while I dabbled with football books and YA stories. Every author says she has the best readers, but I know you all are the best and don't let anyone tell you differently!

Second, that you to all the bloggers, reviewers and readers who take the time not only to read the book but share their thoughts with others. You are the backbone of the publishing community and you all don't get enough credit or thanks.

Thank you to my dear husband who is taking on so many other duties so I can find the time to write and to my wonderful, beautiful, sweet daughter who is growing up into this amazing young woman.

To my friends Daphne, Jill, Elyssa, Jeanette (again), Melissa, Meljean, and Lea, thank you for all your support and friendship. I'm not able to do any of this without friends.

To Elle and Meljean, thank you for helping me whip this book into shape.

To Nina for taking on the huge task of spreading the good word about this series and all the other ones.

To Natasha and Nicole who help keep track of my head. I'd be lost without the two of you.

UNDECLARED

BY JEN FREDERICK

Available Now

For four years, Grace Sullivan wrote to a Marine she never met, and fell in love. But when his deployment ended, so did the letters. Ever since that day, Grace has been coasting, academically and emotionally. The one thing she's decided? No way is Noah Jackson—or any man—ever going to break her heart again.

Noah has always known exactly what he wants out of life. Success. Stability. Control. That's why he joined the Marines and that's why he's fighting his way—literally—through college. Now that he's got the rest of his life on track, he has one last conquest: Grace Sullivan. But since he was the one who stopped writing, he knows that winning her back will be his biggest battle yet.

UNSPOKEN

BY JEN FREDERICK

Available Now

Whore. Slut. Typhoid Mary.

I've been called all these at Central College. One drunken night, one act of irresponsible behavior, and my reputation was ruined. Guys labeled me as easy and girls shied away. To cope, I stayed away from Central social life and away from Central men, so why is it that my new biology lab partner is so irresistible to me?

He's everything I shouldn't want. A former Marine involved in illegal fighting with a quick trigger temper and an easy smile for all the women. His fists aren't the danger to me, though, it's his charm. He's sliding his way into my heart and I'm afraid that he's going to be the one to break me.

Impulsive. Unthinking. Hot tempered.

I allow instinct to rule my behavior. If it feels good, do it, has been my motto because if I spend too much time thinking, I'll begin to remember exactly where I came from. At Central College, I've got fighting and I've got women and I thought I was satisfied until I met her.

She's everything I didn't realize I wanted and the more time I spend with her, the more I want her. But she's been hurt too much in the past and I don't want to be the one to break her. I know I should walk away, but I just can't.

UNRAVELED

BY JEN FREDERICK

Available Now

Twenty-five-year-old Sgt. Gray Phillips is at a crossroads in his life: stay in the Marine Corps or get out and learn to be a civilian? He's got forty-five days of leave to make up his mind but the people in his life aren't making the decision any easier. His dad wants him to get out; his grandfather wants him to stay in. And his growing feelings for Sam Anderson are wreaking havoc with his heart...and his mind. He believes relationships get ruined when a Marine goes on deployment. So now he's got an even harder decision to make: take a chance on Sam or leave love behind and give his all to the Marines.

Twenty-two year old Samantha Anderson lost her husband to an IED in Afghanistan just two months after their vows. Two years later, Sam is full of regrets—that she didn't move with her husband to Alaska; that she allowed her friends to drift away; that she hasn't taken many chances in life. Now, she's met Gray and taking a risk on this Marine could be her one opportunity to feel alive and in love again. But how can she risk her heart on another military man who could share the same tragic fate as her husband?

UNDRESSED

BY JEN FREDERICK

Available Now

Noah and Grace's happy ever after hits a stumbling block in the form of one shady professor threatening Noah's scholarship eligibility. Noah is given the choice of throwing his New Year's MMA fight for a big payoff or accepting that the true meaning of love isn't measured by the thickness of his wallet but the depth of Grace's big heart.

UNREQUITED

BY JEN FREDERICK

Available Now

Winter Donovan loves two things: her sister and her sister's ex boyfriend. She's spent her whole life doing the right thing except that one time, that night when Finn O'Malley looked hollowed out by his father's death. Then she did something very wrong that felt terribly right.

Finn can't stop thinking about Winter and the night and he'll do anything to make her a permanent part of his life, even if it means separating Winter from the only family she has.

Their love was supposed to be unrequited but one grief stricken guy and one girl with too big of a heart results in disastrous consequences.

THE CHARLOTTE CHRONICLES

BY JEN FREDERICK

Available Now

Charlotte Randolph was only fifteen when she fell in love with her best friend's gorgeous older brother—but she wasn't foolish enough to hope he could ever love her back. Nate Jackson always viewed her as a pesky kid...until the day she got sick. The one bright spot during her illness? He realized she was all grown up. But just when she allows herself to believe that dreams *can* come true, Nate disappears from her life, taking her heart with him.

Nate knows he lost more than his best friend when he deserted Charlotte to enlist in the Navy. He thought he was doing the right thing, sparing the girl he loves from the shame and humiliation of his actions. Nine years later, it's time to right his wrongs. He returns home determined to win back his first love...only to find that Charlotte's moved on without him.

But if there's one thing that being a Navy SEAL has taught Nate?

Never give up, even when all hope seems lost. And Nate's never going to give up on Charlotte. Ever.

#GETSACKED

BY JEN FREDERICK

Available Now

What he wants he gets...

Knox Masters is a quarterback's worst nightmare. Warrior. Champion. And...virgin. Knox knows what he wants--and he gets it. All American Football player? Check. NFL pros scouting him? Check. Now, he's set his sight on two things. The national title. And Ellie Campbell. Sure, she's the sister of his fellow teammate, but that's not going to stop him. Especially not when he's convinced Ellie is the one.

...but he's never met her before.

But Ellie isn't as sure. She's trying to start a new life and she's not interested in a relationship...with anyone. Beside it's not just her cardinal rule of never dating her brother's teammates that keeps her away, but Ellie has a dark secret that would jeopardize everything Knox is pursuing.

Knox has no intention of losing. Ellie has no intention of giving in.

#GETJOCKBLOCKED

BY JEN FREDERICK

Available Now

She's always played it safe...

College junior Lucy Washington abides by one rule—avoid risk at all costs. She's cautious in every aspect of her life, from her health, to her mock trial team, to the boring guys she dates. When a brash, gorgeous jock walks into the campus coffeeshop and turns his flirt on, Lucy is stunned by the force of attraction. For the first time ever, she's willing to step out of her comfort zone, but can she really trust the guy who's determined to sweep her off her feet?

He's always played around...

Entering his last year of college eligibility, linebacker Matthew "Matty" Iverson has the team captaincy in his sights. And it's his for the taking, if he can convince his quarterback Ace Anderson to give up the starting position. Luckily, Matty already has an edge—the hottie he's lusting over just happens to be Ace's childhood best friend. Getting Lucy on his side and in his bed? Hell yeah. Matty is more than confident he can have both, but when he falls hard for Lucy, it's time for a new game plan: convince the woman of his dreams that she's not sleeping with the enemy.

#GETDOWNED

BY JEN FREDERICK

Available Now

He's the guy no one likes...

Despite winning two national championships, JR "Ace" Anderson was sent packing from his old school after losing the trust of his coach. At Southern U, he has a second chance to prove that his college legacy isn't endless debauchery and selfishness. But his reputation precedes him, and his teammates offer a chilly welcome in the locker room. The one person who is willing to accept him is the very woman he should stay away from—his new coach's daughter.

She's the girl everyone loves...

Bryant Johnson's only goal in life is to make others happy, even at her own expense. One look at her father's new star quarterback, and she knows that Ace is her next project. With a reputation for being a "jerk whisperer", Bryant has spent her last three years at college reforming sorry behavior and turning bad boys into the best boyfriends ever. In Ace, though, she's met with surly resistance and a sizzling attraction she doesn't expect. Fixing this wounded warrior will be her biggest challenge yet. Not falling for him will be even harder.

Between her big heart and his damaged one, a battle is ensuing. In this game of love, every defense will crumble.

ABOUT THE AUTHOR

Jen Frederick is a *USA Today* bestselling author. She lives in the Midwest with her husband, who keeps track of life's details while she's writing; a daughter, who understands when Mom disappears into her office for hours at a time; and a rambunctious dog who does neither. Jen loves to hear from readers so drop her a line!

Contact Me:

jenfrederick.com

jen@jenfrederick.com

Made in the USA
Columbia, SC
05 June 2017